D0441001

RECEIVED

DEC   2018

By_____

ALSO BY STEPHEN KING

STEPHEN KING

APT PUPIL

SCRIBNER

New York   London   Toronto   Sydney   New Delhi

Scribner

An Imprint of Simon & Schuster, Inc.

1230 Avenue of the Americas

New York, NY 10020

This Scribner trade paperback edition December 2018

SCRIBNER and design are registered trademarks of The Gale Group, Inc., used under license by Simon & Schuster, Inc., the publisher of this work.

For information about special discounts for bulk purchases, please contact Simon & Schuster Special Sales at 1-866-506-1949 or business@simonandschuster.com.

The Simon & Schuster Speakers Bureau can bring authors to your live event. For more information or to book an event, contact the Simon & Schuster Speakers Bureau at 1-866-248-3049 or visit our website at www.simonspeakers.com.

Manufactured in the United States of America

1   3   5   7   9   10   8   6   4   2

Library of Congress Cataloging-in-Publication Data is available.

ISBN 978-1-9821-1544-9

ISBN 978-1-9821-1545-6 (ebook)

For Elaine Koster and Herbert Schnall

He looked like the total all-American kid as he pedaled his twenty-six-inch Schwinn with the apehanger handlebars up the residential suburban street, and that's just what he was: Todd Bowden, thirteen years old, five-feet-eight and a healthy one hundred and forty pounds, hair the color of ripe corn, blue eyes, white even teeth, lightly tanned skin marred by not even the first shadow of adolescent acne.

He was smiling a summer vacation smile as he pedaled through the sun and shade not too far from his own house. He looked like the kind of kid who might have a paper route, and as a matter of fact, he did—he delivered the Santo Donato *Clarion*. He also looked like the kind of kid who might sell greeting cards for premiums, and he had done that, too. They were the kind that come with your name printed inside—JACK AND MARY BURKE, OR DON AND SALLY, OR THE MURCHISONS. He looked like the sort of boy who might whistle while he worked, and he often did so. He whistled quite prettily, in fact. His dad was an architectural engineer who made forty thousand dollars a year. His mom had majored in French in college and had met Todd's father when he desperately needed a tutor. She typed manuscripts in her spare time. She had kept all of Todd's old school report cards in a folder. Her favorite was his final fourth-grade card, on which Mrs. Upshaw had scratched: "Todd is an extremely apt pupil." He was, too. Straight A's and B's all the way up the line. If he'd done any better—straight A's, for example—his friends might have begun to think he was weird.

Now he brought his bike to a halt in front of 963 Claremont Street and stepped off it. The house was a small bungalow set discreetly back on its lot. It was white with green shutters and green trim. A hedge ran around the front. The hedge was well-watered and well-clipped.

Todd brushed his blonde hair out of his eyes and walked the Schwinn up the cement path to the steps. He was still smiling, and his smile was open and expectant and beautiful. He pushed down the bike's kickstand with the toe of one Nike running-shoe and then picked the folded newspaper off the bottom step. It wasn't the *Clarion;* it was the *L.A. Times.* He put it under his arm and mounted the steps. At the top was a heavy wooden door with no window inside of a latched screen door. There was a doorbell on the right-hand doorframe, and below the bell were two small signs, each neatly screwed into the wood and covered with protective plastic so they wouldn't yellow or waterspot. German efficiency, Todd thought, and his smile widened a little. It was an adult thought, and he always mentally congratulated himself when he had one of those.

The top sign said ARTHUR DENKER.

The bottom one said NO SOLICITORS, NO PEDDLERS, NO SALESMEN.

Smiling still, Todd rang the bell.

He could barely hear its muted burring, somewhere far off inside the small house. He took his finger off the bell and cocked his head a little, listening for footsteps. There were none. He looked at his Timex watch (one of the premiums he had gotten for selling personalized greeting cards) and saw that it was twelve past ten. The guy should be up by now. Todd himself was always up by seven-thirty at the latest, even during summer vacation. The early bird catches the worm.

He listened for another thirty seconds and when the house remained silent he leaned on the bell, watching the sweep second hand on his Timex as he did so. He had been pressing the doorbell for exactly seventy-one seconds when he finally heard shuffling footsteps. Slippers, he deduced from the soft *wish-wish* sound. Todd was into deductions. His current ambition was to become a private detective when he grew up.

2

"All right! All right!" the man who was pretending to be Arthur Denker called querulously. "I'm coming! Let it go! I'm coming!"

Todd stopped pushing the doorbell button.

A chain and bolt rattled on the far side of the windowless inner door. Then it was pulled open.

An old man, hunched inside a bathrobe, stood looking out through the screen. A cigarette smouldered between his fingers. Todd thought the man looked like a cross between Albert Einstein and Boris Karloff. His hair was long and white but beginning to yellow in an unpleasant way that was more nicotine than ivory. His face was wrinkled and pouched and puffy with sleep, and Todd saw with some distaste that he hadn't bothered shaving for the last couple of days. Todd's father was fond of saying, "A shave puts a shine on the morning." Todd's father shaved every day, whether he had to work or not.

The eyes looking out at Todd were watchful but deeply sunken, laced with snaps of red. Todd felt an instant of deep disappointment. The guy *did* look a little bit like Albert Einstein, and he *did* look a little bit like Boris Karloff, but what he looked like more than anything else was one of the seedy old winos that hung around down by the railroad yard.

But of course, Todd reminded himself, the man had just gotten up. Todd had seen Denker many times before today (although he had been very careful to make sure that Denker hadn't seen *him*, no *way*, Jose), and on his public occasions, Denker looked very natty, every inch an officer in retirement, you might say, even though he was seventy-six if the articles Todd had read at the library had his birth-date right. On the days when Todd had shadowed him to the Shoprite where Denker did his shopping or to one of the three movie theaters on the bus line—Denker had no car—he was always dressed in one of three neatly kept suits, no matter how warm the weather. If the weather looked threatening he carried a furled umbrella under one arm like a swagger stick. He sometimes wore a trilby hat. And on the occasions when Denker went out, he was always neatly shaved and his white moustache (worn to conceal an imperfectly corrected harelip) was carefully trimmed.

"A boy," he said now. His voice was thick and sleepy. Todd saw with new disappointment that his robe was faded and tacky. One rounded collar point stood up at a drunken angle to poke at his wattled neck. There was a splotch of something that might have been chili or possibly A-1 Steak Sauce on the left lapel, and he smelled of cigarettes and stale booze.

"A boy," he repeated. "I don't need anything, boy. Read the sign. You can read, can't you? Of course you can. All American boys can read. Don't be a nuisance, boy. Good day."

The door began to close.

He might have dropped it right there, Todd thought much later on one of the nights when sleep was hard to find. His disappointment at seeing the man for the first time at close range, seeing him with his street-face put away—hanging in the closet, you might say, along with his umbrella and his trilby—might have done it. It could have ended in that moment, the tiny, unimportant snicking sound of the latch cutting off everything that happened later as neatly as a pair of shears. But, as the man himself had observed, he was an American boy, and he had been taught that persistence is a virtue.

"Don't forget your paper, Mr. Dussander," Todd said, holding the *Times* out politely.

The door stopped dead in its swing, still inches from the jamb. A tight and watchful expression flitted across Kurt Dussander's face and was gone at once. There might have been fear in that expression. It was good, the way he had made that expression disappear, but Todd was disappointed for the third time. He hadn't expected Dussander to be good; he had expected Dussander to be *great*.

Boy, Todd thought with real disgust. *Boy oh boy.*

4

He pulled the door open again. One hand, bunched with arthritis, unlatched the screen door. The hand pushed the screen door open just enough to wriggle through like a spider and close over the edge of the paper Todd was holding out. The boy saw with distaste that the old man's fingernails were long and yellow and horny. It was a hand that had spent most of its waking hours holding one cigarette after another. Todd thought smoking was a filthy dangerous habit, one he himself would never take up. It really was a wonder that Dussander had lived as long as he had.

The old man tugged. "Give me my paper."

"Sure thing, Mr. Dussander." Todd released his hold on the paper. The spider-hand yanked it inside. The screen closed.

"My name is Denker," the old man said. "Not this Doo-Zander. Apparently you cannot read. What a pity. Good day."

The door started to close again. Todd spoke rapidly into the narrowing gap. "Bergen-Belsen, January 1943 to June 1943. Auschwitz, June 1943 to June of 1944, *Unterkommandant*. Patin—"

The door stopped again. The old man's pouched and pallid face hung in the gap like a wrinkled, half-deflated balloon. Todd smiled.

"You left Patin just ahead of the Russians. You got to Buenos Aires. Some people say you got rich there, investing the gold you took out of Germany in the drug trade. Whatever, you were in Mexico City from 1950 to 1952. Then—"

"Boy, you are crazy like a cuckoo bird." One of the arthritic fingers twirled circles around a misshapen ear. But the toothless mouth was quivering in an infirm, panicky way.

"From 1952 until 1958, I don't know," Todd said, smiling more widely still. "No one does, I guess, or at least they're not telling. But an Israeli agent spotted you in Cuba, working as the concierge in a big hotel just before Castro took over. They lost you when the rebels came into Havana. You popped up in West Berlin in 1965. They almost got you." He pronounced

5

the last two words as one: *gotcha.* At the same time he squeezed all of his fingers together into one large, wriggling fist. Dussander's eyes dropped to those well-made and well-nourished American hands, hands that were made for building soapbox racers and Aurora models. Todd had done both. In fact, the year before, he and his dad had built a model of the *Titanic.* It had taken almost four months, and Todd's father kept it in his office.

"I don't know what you are talking about," Dussander said. Without his false teeth, his words had a mushy sound Todd didn't like. It didn't sound . . . well, authentic. Colonel Klink on *Hogan's Heroes* sounded more like a Nazi than Dussander did. But in his time he must have been a real whiz. In an article on the death-camps in *Men's Action,* the writer had called him The Blood-Fiend of Patin. "Get out of here, boy. Before I call the police."

"Gee, I guess you better call them, Mr. Dussander. Or Herr Dussander, if you like that better." He continued to smile, showing perfect teeth that had been fluoridated since the beginning of his life and bathed thrice a day in Crest toothpaste for almost as long. "After 1965, no one saw you again . . . until I did, two months ago, on the downtown bus."

"You're insane."

"So if you want to call the police," Todd said, smiling, "you go right ahead. I'll wait on the stoop. But if you don't want to call them right away, why don't I come in? We'll talk."

There was a long moment while the old man looked at the smiling boy. Birds twitted in the trees. On the next block a power mower was running, and far off, on busier streets, horns honked out their own rhythm of life and commerce.

In spite of everything, Todd felt the onset of doubt. He couldn't be wrong, could he? Was there some mistake on his part? He didn't think so, but this was no schoolroom exercise. It was real life. So he felt a surge of relief (*mild* relief, he assured himself later) when Dussander said: "You may come in for a moment, if you like. But only because I do not wish to make trouble for you, you understand?"

"Sure, Mr. Dussander," Todd said. He opened the screen and came into the hall. Dussander closed the door behind them, shutting off the morning.

The house smelled stale and slightly malty. It smelled the way Todd's own house smelled sometimes the morning after his folks had thrown a party and before his mother had had a chance to air it out. But this smell was worse. It was lived-in and ground-in. It was liquor, fried food, sweat, old clothes, and some stinky medicinal smell like Vick's or Mentholatum. It was dark in the hallway, and Dussander was standing too close, his head hunched into the collar of his robe like the head of a vulture waiting for some hurt animal to give up the ghost. In that instant, despite the stubble and the loosely hanging flesh, Todd could see the man who had stood inside the black SS uniform more clearly than he had ever seen him on the street. And he felt a sudden lancet of fear slide into his belly. *Mild* fear, he amended later.

"I should tell you that if anything happens to me—" he began, and then Dussander shuffled past him and into the living room, his slippers *wish-wishing* on the floor. He flapped a contemptuous hand at Todd, and Todd felt a flush of hot blood mount into his throat and cheeks.

Todd followed him, his smile wavering for the first time. He had not pictured it happening quite like this. But it would work out. Things would come into focus. Of course they would. Things always did. He began to smile again as he stepped into the living room.

It was another disappointment—and how!—but one he supposed he should have been prepared for. There was of course no oil portrait of Hitler with his forelock dangling and eyes that followed you. No medals in cases, no ceremonial sword mounted on the wall, no Luger or PPK Walther on the mantel (there was, in fact, no mantel). Of course,

Todd told himself, the guy would have to be crazy to put any of those things out where people could see them. Still, it was hard to put everything you saw in the movies or on TV out of your head. It looked like the living room of any old man living alone on a slightly frayed pension. The fake fireplace was faced with fake bricks. A Westclox hung over it. There was a black and white Motorola TV on a stand; the tips of the rabbit ears had been wrapped in aluminum foil to improve reception. The floor was covered with a gray rug; its nap was balding. The magazine rack by the sofa held copies of *National Geographic, Reader's Digest,* and the *L.A. Times.* Instead of Hitler or a ceremonial sword hung on the wall, there was a framed certificate of citizenship and a picture of a woman in a funny hat. Dussander later told him that sort of hat was called a cloche, and they had been popular in the twenties and thirties.

"My wife," Dussander said sentimentally. "She died in 1955 of a lung disease. At that time I was working at the Menschler Motor Works in Essen. I was heartbroken."

Todd continued to smile. He crossed the room as if to get a better look at the woman in the picture. Instead of looking at the picture, he fingered the shade on a small table-lamp.

"Stop that!" Dussander barked harshly. Todd jumped back a little.

"That was good," he said sincerely. "Really commanding. It was Ilse Koch who had the lampshades made out of human skin, wasn't it? And she was the one who had the trick with the little glass tubes."

"I don't know what you're talking about," Dussander said. There was a package of Kools, the kind with no filter, on top of the TV. He offered them to Todd. "Cigarette?" he asked, and grinned. His grin was hideous.

"No. They give you lung cancer. My dad used to smoke, but he gave it up. He went to Smokenders."

"Did he." Dussander produced a wooden match from the

pocket of his robe and scratched it indifferently on the plastic case of the Motorola. Puffing, he said: "Can you give me one reason why I shouldn't call the police and tell them of the monstrous accusations you've just made? One reason? Speak quickly, boy. The telephone is just down the hall. Your father would spank you, I think. You would sit for dinner on a cushion for a week or so, eh?"

"My parents don't believe in spanking. Corporal punishment causes more problems than it cures." Todd's eyes suddenly gleamed. "Did you spank any of them? The women? Did you take off their clothes and—"

With a muffled exclamation, Dussander started for the phone.

Todd said coldly: "You better not do that."

Dussander turned. In measured tones that were spoiled only slightly by the fact that his false teeth were not in, he said: "I tell you this once, boy, and once only. My name is Arthur Denker. It has never been anything else; it has not even been Americanized. I was in fact named Arthur by my father, who greatly admired the stories of Arthur Conan Doyle. It has never been Doo-Zander, or Himmler, or Father Christmas. I was a reserve lieutenant in the war. I never joined the Nazi party. In the battle of Berlin I fought for three weeks. I will admit that in the late thirties, when I was first married, I supported Hitler. He ended the depression and returned some of the pride we had lost in the aftermath of the sickening and unfair Treaty of Versailles. I suppose I supported him mostly because I got a job and there was tobacco again, and I didn't need to hunt through the gutters when I needed to smoke. I thought, in the late thirties, that he was a great man. In his own way, perhaps he was. But at the end he was mad, directing phantom armies at the whim of an astrologer. He even gave Blondi, his dog, a death-capsule. The act of a madman; by the end they were all madmen, singing the 'Horst Wessel Song' as they fed poison to their children. On May 2nd, 1945, my regiment gave up to the Americans. I remember that a private soldier named Hackermeyer gave me a chocolate bar. I wept. There was no reason to fight on; the war was over, and really had been since February. I was interned at Essen and was treated very well. We listened to the Nuremberg trials on the radio, and when Goering committed suicide, I traded fourteen American cigarettes for half a bottle of *Schnaps* and got drunk. When I was released, I put wheels on cars at the Essen Motor Works until 1963, when I retired. Later I emigrated to the United States. To come here was a lifelong ambition. In 1967 I became a citizen. I am an American. I vote. No Buenos Aires. No drug dealing. No Berlin. No Cuba." He pronounced it *Koo-ba*. "And now, unless you leave, I make my telephone call."

He watched Todd do nothing. Then he went down the hall and picked up the telephone. Still Todd stood in the living room, beside the table with the small lamp on it.

Dussander began to dial. Todd watched him, his heart speeding up until it was drumming in his chest. After the fourth number, Dussander turned and looked at him. His shoulders sagged. He put the phone down.

"A boy," he breathed, "A *boy*."

Todd smiled widely but rather modestly.

"How did you find out?"

"One piece of luck and a lot of hard work," Todd said. "There's this friend of mine, Harold Pegler his name is, only all the kids call him Foxy. He plays second base for our team. His dad's got all these magazines out in his garage. Great big stacks of them. War magazines. They're old. I looked for some new ones, but the guy who runs the newsstand across from the school says most of them went out of business. In most of them there's pictures of krauts—German soldiers, I mean— and Japs torturing these women. And articles about the concentration camps. I really groove on all that concentration camp stuff."

"You . . . groove on it." Dussander was staring at him, one

hand rubbing up and down on his cheek, producing a very small sandpapery sound.

"Groove. You know. I get off on it. I'm interested."

He remembered that day in Foxy's garage as clearly as anything in his life—more clearly, he suspected. He remembered in the fifth grade, before Careers Day, how Mrs. Anderson (all the kids called her Bugs because of her big front teeth) had talked to them about what she called finding YOUR GREAT INTEREST.

"It comes all at once," Bugs Anderson had rhapsodized. "You see something for the first time, and right away you know you have found YOUR GREAT INTEREST. It's like a key turning in a lock. Or falling in love for the first time. That's why Careers Day is so important, children—it may be the day on which you find YOUR GREAT INTEREST." And she had gone on to tell them about her own GREAT INTEREST, which turned out not to be teaching the fifth grade but collecting nineteenth-century postcards.

Todd had thought Mrs. Anderson was full of bullspit at the time, but that day in Foxy's garage, he remembered what she had said and wondered if maybe she hadn't been right after all.

The Santa Anas had been blowing that day, and to the east there were brush-fires. He remembered the smell of burning, hot and greasy. He remembered Foxy's crewcut, and the flakes of Butch Wax clinging to the front of it. He remembered *everything*.

"I know there's comics here someplace," Foxy had said. His mother had a hangover and had kicked them out of the house for making too much noise. "Neat ones. They're Westerns, mostly, but there's some *Turok, Son of Stone* and—"

"What are those?" Todd asked, pointing at the bulging cardboard cartons under the stairs.

"Ah, they're no good," Foxy said. "True war stories, mostly. Boring."

"Can I look at some?"

11

"Sure. I'll find the comics."

But by the time fat Foxy Pegler found them, Todd no longer wanted to read comics. He was lost. Utterly lost.

It's like a key turning in a lock. Or falling in love for the first time.

It *had* been like that. He had known about the war, of course—not the stupid one going on now, where the Americans had gotten the shit kicked out of them by a bunch of gooks in black pajamas—but World War II. He knew that the Americans wore round helmets with net on them and the krauts wore sort of square ones. He knew that the Americans won most of the battles and that the Germans had invented rockets near the end and shot them from Germany onto London. He had even known something about the concentration camps.

The difference between all of that and what he found in the magazines under the stairs in Foxy's garage was like the difference between being *told* about germs and then actually *seeing* them in a microscope, squirming around and alive.

Here was Ilse Koch. Here were crematoriums with their doors standing open on their soot-clotted hinges. Here were officers in SS uniforms and prisoners in striped uniforms. The smell of the old pulp magazines was like the smell of the brush-fires burning out of control on the east of Santo Donato, and he could feel the old paper crumbling against the pads of his fingers, and he turned the pages, no longer in Foxy's garage but caught somewhere crosswise in time, trying to cope with the idea that *they had really done those things,* that *somebody had really done those things,* and that *somebody had let them do those things,* and his head began to ache with a mixture of revulsion and excitement, and his eyes were hot and strained, but he read on, and from a column of print beneath a picture of tangled bodies at a place called Dachau, this figure jumped out at him:

6,000,000.

And he thought: *Somebody goofed there, somebody added a zero or two, that's twice as many people as there are in L.A.!* But then, in another magazine (the cover of this one showed a woman chained to a wall while a guy in a Nazi uniform approached her with a poker in his hand and a grin on his face), he saw it again:

6,000,000.

His headache got worse. His mouth went dry. Dimly, from some distance, he heard Foxy saying he had to go in for supper. Todd asked Foxy if he could stay here in the garage and read while Foxy ate. Foxy gave him a look of mild puzzlement, shrugged, and said sure. And Todd read, hunched over the boxes of the old true war magazines, until his mother called and asked if he was *ever* going to go home.

Like a key turning in a lock.

All the magazines said it was bad, what had happened. But all the stories were continued at the back of the book, and when you turned to those pages, the words saying it was bad were surrounded by ads, and these ads sold German knives and belts and helmets as well as Magic Trusses and Guaranteed Hair Restorer. These ads sold German flags emblazoned with swastikas and Nazi Lugers and a game called Panzer Attack as well as correspondence lessons and offers to make you rich selling elevator shoes to short men. They said it was bad, but it seemed like a lot of people must not mind.

Like falling in love.

Oh yes, he remembered that day very well. He remembered everything about it—a yellowing pin-up calendar for a defunct year on the back wall, the oil-stain on the cement floor, the way the magazines had been tied together with orange twine. He remembered how his headache had gotten a little worse each time he thought of that incredible number,

6,000,000.

He remembered thinking: *I want to know about everything that happened in those places. Everything. And I want to know which is more true—the words, or the ads they put beside the words.*

He remembered Bugs Anderson as he at last pushed the boxes back under the stairs and thought: *She was right. I've found my GREAT INTEREST.*

Dussander looked at Todd for a long time. Then he crossed the living room and sat down heavily in a rocking chair. He looked at Todd again, unable to analyze the slightly dreamy, slightly nostalgic expression on the boy's face.

"Yeah. It was the magazines that got me interested, but I figured a lot of what they said was just, you know, bullspit. So I went to the library and found out a lot more stuff. Some of it was even neater. At first the crummy librarian didn't want me to look at any of it because it was in the adult section of the library, but I told her it was for school. If it's for school they have to let you have it. She called my dad, though." Todd's eyes turned up scornfully. "Like she thought Dad didn't know what I was doing, if you can dig that."

"He did know?"

"Sure. My dad thinks kids should find out about life as soon as they can—the bad as well as the good. Then they'll be ready for it. He says life is a tiger you have to grab by the tail, and if you don't know the nature of the beast it will eat you up."

"Mmmm," Dussander said.

"My mom thinks the same way."

"Mmmmm." Dussander looked dazed, not quite sure where he was.

"Anyhow," Todd said, "the library stuff was real good. They must have had a hundred books with stuff in them about the Nazi concentration camps, just here in the Santo Donato library. A *lot* of people must like to read about that stuff. There weren't as many pictures as in Foxy's dad's magazines, but the other stuff was real gooshy. Chairs with spikes sticking up through the seats. Pulling out gold teeth with pliers. Poison gas that came out of the showers." Todd shook his head. "You guys just went overboard, you know that? You really did."

"Gooshy," Dussander said heavily.

"I really *did* do a research paper, and you know what I got on it? An A-plus. Of course I had to be careful. You have to write that stuff in a certain way. You got to be careful."

"Do you?" Dussander asked. He took another cigarette with a hand that trembled.

"Oh yeah. All those library books, they read a certain way. Like the guys who wrote them got puking sick over what they were writing about." Todd was frowning, wrestling with the thought, trying to bring it out. The fact that *tone,* as that word is applied to writing, wasn't yet in his vocabulary, made it more difficult. "They all write like they lost a lot of sleep over it. How we've got to be careful so nothing like that ever happens again. I made my paper like that, and I guess the teacher gave me an A just cause I read the source material without losing my lunch." Once more, Todd smiled winningly.

Dussander dragged heavily on his unfiltered Kool. The tip trembled slightly. As he feathered smoke out of his nostrils, he coughed an old man's dank, hollow cough. "I can hardly believe this conversation is taking place," he said. He leaned forward and peered closely at Todd. "Boy, do you know the word 'existentialism'?"

Todd ignored the question. "Did you ever meet Ilse Koch?"

"Ilse Koch?" Almost inaudibly, Dussander said: "Yes, I met her."

"Was she beautiful?" Todd asked eagerly. "I mean . . ." His hands described an hourglass in the air.

"Surely you have seen her photograph?" Dussander asked. "An aficionado such as yourself?"

"What's an af . . . aff . . ."

"An aficionado," Dussander said, "is one who grooves. One who . . . gets off on something."

15

"Yeah? Cool." Todd's grin, puzzled and weak for a moment, shone out triumphantly again. "Sure, I've seen her picture. But you know how they are in those books." He spoke as if Dussander had them all. "Black and white, fuzzy . . . just snapshots. None of those guys knew they were taking pictures for, you know, *history.* Was she really stacked?"

"She was fat and dumpy and she had bad skin," Dussander said shortly. He crushed his cigarette out half-smoked in a Table Talk pie-dish filled with dead butts.

"Oh. Golly." Todd's face fell.

"Just luck," Dussander mused, looking at Todd. "You saw my picture in a war-adventures magazine and happened to ride next to me on the bus. *Tcha!*" He brought a fist down on the arm of his chair, but without much force.

"No sir, Mr. Dussander. There was more to it than that. A *lot,*" Todd added earnestly, leaning forward.

"Oh? Really?" The bushy eyebrows rose, signalling polite disbelief.

"Sure. I mean, the pictures of you in my scrapbook were all thirty years old, at least. I mean, it *is* 1974."

"You keep a . . . a scrapbook?"

"Oh, yes, sir! It's a good one. Hundreds of pictures. I'll show it to you sometime. You'll go ape."

Dussander's face pulled into a revolted grimace, but he said nothing.

"The first couple of times I saw you, I wasn't sure at all. And then you got on the bus one day when it was raining, and you had this shiny black slicker on—"

"That," Dussander breathed.

"Sure. There was a picture of you in a coat like that in one of the magazines out in Foxy's garage. Also, a photo of you in your SS greatcoat in one of the library books. And when I saw you that day, I just said to myself, 'It's for sure. That's Kurt Dussander.' So I started to shadow you—"

"You did *what?*"

"Shadow you. Follow you. My ambition is to be a private detective like Sam Spade in the books, or Mannix on TV. Anyway, I was super careful. I didn't want you to get wise. Want to look at some pictures?"

Todd took a folded-over manila envelope from his back pocket. Sweat had stuck the flap down. He peeled it back carefully. His eyes were sparkling like a boy thinking about his birthday, or Christmas, or the firecrackers he will shoot off on the Fourth of July.

"You took pictures of me?"

"Oh, you bet. I got this little camera. A Kodak. It's thin and flat and fits right into your hand. Once you get the hang of it, you can take pictures of the subject just by holding the camera in your hand and spreading your fingers enough to let the lens peek through. Then you hit the button with your thumb." Todd laughed modestly. "I got the hang of it, but I took a lot of pictures of my fingers while I did. I hung right in there, though. I think a person can do anything if they try hard enough, you know it? It's corny but true."

Kurt Dussander had begun to look white and ill, shrunken inside his robe. "Did you have these pictures finished by a commercial developer, boy?"

"Huh?" Todd looked shocked and startled, then contemptuous. "No! What do you think I am, stupid? My dad's got a darkroom. I've been developing my own pictures since I was nine."

Dussander said nothing, but he relaxed a little and some color came back into his face.

Todd handed him several glossy prints, the rough edges confirming that they had been home-developed. Dussander went through them, silently grim. Here he was sitting erect in a window seat of the downtown bus, with a copy of the latest James Michener, *Centennial,* in his hands. Here he was at the Devon Avenue bus stop, his umbrella under his arm and his head cocked back at an angle which suggested De Gaulle at his most imperial. Here he was standing on line just under the marquee of the Majestic Theater, erect and silent, conspicuous among the leaning teenagers and blank-faced housewives in curlers by his height and his bearing. Finally, here he was peering into his own mailbox.

"I was scared you might see me on that one," Todd said. "It was a calculated risk. I was right across the street. Boy oh boy, I wish I could afford a Minolta with a telephoto lens. Someday . . ." Todd looked wistful.

"No doubt you had a story ready, just in case."

"I was going to ask you if you'd seen my dog. Anyway, after I developed the pix, I compared them to these."

He handed Dussander three Xeroxed photographs. He had seen them all before, many times. The first showed him in his office at the Patin resettlement camp; it had been cropped so nothing showed but him and the Nazi flag on its stand by his desk. The second was a picture that had been taken on the day of his enlistment. The last showed him shaking hands with Heinrich Gluecks, who had been subordinate only to Himmler himself.

"I was pretty sure then, but I couldn't see if you had the harelip because of your goshdamn moustache. But I had to be sure, so I got this."

He handed over the last sheet from his envelope. It had been folded over many times. Dirt was grimed into the creases. The corners were lopped and milled—the way papers get when they spend a long time in the pockets of young boys who have no shortage of things to do and places to go. It was a copy of the Israeli want-sheet on Kurt Dussander. Holding it in his hands, Dussander reflected on corpses that were unquiet and refused to stay buried.

"I took your fingerprints," Todd said, smiling. "And then I did the compares to the one on the sheet."

Dussander gaped at him and then uttered the German word for shit. "You did not!"

"Sure I did. My mom and dad gave me a fingerprint set for Christmas last year. A real one, not just a toy. It had the powder and three brushes for three different surfaces and special paper for lifting them. My folks know I want to be a PI when I grow up. Of course, they think I'll grow out of it." He dismissed this idea with a disinterested lift and drop of his shoulders. "The book explained all about whorls and lands and points of similarity. They're called *compares*. You need eight compares for a fingerprint to get accepted in court.

"So anyway, one day when you were at the movies, I came here and dusted your mailbox and doorknob and lifted all the prints I could. Pretty smart, huh?"

Dussander said nothing. He was clutching the arms of his chair, and his toothless, deflated mouth was trembling. Todd didn't like that. It made him look like he was on the verge of tears. That, of course, was ridiculous. The Blood-Fiend of Patin in tears? You might as well expect Chevrolet to go bankrupt or McDonald's to give up burgers and start selling caviar and truffles.

"I got two sets of prints," Todd said. "One of them didn't look anything like the ones on the wanted poster. I figured those were the postman's. The rest were yours. I found more than eight compares. I found fourteen good ones." He grinned. "And that's how I did it."

"You are a little *bastard*," Dussander said, and for a moment his eyes shone dangerously. Todd felt a tingling little thrill, as he had in the hall. Then Dussander slumped back again.

"Whom have you told?"

"No one."

"Not even this friend? This Cony Pegler?"

"Foxy. Foxy Pegler. Nah, he's a blabbermouth. I haven't told anybody. There's nobody I trust that much."

"What do you want? Money? There is none, I'm afraid. In South America there was, although it was nothing as romantic or dangerous as the drug trade. There is—there *was*—a

19

kind of 'old boy network' in Brazil and Paraguay and Santo
Domingo. Fugitives from the war. I became part of their circle
and did modestly well in minerals and ores—tin, copper, baux-
ite. Then the changes came. Nationalism, anti-Americanism.
I might have ridden out the changes, but then Wiesenthal's
men caught my scent. Bad luck follows bad luck, boy, like
dogs after a bitch in heat. Twice they almost had me; once I
heard the Jew-bastards in the next room.

"They hanged Eichmann," he whispered. One hand went to
his neck, and his eyes had become as round as the eyes of a child
listening to the darkest passage of a scary tale—"Hansel and
Gretel," perhaps, or "Bluebeard." "He was an old man, of no
danger to anyone. He was apolitical. Still, they hanged him."

Todd nodded.

"At last, I went to the only people who could help me. They
had helped others, and I could run no more."

"You went to the Odessa?" Todd asked eagerly.

'To the Sicilians," Dussander said dryly, and Todd's face fell
again. "It was arranged. False papers, false past. Would you
care for a drink, boy?"

"Sure. You got a Coke?"

"No Coke." He pronounced it *Kök*.

"Milk?"

"Milk." Dussander went through the archway and into the
kitchen. A fluorescent bar buzzed into life. "I live now on
stock dividends," his voice came back. "Stocks I picked up
after the war under yet another name. Through a bank in the
State of Maine, if you please. The banker who bought them for
me went to jail for murdering his wife a year after I bought
them . . . life is sometimes strange, boy, *hein?*"

A refrigerator door opened and closed.

"The Sicilian jackals didn't know about those stocks," he
said. "Today the Sicilians are everywhere, but in those days,
Boston was as far north as they could be found. If they had
known, they would have had those as well. They would have

picked me clean and sent me to America to starve on welfare and food stamps."

Todd heard a cupboard door opened; he heard liquid poured into a glass.

"A little General Motors, a little American Telephone and Telegraph, a hundred and fifty shares of Revlon. All this banker's choices. Dufresne, his name was—I remember, because it sounds a little like mine. It seems he was not so smart at wife-killing as he was at picking growth stocks. The *crime passionel*, boy. It only proves that all men are donkeys who can read."

He came back into the room, slippers whispering. He held two green plastic glasses that looked like the premiums they sometimes gave out at gas station openings. When you filled your tank, you got a free glass. Dussander thrust a glass at Todd.

"I lived adequately on the stock portfolio this Dufresne had set up for me for the first five years I was here. But then I sold my Diamond Match stock in order to buy this house and a small cottage not far from Big Sur. Then, inflation. Recession. I sold the cottage and one by one I sold the stocks, many of them at fantastic profits. I wish to God I had bought more. But I thought I was well-protected in other directions; the stocks were, as you Americans say, a 'flier . . .'" He made a toothless hissing sound and snapped his fingers.

Todd was bored. He had not come here to listen to Dussander whine about his money or mutter about his stocks. The thought of blackmailing Dussander had never even crossed Todd's mind. Money? What would he do with it? He had his allowance; he had his paper route. If his monetary needs went higher than what these could provide during any given week, there was always someone who needed his lawn mowed.

Todd lifted his milk to his lips and then hesitated. His smile shone out again . . . an admiring smile. He extended the gas station premium glass to Dussander.

"*You* have some of it," he said slyly.

Dussander stared at him for a moment, uncomprehending, and then rolled his bloodshot eyes. *"Grüss Gott!"* He took the glass, swallowed twice, and handed it back. "No gasping for breath. No clawing at the t'roat. No smell of bitter almonds. It is milk, boy. *Milk.* From the Dairylea Farms. On the carton is a picture of a smiling cow."

Todd watched him warily for a moment, then took a small sip. Yes, it *tasted* like milk, sure did, but somehow he didn't feel very thirsty anymore. He put the glass down. Dussander shrugged, raised his own glass, and took a swallow. He smacked his lips over it.

"Schnaps?" Todd asked.

"Bourbon. Ancient Age. Very nice. And cheap."

Todd fiddled his fingers along the seams of his jeans.

"So," Dussander said, "if you have decided to have a 'flier' of your own, you should be aware that you have picked a worthless stock."

"Huh?"

"Blackmail," Dussander said. "Isn't that what they call it on *Mannix* and *Hawaii Five-0* and *Barnaby Jones?* Extortion. If that was what—"

But Todd was laughing—hearty, boyish laughter. He shook his head, tried to speak, could not, and went on laughing.

"No," Dussander said, and suddenly he looked gray and more frightened than he had since he and Todd had begun to speak. He took another large swallow of his drink, grimaced, and shuddered. "I see that is not it . . . at least, not the extortion of money. But, though you laugh, I smell extortion in it somewhere. What is it? Why do you come here and disturb an old man? Perhaps, as you say, I was once a Nazi. SS, even. Now I am only old, and to have a bowel movement I have to use a suppository. So what do you want?"

Todd had sobered again. He stared at Dussander with an open and appealing frankness. "Why . . . I want to hear about it. That's all. That's all I want. Really."

"*Hear* about it?" Dussander echoed. He looked utterly perplexed.

Todd leaned forward, tanned elbows on bluejeaned knees. "Sure. The firing squads. The gas chambers. The ovens. The guys who had to dig their own graves and then stand on the ends so they'd fall into them. The . . ." His tongue came out and wetted his lips. "The examinations. The experiments. Everything. All the gooshy stuff."

Dussander stared at him with a certain amazed detachment, the way a veterinarian might stare at a cat who was giving birth to a succession of two-headed kittens. "You are a monster," he said softly.

Todd sniffed. "According to the books I read for my report, *you're* the monster, Mr. Dussander. Not me. You sent them to the ovens, not me. Two thousand a day at Patin before you came, three thousand after, thirty-five hundred before the Russians came and made you stop. Himmler called you an efficiency expert and gave you a medal. So you call me a monster. Oh *boy*."

"All of that is a filthy American lie," Dussander said, stung. He set his glass down with a bang, slopping bourbon onto his hand and the table. "The problem was not of my making, nor was the solution. I was given orders and directives, which I followed."

Todd's smile widened; it was now almost a smirk.

"Oh, I know how the Americans have distorted that," Dussander muttered. "But your own politicians make our Dr. Goebbels look like a child playing with picture books in a kindergarten. They speak of morality while they douse screaming children and old women in burning napalm. Your draft-resisters are called cowards and 'peaceniks.' For refusing to follow orders they are either put in jails or scourged from the country. Those who demonstrate against this country's unfortunate Asian adventure are clubbed down in the streets. The GI soldiers who kill the innocent are decorated by

Presidents, welcomed home from the bayoneting of children and the burning of hospitals with parades and bunting. They are given dinners, Keys to the City, free tickets to pro football games." He toasted his glass in Todd's direction. "Only those who lose are tried as war criminals for following orders and directives." He drank and then had a coughing fit that brought thin color to his cheeks.

Through most of this Todd fidgeted the way he did when his parents discussed whatever had been on the news that night—good old Walter Klondike, his dad called him. He didn't care about Dussander's politics any more than he cared about Dussander's stocks. His idea was that people made up politics so they could do things. Like when he wanted to feel around under Sharon Ackerman's dress last year. Sharon said it was bad for him to want to do that, even though he could tell from her tone of voice that the idea sort of excited her. So he told her he wanted to be a doctor when he grew up and then she let him. That was politics. He wanted to hear about German doctors trying to mate women with dogs, putting identical twins into refrigerators to see whether they would die at the same time or if one of them would last longer, and electroshock therapy, and operations without anesthetic, and German soldiers raping all the women they wanted. The rest was just so much tired bullspit to cover up the gooshy stuff after someone came along and put a stop to it.

"If I hadn't followed orders, I would have been dead." Dussander was breathing hard, his upper body rocking back and forth in the chair, making the springs squeak. A little cloud of liquor-smell hung around him. "There was always the Russian front, *nicht wahr*? Our leaders were madmen, granted, but does one argue with madmen . . . especially when the maddest of them all has the luck of Satan. He escaped a brilliant assassination attempt by inches. Those who conspired were strangled with piano-wire, strangled slowly. Their death-agonies were filmed for the edification of the elite—"

"Yeah! Neat!" Todd cried impulsively. "Did you see that movie?"

"Yes. I saw. We all saw what happened to those unwilling or unable to run before the wind and wait for the storm to end. What we did then was the right thing. For that time and that place, it was the right thing. I would do it again. But . . ."

His eyes dropped to his glass. It was empty.

". . . but I don't wish to speak of it, or even think of it. What we did was motivated only by survival, and nothing about survival is pretty. I had dreams . . ." He slowly took a cigarette from the box on the TV. "Yes. For years I had them. Blackness, and sounds in the blackness. Tractor engines. Bulldozer engines. Gunbutts thudding against what might have been frozen earth, or human skulls. Whistles, sirens, pistol-shots, screams. The doors of cattle-cars rumbling open on cold winter afternoons.

"Then, in my dreams, all sounds would stop—and eyes would open in the dark, gleaming like the eyes of animals in a rainforest. For many years I lived on the edge of the jungle, and I suppose that is why it is always the jungle I smelled and felt in those dreams. When I woke from them I would be drenched with sweat, my heart thundering in my chest, my hand stuffed into my mouth to stifle the screams. And I would think: *The dream is the truth.* Brazil, Paraguay, Cuba . . . those places are the dream. In the reality I am still at Patin. The Russians are closer today than yesterday. Some of them are remembering that in 1943 they had to eat frozen German corpses to stay alive. Now they long to drink hot German blood. There were rumors, boy, that some of them did just that when they crossed into Germany: cut the t'roats of some prisoners and drank their blood out of a boot. I would wake up and think: *The work must go on, if only so there is no evidence of what we did here, or so little that the world, which doesn't want to believe it, won't have to.* I would think: *The work must go on if we are to survive.*"

Todd listened to this with close attention and great interest.

25

This was pretty good, but he was sure there would be better stuff in the days ahead. All Dussander needed was a little prodding. Heck, he was lucky. Lots of men his age were senile.

Dussander dragged deeply on his cigarette. "Later, after the dreams went away, there were days when I would think I had seen someone from Patin. Never guards or fellow officers, always inmates. I remember one afternoon in West Germany, ten years ago. There was an accident on the Autobahn. Traffic was frozen in every lane. I sat in my Morris, listening to the radio, waiting for the traffic to move. I looked to my right. There was a very old Simca in the next lane, and the man behind the wheel was looking at me. He was perhaps fifty, and he looked ill. There was a scar on his cheek. His hair was white, short, cut badly. I looked away. The minutes passed and still the traffic didn't move. I began snatching glances at the man in the Simca. Every time I did, he was looking at me, his face as still as death, his eyes sunken in their sockets. I became convinced he had been at Patin. He had been there and he had recognized me."

Dussander wiped a hand across his eyes.

"It was winter. The man was wearing an overcoat. But I was convinced that if I got out of my car and went to him, made him take off his coat and push up his shirtsleeves, I would see the number on his arm.

"At last the traffic began to move again. I pulled away from the Simca. If the jam had lasted another ten minutes, I believe I would have gotten out of my car and pulled the old man out of his. I would have beaten him, number or no number. I would have beaten him for looking at me that way.

"Shortly after that, I left Germany forever."

"Lucky for you," Todd said.

Dussander shrugged. "It was the same everywhere. Havana, Mexico City, Rome. I was in Rome for three years, you know. I would see a man looking at me over his *cappucino* in a café . . . a woman in a hotel lobby who seemed more interested in me than in her magazine . . . a waiter in a restaurant who would keep glancing at me no matter whom he was serving. I would become convinced that these people were studying me, and that night the dream would come—the sounds, the jungle, the eyes.

"But when I came to America I put it out of my mind. I go to movies. I eat out once a week, always at one of those fast-food places that are so clean and so well-lighted by fluorescent bars. Here at my house I do jigsaw puzzles and I read novels—most of them bad ones—and watch TV. At night I drink until I'm sleepy. The dreams don't come anymore. When I see someone looking at me in the supermarket or the library or the tobacconist's, I think it must be because I look like their grandfather . . . or an old teacher . . . or a neighbor in a town they left some years ago." He shook his head at Todd. "Whatever happened at Patin, it happened to another man. Not to me."

"Great!" Todd said. "I want to hear all about it."

Dussander's eyes squeezed closed, and then opened slowly. "You don't understand. I do not wish to speak of it."

"You will, though. If you don't, I'll tell everyone who you are."

Dussander stared at him, gray-faced. "I knew," he said, "that I would find the extortion sooner or later."

"Today I want to hear about the gas ovens," Todd said. "How you baked them after they were dead." His smile beamed out, rich and radiant. "But put your teeth in before you start. You look better with your teeth in."

Dussander did as he was told. He talked to Todd about the gas ovens until Todd had to go home for lunch. Every time he tried to slip over into generalities, Todd would frown severely and ask him specific questions to get him back on the track. Dussander drank a great deal as he talked. He didn't smile. Todd smiled. Todd smiled enough for both of them.

2

August, 1974.

They sat on Dussander's back porch under a cloudless, smiling sky. Todd was wearing jeans, Keds, and his Little League shirt. Dussander was wearing a baggy gray shirt and shapeless khaki pants held up with suspenders—wino-pants, Todd thought with private contempt; they looked like they had come straight from a box in the back of the Salvation Army store downtown. He was really going to have to do something about the way Dussander dressed when he was at home. It spoiled some of the fun.

The two of them were eating Big Macs that Todd had brought in his bike-basket, pedaling fast so they wouldn't get cold. Todd was sipping a Coke through a plastic straw. Dussander had a glass of bourbon.

His old man's voice rose and fell, papery, hesitant, sometimes nearly inaudible. His faded blue eyes, threaded with the usual snaps of red, were never still. An observer might have thought them grandfather and grandson, the latter perhaps attending some rite of passage, a handing down.

"And that's all I remember," Dussander finished presently, and took a large bite of his sandwich. McDonald's Secret Sauce dribbled down his chin.

"You can do better than that," Todd said softly.

Dussander took a large swallow from his glass. "The uniforms were made of paper," he said finally, almost snarling. "When one inmate died, the uniform was passed on if it could still be worn. Sometimes one paper uniform could dress as many as forty inmates. I received high marks for my frugality."

"From Gluecks?"

"From Himmler."

"But there was a clothing factory in Patin. You told me that

28

just last week. Why didn't you have the uniforms made there? The inmates themselves could have made them."

"The job of the factory in Patin was to make uniforms for German soldiers. And as for us . . ." Dussander's voice faltered for a moment, and then he forced himself to go on. "We were not in the business of rehabilitation," he finished.

Todd smiled his broad smile.

"Enough for today? Please? My throat is sore."

"You shouldn't smoke so much, then," Todd said, continuing to smile. "Tell me some more about the uniforms."

"Which? Inmate or SS?" Dussander's voice was resigned.

Smiling, Todd said: "Both."

3

September, 1974.

Todd was in the kitchen of his house, making himself a peanut butter and jelly sandwich. You got to the kitchen by going up half a dozen redwood steps to a raised area that gleamed with chrome and stainless steel. His mother's electric typewriter had been going steadily ever since Todd had gotten home from school. She was typing a master's thesis for a grad student. The grad student had short hair, wore thick glasses, and looked like a creature from outer space, in Todd's humble opinion. The thesis was on the effect of fruit-flies in the Salinas Valley after World War II, or some good shit like that. Now her typewriter stopped and she came out of her office.

"Todd-baby," she greeted him.

"Monica-baby," he hailed back, amiably enough.

His mother wasn't a bad-looking chick for thirty-six, Todd thought; blonde hair that was streaked ash in a couple of places, tall, shapely, now dressed in dark red shorts and a sheer blouse of a warm whiskey color—the blouse was casually knotted below her breasts, putting her flat, unlined midriff on show. A typewriter eraser was tucked into her hair, which had been pinned carelessly back with a turquoise clip.

"So how's school?" she asked him, coming up the steps into the kitchen. She brushed his lips casually with hers and then slid onto one of the stools in front of the breakfast counter.

"School's cool."

"Going to be on the honor roll again?"

"Sure." Actually, he thought his grades might slip a notch this first quarter. He had been spending a lot of time with Dussander, and when he wasn't actually with the old kraut, he was thinking about the things Dussander had told him. Once or twice he had dreamed about the things Dussander had told him. But it was nothing he couldn't handle.

"Apt pupil," she said, ruffling his shaggy blonde hair. "How's that sandwich?"

"Good," he said.

"Would you make me one and bring it into my office?"

"Can't," he said, getting up. "I promised Mr. Denker I'd come over and read to him for an hour or so."

"Are you still on *Robinson Crusoe?*"

"Nope." He showed her the spine of a thick book he had bought in a junkshop for twenty cents. *"Tom Jones."*

"Ye gods and little fishes! It'll take you the whole school-year to get through that, Toddy-baby. Couldn't you at least find an abridged edition, like with *Crusoe!*"

"Probably, but he wanted to hear all of this one. He said so."

"Oh." She looked at him for a moment, then hugged him. It was rare for her to be so demonstrative, and it made Todd a little uneasy. "You're a peach to be taking so much of your spare time to read to him. Your father and I think it's just . . . just exceptional."

Todd cast his eyes down modestly.

"And to not want to tell anybody," she said. "Hiding your light under a bushel."

"Oh, the kids I hang around with—they'd probably think I was some kind of weirdo," Todd said, smiling modestly down at the floor. "All that good shit."

"Don't say that," she admonished absently. Then: "Do you think Mr. Denker would like to come over and have dinner with us some night?"

"Maybe," Todd said vaguely. "Listen, I gotta put an egg in my shoe and beat it."

"Okay. Supper at six-thirty. Don't forget."

"I won't."

"Your father's got to work late so it'll just be me and thee again, okay?"

"Crazy, baby."

She watched him go with a fond smile, hoping there was nothing in *Tom Jones* he shouldn't be reading; he was only thirteen. She didn't suppose there was. He was growing up in a society where magazines like *Penthouse* were available to anyone with a dollar and a quarter, or to any kid who could reach up to the top shelf of the magazine rack and grab a quick peek before the clerk could shout for him to put that up and get lost. In a society that seemed to believe most of all in the creed of hump thy neighbor, she didn't think there could be much in a book two hundred years old to screw up Todd's head—although she supposed the old man might get off on it a little. And as Richard liked to say, for a kid the whole world's a laboratory. You have to let them poke around in it. And if the kid in question has a healthy home life and loving parents, he'll be all the stronger for having knocked around a few strange corners.

And there went the healthiest kid she knew, pedaling up the street on his Schwinn. *We did okay by the lad,* she thought, turning to make her sandwich. *Damned if we didn't do okay.*

4

October, 1974.

Dussander had lost weight. They sat in the kitchen, the shopworn copy of *Tom Jones* between them on the oilcloth-covered table (Todd, who tried never to miss a trick, had purchased the Cliff's Notes on the book with part of his allowance and had carefully read the entire summary against the possibility that his mother or father might ask him questions about the plot). Todd was eating a Ring Ding he had bought at the market. He had bought one for Dussander, but Dussander hadn't touched it. He only looked at it morosely from time to time as he drank his bourbon. Todd hated to see anything as tasty as Ring Dings go to waste. If he didn't eat it pretty quick, Todd was going to ask him if he could have it.

"So how did the stuff get to Patin?" he asked Dussander.

"In railroad cars," Dussander said. "In railroad cars labelled medical supplies. It came in long crates that looked like coffins. Fitting, I suppose. The inmates off-loaded the crates and stacked them in the infirmary. Later, our own men stacked them in the storage sheds. They did it at night. The storage sheds were behind the showers."

"Was it always Zyklon-B?"

"No, from time to time we would be sent something else. Experimental gases. The High Command was always interested in improving efficiency. Once they sent us a gas code-named PEGASUS. A nerve-gas. Thank God they never sent it again. It—" Dussander saw Todd lean forward, saw those eyes sharpen, and he suddenly stopped and gestured casually with his gas station premium glass. "It didn't work very well," he said. "It was . . . quite boring."

But Todd was not fooled, not in the least. "What did it do?"

"It killed them—what did you think it did, made them walk on water? It killed them, that's all."

'Tell me."

"No," Dussander said, now unable to hide the horror he felt. He hadn't thought of PEGASUS in . . . how long? Ten years? Twenty? "I won't tell you! I refuse!"

"Tell me," Todd repeated, licking chocolate icing from his fingers. "Tell me or you know what."

Yes, Dussander thought. *I know what. Indeed I do, you putrid little monster.*

"It made them dance," he said reluctantly.

"Dance?"

"Like the Zyklon-B, it came in through the shower-heads. And they . . . they began to leap about. Some were screaming. Most of them were laughing. They began to vomit, and to . . . to defecate helplessly."

"Wow," Todd said. "Shit themselves, huh?" He pointed at the Ring Ding on Dussander's plate. He had finished his own. "You going to eat that?"

Dussander didn't reply. His eyes were hazed with memory. His face was far away and cold, like the dark side of a planet which does not rotate. Inside his mind he felt the *queerest* combination of revulsion and—could it be?—*nostalgia?*

"They began to twitch all over and to make high, strange sounds in their throats. My men . . . they called PEGASUS the Yodeling Gas. At last they all collapsed and just lay there on the floor in their own filth, they lay there, yes, they lay there on the concrete, screaming and yodeling, with bloody noses. But I lied, boy. The gas didn't kill them, either because it wasn't strong enough or because we couldn't bring ourselves to wait long enough. I suppose it was that. Men and women like that could not have lived long. Finally I sent in five men with rifles to end their agonies. It would have looked bad on my record if it had shown up, I've no doubt of that—it would have looked like a waste of cartridges at a time when the Fuehrer had declared every cartridge a national resource. But those five men I trusted. There were times, boy, when I thought I would never forget the sound they made. The yodeling sound. The laughing."

"Yeah, I bet," Todd said. He finished Dussander's Ring Ding in two bites. Waste not, want not, Todd's mother said on the rare occasions when Todd complained about left-overs. "That was a good story, Mr. Dussander. You always tell them good. Once I get you going."

Todd smiled at him. And incredibly—certainly not because he wanted to—Dussander found himself smiling back.

5

November, 1974.

Dick Bowden, Todd's father, looked remarkably like a movie and TV actor named Lloyd Bochner. He—Bowden, not Bochner—was thirty-eight. He was a thin, narrow man who liked to dress in Ivy League–style shirts and solid-color suits, usually dark. When he was on a construction site, he wore khakis and a hard-hat that was a souvenir of his Peace Corps days, when he had helped to design and build two dams in Africa. When he was working in his study at home, he wore half-glasses that had a way of slipping down to the end of his nose and making him look like a college dean. He was wearing these glasses now as he tapped his son's first-quarter report card against his desk's gleaming glass top.

"One B. Four C's. One D. A *D*, for Christ's sake! Todd, your mother's not showing it, but she's really upset."

Todd dropped his eyes. He didn't smile. When his dad swore, that wasn't exactly the best of news.

"My God, you've *never* gotten a report like this. A *D* in Beginning Algebra? What *is* this?"

"I don't know, Dad." He looked humbly at his knees.

"Your mother and I think that maybe you've been spending a little too much time with Mr. Denker. Not hitting the books enough. We think you ought to cut it down to weekends, slugger. At least until we see where you're going academically . . ."

Todd looked up, and for a single second Bowden thought he saw a wild, pallid anger in his son's eyes. His own eyes widened, his fingers clenched on Todd's buff-colored report card . . . and then it was just Todd, looking at him openly if rather unhappily. Had that anger really been there? Surely not. But the moment had unsettled him, made it hard for him to know exactly how to proceed. Todd hadn't been mad, and Dick Bowden didn't want to *make* him mad. He and his son were friends, always had been friends, and Dick wanted things to stay that way. They had no secrets from each other, none at all (except for the fact that Dick Bowden was sometimes unfaithful with his secretary, but that wasn't exactly the sort of thing you told your thirteen-year-old son, was it? . . . and besides, that had absolutely no bearing on his home life, his *family* life). That was the way it was supposed to be, the way it *had* to be in a cockamamie world where murderers went unpunished, high school kids skin-popped heroin, and junior high schoolers—kids Todd's age—turned up with VD.

"No, Dad, please don't do that. I mean, don't punish Mr. Denker for something that's my fault. I mean, he'd be lost without me. I'll do better. Really. That algebra . . . it just threw me to start with. But I went over to Ben Tremaine's, and after we studied together for a few days, I started to get it. I just . . . I dunno, I sorta choked at first."

"I think you're spending too much time with him," Bowden said, but he was weakening. It was hard to refuse Todd, hard to disappoint him, and what he said about punishing the old man for Todd's falling-off . . . goddammit, it made sense. The old man looked forward to his visits so much.

"That Mr. Storrman, the algebra teacher, is really hard," Todd said. "Lots of kids got D's. Three or four got F's."

Bowden nodded thoughtfully.

"I won't go Wednesdays anymore. Not until I bring my

grades up." He had read his father's eyes. "And instead of going out for anything at school, I'll stay after every day and study. I promise."

"You really like the old guy that much?"

"He's really neat," Todd said sincerely.

"Well . . . okay. We'll try it your way, slugger. But I want to see a big improvement in your marks come January, you understand me? I'm thinking of your future. You may think junior high's too soon to start thinking about that, but it's not. Not by a long chalk." As his mother liked to say *Waste not, want not,* so Dick Bowden liked to say *Not by a long chalk.*

"I understand, Dad," Todd said gravely. Man-to-man stuff.

"Get out of here and give those books a workout then." He pushed his half-glasses up on his nose and clapped Todd on the shoulder.

Todd's smile, broad and bright, broke across his face. "Right on, Dad!"

Bowden watched Todd go with a prideful smile of his own. One in a million. And that hadn't been anger on Todd's face. For sure. Pique, maybe . . . but not that high-voltage emotion he had at first thought he'd seen there. If Todd was that mad, he would have known; he could read his son like a book. It had always been that way.

Whistling, his fatherly duty discharged, Dick Bowden unrolled a blueprint and bent over it.

6

December, 1974.

The face that came in answer to Todd's insistent finger on the bell was haggard and yellowed. The hair, which had been lush in July, had now begun to recede from the bony brow; it looked lusterless and brittle. Dussander's body, thin to begin with, was now gaunt . . . although, Todd thought, he was nowhere near as gaunt as the inmates who had once been delivered into his hands.

Todd's left hand had been behind his back when Dussander came to the door. Now he brought it out and handed a wrapped package to Dussander. "Merry Christmas!" he yelled.

Dussander had cringed from the box; now he took it with no expression of pleasure or surprise. He handled it gingerly, as if it might contain explosive. Beyond the porch, it was raining. It had been raining off and on for almost a week, and Todd had carried the box inside his coat. It was wrapped in gay foil and ribbon.

"What is it?" Dussander asked without enthusiasm as they went to the kitchen.

"Open it and see."

Todd took a can of Coke from his jacket pocket and put it on the red and white checked oilcloth that covered the kitchen table. "Better pull down the shades," he said confidentially.

Distrust immediately leaked onto Dussander's face. "Oh? Why?"

"Well . . . you can never tell who's lookin," Todd said, smiling. "Isn't that how you got along all those years? By seeing the people who might be lookin before they saw you?"

Dussander pulled down the kitchen shades. Then he poured himself a glass of bourbon. Then he pulled the bow off the package. Todd had wrapped it the way boys so often wrap Christmas packages—boys who have more important things on their minds, things like football and street hockey and the Friday Nite Creature Feature you'll watch with a friend who's sleeping over, the two of you wrapped in a blanket and crammed together on one end of the couch, laughing. There were a lot of ragged corners, a lot of uneven seams, a lot of Scotch tape. It spoke of impatience with such a womanly thing.

Dussander was a little touched in spite of himself. And later, when the horror had receded a little, he thought: *I should have known.*

It was a uniform. An SS uniform. Complete with jackboots.

He looked numbly from the contents of the box to its cardboard cover: PETER'S QUALITY COSTUME CLOTHIERS—AT THE SAME LOCATION SINCE 1951!

"No," he said softly. "I won't put it on. This is where it ends, boy. I'll die before I put it on."

"Remember what they did to Eichmann," Todd said solemnly. "He was an old man and he had no politics. Isn't that what you said? Besides, I saved the whole fall for it. It cost over eighty bucks, with the boots thrown in. You didn't mind wearing it in 1944, either. Not at all."

"You little *bastard*!" Dussander raised one fist over his head. Todd didn't flinch at all. He stood his ground, eyes shining.

"Yeah," he said softly. "Go ahead and touch me. You just touch me *once*."

Dussander lowered the hand. His lips were quivering. "You are a fiend from hell," he muttered.

"Put it on," Todd invited.

Dussander's hands went to the tie of his robe and paused there. His eyes, sheeplike and begging, looked into Todd's. "Please," he said. "I am an old man. No more."

Todd shook his head slowly but firmly. His eyes were still shining. He liked it when Dussander begged. The way they must have begged him once. The inmates at Patin.

Dussander let the robe fall to the floor and stood naked except for his slippers and his boxer shorts. His chest was sunken, his belly slightly bloated. His arms were scrawny old man's arms. But the uniform, Todd thought. The uniform will make a difference.

Slowly, Dussander took the tunic out of the box and began to put it on.

Ten minutes later he stood fully dressed in the SS uniform. The cap was slightly askew, the shoulders slumped, but still the death's-head insignia stood out clearly. Dussander had a

dark dignity—at least in Todd's eyes—that he had not possessed earlier. In spite of his slump, in spite of the cockeyed
angle of his feet, Todd was pleased. For the first time Dussander looked to Todd as Todd believed he should look. Older,
yes. Defeated, certainly. But in uniform again. Not an old man
spinning away his sunset years watching Lawrence Welk on a
cruddy black and white TV with tinfoil on the rabbit ears, but
Kurt Dussander, The Blood-Fiend of Patin.

As for Dussander, he felt disgust, discomfort . . . and a mild,
sneaking sense of relief. He partly despised this latter emotion,
recognizing it as the truest indicator yet of the psychological domination the boy had established over him. He was the
boy's prisoner, and every time he found he could live through
yet another indignity, every time he felt that mild relief, the
boy's power grew. And yet he *was* relieved. It was only cloth
and buttons and snaps . . . and it was a sham at that. The fly
was a zipper; it should have been buttons. The marks of rank
were wrong, the tailoring sloppy, the boots a cheap grade of
imitation leather. It was only a trumpery uniform after all, and
it wasn't exactly *killing* him, was it? No. It—

"Straighten your cap!" Todd said loudly.

Dussander blinked at him, startled.

"Straighten your cap, soldier!"

Dussander did so, unconsciously giving it that final small
insolent twist that had been the trademark of his *Oberleut-
nants*—and, sadly wrong as it was, this was an *Oberleutnant's*
uniform.

"Get those feet together!"

He did so, bringing the heels together with a smart rap,
doing the correct thing with hardly a thought, doing it as if
the intervening years had slipped off along with his bathrobe.

"Achtung!"

He snapped to attention, and for a moment Todd was
scared—really scared. He felt like the sorcerer's apprentice,
who had brought the brooms to life but who had not possessed

enough wit to stop them once they got started. The old man living in genteel poverty was gone. Dussander was here.

Then his fear was replaced by a tingling sense of power.

"*About face!*"

Dussander pivoted neatly, the bourbon forgotten, the torment of the last four months forgotten. He heard his heels click together again as he faced the grease-splattered stove. Beyond it, he could see the dusty parade ground of the military academy where he had learned his soldier's trade.

"*About face!*"

He whirled again, this time not executing the order as well, losing his balance a little. Once it would have been ten demerits and the butt of a swagger stick in his belly, sending his breath out in a hot and agonized gust. Inwardly he smiled a little. The boy didn't know all the tricks. No indeed.

"Now *march!*" Todd cried. His eyes were hot, glowing.

The iron went out of Dussander's shoulders; he slumped forward again. "No," he said. "Please—"

"*March! March! March, I said!*"

With a strangled sound, Dussander began to goose-step across the faded linoleum of his kitchen floor. He right-faced to avoid the table, right-faced again as he approached the wall. His face was uptilted slightly, expressionless. His legs rammed out before him, then crashed down, making the cheap china rattle in the cabinet over the sink. His arms moved in short arcs.

The image of the walking brooms recurred to Todd, and his fright recurred with it. It suddenly struck him that he didn't want Dussander to be enjoying any part of this, and that perhaps—just perhaps—he had wanted to make Dussander appear ludicrous even more than he had wanted to make him appear authentic. But somehow, despite the man's age and the cheap dime-store furnishings of the kitchen, he didn't look ludicrous in the least. He looked frightening. For the first time the corpses in the ditches and the crematoriums seemed to take on their own reality for Todd. The photographs of the tangled arms and legs and torsos, fishbelly white in the cold spring rains of Germany, were not something staged like a scene in a horror film—a pile of bodies created from department-store dummies, say, to be picked up by the grips and propmen when the scene was done—but simply a real fact, stupendous and inexplicable and evil. For a moment it seemed to him that he could smell the bland and slightly smoky odor of decomposition.

Terror gathered him in.

"Stop!" he shouted.

Dussander continued to goose-step, his eyes blank and far away. His head had come up even more, pulling the scrawny chicken-tendons of his throat tight, tilting his chin at an arrogant angle. His nose, blade-thin, jutted obscenely.

Todd felt sweat in his armpits. *"Halt!"* he cried out.

Dussander halted, right foot forward, left coming up and then down beside the right with a single pistonlike stamp. For a moment the cold lack of expression held on his face— robotic, mindless—and then it was replaced by confusion. Confusion was followed by defeat. He slumped.

Todd let out a silent breath of relief and for a moment he was furious with himself. *Who's in charge here, anyway?* Then his self-confidence flooded back in. *I am, that's who. And he better not forget it.*

He began to smile again. "Pretty good. But with a little practice, I think you'll be a lot better."

Dussander stood mute, panting, his head hanging.

"You can take it off now," Todd added generously . . . and couldn't help wondering if he really wanted Dussander to put it on again. For a few seconds there—

7

January, 1975.

Todd left school by himself after the last bell, got his bike,

41

and pedaled down to the park. He found a deserted bench, set his Schwinn up on its kickstand, and took his report card out of his hip pocket. He took a look around to see if there was anyone in the area he knew, but the only other people in sight were two high school kids making out by the pond and a pair of gross-looking winos passing a paper bag back and forth. Dirty fucking winos, he thought, but it wasn't the winos that had upset him. He opened his card.

English: C. American History: C. Earth Science: D. Your Community and You: B. Primary French: F. Beginning Algebra: F.

He stared at the grades, unbelieving. He had known it was going to be bad, but this was disaster.

Maybe that's best, an inner voice spoke up suddenly. *Maybe you even did it on purpose, because a part of you wants it to end. Needs for it to end. Before something bad happens.*

He shoved the thought roughly aside. Nothing bad was going to happen. Dussander was under his thumb. Totally under his thumb. The old man thought one of Todd's friends had a letter, but he didn't know which friend. If anything happened to Todd—*anything*—that letter would go to the police. Once he supposed Dussander might have tried it anyway. Now he was too old to run, even with a head start.

"He's under control, dammit," Todd whispered, and then pounded his thigh hard enough to make the muscle knot. Talking to yourself was bad shit—crazy people talked to themselves. He had picked up the habit over the last six weeks or so, and didn't seem able to break it. He'd caught several people looking at him strangely because of it. A couple of them had been teachers. And that asshole Bernie Everson had come right out and asked him if he was going fruitcrackers. Todd had come very, very close to punching the little pansy in the mouth, and that sort of stuff—brawls, scuffles, punch-outs— was no good. That sort of stuff got you noticed in all the wrong ways. Talking to yourself was bad, right, okay, but—

"The dreams are bad, too," he whispered. He didn't catch himself that time.

Just lately the dreams had been very bad. In the dreams he was always in uniform, although the type varied. Sometimes it was a paper uniform and he was standing in line with hundreds of gaunt men; the smell of burning was in the air and he could hear the choppy roar of bulldozer engines. Then Dussander would come up the line, pointing out this one or that one. They were left. The others were marched away toward the crematoriums. Some of them kicked and struggled, but most were too undernourished, too exhausted. Then Dussander was standing in front of Todd. Their eyes met for a long, paralyzing moment, and then Dussander levelled a faded umbrella at Todd.

"Take this one to the laboratories," Dussander said in the dream. His lip curled back to reveal his false teeth. "Take this American *boy*."

In another dream he wore an SS uniform. His jackboots were shined to a mirrorlike reflecting surface. The death's-head insignia and the lightning-bolts glittered. But he was standing in the middle of Santo Donato Boulevard and everyone was looking at him. They began to point. Some of them began to laugh. Others looked shocked, angry, or revolted. In this dream an old car came to a squalling, creaky halt and Dussander peered out at him, a Dussander who looked two hundred years old and nearly mummified, his skin a yellowed scroll.

"I know you!" the dream-Dussander proclaimed shrilly. He looked around at the spectators and then back to Todd. "You were in charge at Patin! Look, everybody! This is The Blood-Fiend of Patin! Himmler's 'Efficiency Expert'! I denounce you, murderer! I denounce you, butcher! I denounce you, killer of infants! I denounce you!"

In yet another dream he wore a striped convict's uniform and was being led down a stone-walled corridor by two guards who looked like his parents. Both wore conspicuous yellow armbands with the Star of David on them. Walking behind them was a minister, reading from the Book of Deuteronomy. Todd looked back over his shoulder and saw that the minister was Dussander, and he was wearing the black tunic of an SS officer.

At the end of the stone corridor, double doors opened on an octagonal room with glass walls. There was a scaffold in the center of it. Behind the glass walls stood ranks of emaciated men and women, all naked, all watching with the same dark, flat expression. On each arm was a blue number.

"It's all right," Todd whispered to himself. "It's okay, really, everything's under control."

The couple that had been making out glanced over at him. Todd stared at them fiercely, daring them to say anything. At last they looked back the other way. Had the boy been grinning?

Todd got up, jammed his report card into his hip pocket, and mounted his bike. He pedaled down to a drugstore two blocks away. There he bought a bottle of ink eradicator and a fine-point pen that dispensed blue ink. He went back to the park (the make-out couple was gone, but the winos were still there, stinking the place up) and changed his English grade to a B, American History to A, Earth Science to B, Primary French to C, and Beginning Algebra to B. Your Community and You he eradicated and then simply wrote in again, so the card would have a uniform look.

Uniforms, right.

"Never mind," he whispered to himself. "That'll hold them. That'll hold them, all right."

One night late in the month, sometime after two o'clock, Kurt Dussander awoke struggling with the bedclothes, gasping and moaning, into a darkness that seemed close and terrifying. He felt half-suffocated, paralyzed with fear. It was as if a heavy stone lay on his chest, and he wondered if he could be having a heart attack. He clawed in the darkness for the bedside lamp and almost knocked it off the nightstand turning it on.

I'm in my own room, he thought, my own bedroom, here in Santo Donato, here in California, here in America. See, the same brown drapes pulled across the same window, the same bookshelves filled with dime paperbacks from the bookshop on Soren Street, same gray rug, same blue wallpaper. No heart attack. No jungle. No eyes.

But the terror still clung to him like a stinking pelt, and his heart went on racing. The dream had come back. He had known that it would, sooner or later, if the boy kept on. The cursed boy. He thought the boy's letter of protection was only a bluff, and not a very good one at that; something he had picked up from the TV detective programs. What friend would the boy trust not to open such a momentous letter? No friend, that was who. Or so he thought. If he could be *sure*—

His hands closed with an arthritic, painful snap and then opened slowly.

He took the packet of cigarettes from the table and lit one, scratching the wooden match on the bedpost. The clock's hands stood at 2:41. There would be no more sleep for him this night. He inhaled smoke and then coughed it out in a series of racking spasms. No more sleep unless he wanted to go downstairs and have a drink or two. Or three. And there had been altogether too much drinking over the last six weeks or so. He was no longer a young man who could toss them off one after the other, the way he had when he had been an officer on leave in Berlin in '39, when the scent of victory had been in the air and everywhere you heard the Fuehrer's voice, saw his blazing, commanding eyes—

The boy . . . the cursed boy!

"Be honest," he said aloud, and the sound of his own voice in the quiet room made him jump a little. He was not in the habit of talking to himself, but neither was it the first time he had ever done so. He remembered doing it off and on during the last few weeks at Patin, when everything had come down around their ears and in the east the sound of Russian thunder grew louder first every day and then every hour. It had been natural enough to talk to himself then. He had been under stress, and people under stress often do strange things—cup their testicles through the pockets of their pants, click their teeth together . . . Wolff had been a great teeth-clicker. He grinned as he did it. Huffmann had been a finger-snapper and a thigh-patter, creating fast, intricate rhythms that he seemed utterly unaware of. He, Kurt Dussander, had sometimes talked to himself. But now—

"You are under stress again," he said aloud. He was aware that he had spoken in German this time. He hadn't spoken German in many years, but the language now seemed warm and comfortable. It lulled him, eased him. It was sweet and dark.

"Yes. You are under stress. Because of the boy. But be honest with yourself. It is too early in the morning to tell lies. You have not entirely regretted talking. At first you were terrified that the boy could not or would not keep his secret. He would have to tell a friend, who would tell another friend, and that friend would tell two. But if he has kept it this long, he will keep it longer. If I am taken away, he loses his . . . his talking book. Is that what I am to him? I think so."

He fell silent, but his thoughts went on. He had been lonely—no one would ever know just how lonely. There had been times when he thought almost seriously of suicide. He made a bad hermit. The voices he heard came from the radio. The only people who visited were on the other side of a dirty glass square. He was an old man, and although he was afraid of death, he was more afraid of being an old man who is alone.

His bladder sometimes tricked him. He would be halfway to the bathroom when a dark stain spread on his pants. In wet weather his joints would first throb and then begin to cry out, and there had been days when he had chewed an entire tin of Arthritis Pain Formula between sunrise and sunset . . . and still the aspirin only subdued the aches. Even such acts as taking a book from the shelf or switching the TV channel became an essay in pain. His eyes were bad; sometimes he knocked things over, barked his shins, bumped his head. He lived in fear of breaking a bone and not being able to get to the telephone, and he lived in fear of getting there and having some doctor uncover his real past as he became suspicious of Mr. Denker's nonexistent medical history.

The boy had alleviated some of those things. When the boy was here, he could call back the old days. His memory of those days was perversely clear; he spilled out a seemingly endless catalogue of names and events, even the weather of such and such a day. He remembered Private Henreid, who manned a machine-gun in the northeast tower and the wen Private Henreid had had between his eyes. Some of the men called him Three-Eyes, or Old Cyclops. He remembered Kessel, who had a picture of his girlfriend naked, lying on a sofa with her hands behind her head. Kessel charged the men to look at it. He remembered the names of the doctors and their experiments— thresholds of pain, the brainwaves of dying men and women, physiological retardation, effects of different sorts of radiation, dozens more. *Hundreds* more.

He supposed he talked to the boy as all old men talk, but he guessed he was luckier than most old men, who had impatience, disinterest, or outright rudeness for an audience. *His* audience was endlessly fascinated.

Were a few bad dreams too high a price to pay?

He crushed out his cigarette, lay looking at the ceiling for a moment, and then swung his feet out onto the floor. He and the boy were loathsome, he supposed, feeding off each other . . . eating each other. If his own belly was sometimes sour with the dark but rich food they partook of in his afternoon kitchen, what was the boy's like? Did he sleep well? Perhaps not. Lately Dussander thought the boy looked rather pale, and thinner than when he had first come into Dussander's life.

He walked across the bedroom and opened the closet door.

He brushed hangers to the right, reached into the shadows, and brought out the sham uniform. It hung from his hand like a vulture-skin. He touched it with his other hand. Touched it . . . and then stroked it.

After a very long time he took it down and put it on, dressing slowly, not looking into the mirror until the uniform was completely buttoned and belted (and the sham fly zipped).

He looked at himself in the mirror, then, and nodded.

He went back to bed, lay down, and smoked another cigarette. When it was finished, he felt sleepy again. He turned off the bedlamp, not believing it, that it could be this easy. But he was asleep, five minutes later, and this time his sleep was dreamless.

8

February, 1975.

After dinner, Dick Bowden produced a cognac that Dussander privately thought dreadful. But of course he smiled broadly and complimented it extravagantly. Bowden's wife served the boy a chocolate malted. The boy had been unusually quiet all through the meal. Uneasy? Yes. For some reason the boy seemed very uneasy.

Dussander had charmed Dick and Monica Bowden from the moment he and the boy had arrived. The boy had told his parents that Mr. Denker's vision was much worse than it actually was (which made poor old Mr. Denker in need of a Seeing Eye Dog, Dussander thought dryly), because that explained all the reading the boy had supposedly been doing. Dussander had been very careful about that, and he thought there had been no slips.

He was dressed in his best suit, and although the evening was damp, his arthritis had been remarkably mellow—nothing but an occasional twinge. For some absurd reason the boy had wanted him to leave his umbrella home, but Dussander had insisted. All in all, he had had a pleasant and rather exciting evening. Dreadful cognac or no, he had not been out to dinner in nine years.

During the meal he had discussed the Essen Motor Works, the rebuilding of postwar Germany—Bowden had asked several intelligent questions about that, and had seemed impressed by Dussander's answers—and German writers. Monica Bowden had asked him how he had happened to come to America so late in life and Dussander, adopting the proper expression of myopic sorrow, had explained about the death of his fictitious wife. Monica Bowden was meltingly sympathetic.

And now, over the absurd cognac, Dick Bowden said: "If this is too personal, Mr. Denker, please don't answer . . . but I couldn't help wondering what you did in the war."

The boy stiffened ever so slightly.

Dussander smiled and felt for his cigarettes. He could see them perfectly well, but it was important to make not the tiniest slip. Monica put them in his hand.

"Thank you, dear lady. The meal was superb. You are a fine cook. My own wife never did better."

Monica thanked him and looked flustered. Todd gave her an irritated look.

"Not personal at all," Dussander said, lighting his cigarette and turning to Bowden. "I was in the reserves from 1943 on, as were all able-bodied men too old to be in the active services. By then the handwriting was on the wall for the Third Reich, and for the madmen who created it. One madman in particular, of course."

He blew out his match and looked solemn.

"There was great relief when the tide turned against Hitler. Great relief. Of course," and here he looked at Bowden disarmingly, as man to man, "one was careful not to express such a sentiment. Not aloud."

"I suppose not," Dick Bowden said respectfully.

"No," Dussander said gravely. "Not aloud. I remember one evening when four or five of us, all friends, stopped at a local *Ratskeller* after work for a drink—by then there was not always *Schnaps,* or even beer, but it so happened that night there were both. We had all known each other for upwards of twenty years. One of our number, Hans Hassler, mentioned in passing that perhaps the Fuehrer had been ill-advised to open a second front against the Russians. I said, 'Hans, God in Heaven, watch what you say!' Poor Hans went pale and changed the subject entirely. Yet three days later he was gone. I never saw him again, nor, as far as I know, did anyone else who was sitting at our table that night."

"How awful!" Monica said breathlessly. "More cognac, Mr. Denker?"

"No thank you." He smiled at her. "My wife had a saying from her mother: 'One must never overdo the sublime.'"

Todd's small, troubled frown deepened slightly.

"Do you think he was sent to one of the camps?" Dick asked. "Your friend Hessler?"

"*Hassler,*" Dussander corrected gently. He grew grave. "Many were. The camps . . . they will be the shame of the German people for a thousand years to come. They are Hitler's real legacy."

"Oh, I think that's too harsh," Bowden said, lighting his pipe and puffing out a choking cloud of Cherry Blend. "According to what I've read, the majority of the German people had no idea of what was going on. The locals around Auschwitz thought it was a sausage plant."

"Ugh, how *terrible,*" Monica said, and pulled a grimacing that's-enough-of-that expression at her husband. Then she turned to Dussander and smiled. "I just love the smell of a pipe, Mr. Denker, don't you?"

"Indeed I do, madam," Dussander said. He had just gotten an almost insurmountable urge to sneeze under control.

Bowden suddenly reached across the table and clapped

his son on the shoulder. Todd jumped. "You're awfully quiet tonight, son. Feeling all right?"

Todd offered a peculiar smile that seemed divided between his father and Dussander. "I feel okay. I've heard most of these stories before, remember."

"Todd!" Monica said. "That's hardly—"

"The boy is only being honest," Dussander said. "A privilege of boys which men often have to give up. Yes, Mr. Bowden?"

Dick laughed and nodded.

"Perhaps I could get Todd to walk back to my house with me now," Dussander said. "I'm sure he has his studies."

"Todd is a very apt pupil," Monica said, but she spoke almost automatically, looking at Todd in a puzzled sort of way. "All A's and B's, usually. He got a C this last quarter, but he's promised to bring his French up to snuff on his March report. Right, Todd-baby?"

Todd offered the peculiar smile again and nodded.

"No need for you to walk," Dick said. "I'll be glad to run you back to your place."

"I walk for the air and the exercise," Dussander said. "Really, I must insist . . . unless Todd prefers not to."

"Oh, no, I'd like a walk," Todd said, and his mother and father beamed at him.

They were almost to Dussander's corner when Dussander broke the silence. It was drizzling, and he hoisted his umbrella over both of them. And yet still his arthritis lay quiet, dozing. It was amazing.

"You are like my arthritis," he said.

Todd's head came up. "Huh?"

"Neither of you have had much to say tonight. What's got your tongue, boy? Cat or cormorant?"

"Nothing," Todd muttered. They turned down Dussander's street.

"Perhaps I could guess," Dussander said, not without a

touch of malice. "When you came to get me, you were afraid I might make a slip . . . 'let the cat out of the bag,' you say here. Yet you were determined to go through with the dinner because you had run out of excuses to put your parents off. Now you are disconcerted that all went well. Is that not the truth?"

"Who cares?" Todd said, and shrugged sullenly.

"Why shouldn't it go well?" Dussander demanded. "I was dissembling before you were born. You keep a secret well enough, I give you that. I give it to you most graciously. But did you see me tonight? I charmed them. *Charmed* them!"

Todd suddenly burst out: "You didn't have to do that!"

Dussander came to a complete stop, staring at Todd.

"Not do it? *Not?* I thought that was what you wanted, boy! Certainly they will offer no objections if you continue to come over and 'read' to me."

"You're sure taking a lot for granted!" Todd said hotly. "Maybe I've got all I want from you. Do you think there's anybody *forcing* me to come over to your scuzzy house and watch you slop up booze like those old wino pusbags that hang around the old trainyards? Is that what you think?" His voice had risen and taken on a thin, wavering, hysterical note. "Because there's nobody *forcing* me. If I want to come, I'll come, and if I don't, I won't."

"Lower your voice. People will hear."

"Who cares?" Todd said, but he began to walk again. This time he deliberately walked outside the umbrella's span.

"No, nobody forces you to come," Dussander said. And then he took a calculated shot in the dark: "In fact, you are welcome to stay away. Believe me, boy, I have no scruples about drinking alone. None at all."

Todd looked at him scornfully. "You'd like that, wouldn't you?"

Dussander only smiled noncommittally.

"Well, don't count on it." They had reached the concrete

walk leading up to Dussander's stoop. Dussander fumbled in his pocket for his latchkey. The arthritis flared a dim red in the joints of his fingers and then subsided, waiting. Now Dussander thought he understood what it was waiting for: for him to be alone again. Then it could come out.

"I'll tell you something," Todd said. He sounded oddly breathless. "If they knew what you were, if I ever told them, they'd spit on you and then kick you out on your skinny old ass."

Dussander looked at Todd closely in the drizzling dark. The boy's face was turned defiantly up to his, but the skin was pallid, the sockets under the eyes dark and slightly hollowed—the skin-tones of someone who has brooded long while others are asleep.

"I am sure they would have nothing but revulsion for me," Dussander said, although he privately thought that the elder Bowden might stay his revulsion long enough to ask many of the questions his son had asked already. "Nothing but revulsion. But what would they feel for you, boy, when I told them you had known about me for eight months . . . and said nothing?"

Todd stared at him wordlessly in the dark.

"Come and see me if you please," Dussander said indifferently, "and stay home if you don't. Goodnight, boy."

He went up the walk to his front door, leaving Todd standing in the drizzle and looking after him with his mouth slightly ajar.

The next morning at breakfast, Monica said: "Your dad liked Mr. Denker a lot, Todd. He said he reminded him of your grandfather."

Todd muttered something unintelligible around his toast. Monica looked at her son and wondered if he had been sleeping well. He looked pale. And his grades had taken that inexplicable dip. Todd *never* got C's.

"You feeling okay these days, Todd?"

He looked at her blankly for a moment, and then that radiant smile spread over his face, charming her . . . comforting her. There was a dab of strawberry preserves on his chin. "Sure," he said. "Four-oh."

"Todd-baby," she said.

"Monica-baby," he responded, and they both started to laugh.

9

March, 1975.

"Kitty-kitty," Dussander said. "*Heeere,* kitty-kitty. Puss-puss? Puss-puss?"

He was sitting on his back stoop, a pink plastic bowl by his right foot. The bowl was full of milk. It was one-thirty in the afternoon; the day was hazy and hot. Brush-fires far to the west tinged the air with an autumnal smell that jagged oddly against the calendar. If the boy was coming, he would be here in another hour. But the boy didn't always come now. Instead of seven days a week he came sometimes only four times, or five. An intuition had grown in him, little by little, and his intuition told him that the boy was having troubles of his own.

"Kitty-kitty," Dussander coaxed. The stray cat was at the far end of the yard, sitting in the ragged verge of weeds by Dussander's fence. It was a tom, and every bit as ragged as the weeds it sat in. Every time he spoke, the cat's ears cocked forward. Its eyes never left the pink bowl filled with milk.

Perhaps, Dussander thought, the boy was having troubles with his studies. Or bad dreams. Or both.

That last made him smile.

"Kitty-kitty," he called softly. The cat's ears cocked forward again. It didn't move, not yet, but it continued to study the milk.

Dussander had certainly been afflicted with problems of his

own. For three weeks or so he had worn the SS uniform to bed like grotesque pajamas, and the uniform had warded off the insomnia and the bad dreams. His sleep had been—at first— as sound as a lumberjack's. Then the dreams had returned, not little by little, but all at once, and worse than ever before. Dreams of running as well as the dreams of the eyes. Running through a wet, unseen jungle where heavy leaves and damp fronds struck his face, leaving trickles that felt like sap . . . or blood. Running and running, the luminous eyes always around him, peering soullessly at him, until he broke into a clearing. In the darkness he sensed rather than saw the steep rise that began on the clearing's far side. At the top of that rise was Patin, its low cement buildings and yards surrounded by barbed wire and electrified wire, its sentry towers standing like Martian dreadnoughts straight out of *War of the Worlds.* And in the middle, huge stacks billowed smoke against the sky, and below these brick columns were the furnaces, stoked and ready to go, glowing in the night like the eyes of fierce demons. They had told the inhabitants of the area that the Patin inmates made clothes and candles, and of course the locals had believed that no more than the locals around Auschwitz had believed that the camp was a sausage factory. It didn't matter.

Looking back over his shoulder in the dream, he would at last see *them* coming out of hiding, the restless dead, the *Juden,* shambling toward him with blue numbers glaring from the livid flesh of their outstretched arms, their hands hooked into talons, their faces no longer expressionless but animated with hate, lively with vengeance, vivacious with murder. Toddlers ran beside their mothers and grandfathers were borne up by their middle-aged children. And the dominant expression on all their faces was desperation.

Desperation? Yes. Because in the dreams he knew (and so did they) that if he could climb the hill, he would be safe. Down here in these wet and swampy lowlands, in this jungle where the night-flowering plants extruded blood instead of sap, he was a hunted animal . . . prey. But up there, he was in command. If this was a jungle, then the camp at the top of the hill was a zoo, all the wild animals safely in cages, he the head keeper whose job it was to decide which would be fed, which would live, which would be handed over to the vivisectionists, which would be taken to the knacker's in the remover's van.

He would begin to run up the hill, running in all the slowness of nightmare. He would feel the first skeletal hands close about his neck, feel their cold and stinking breath, smell their decay, hear their birdlike cries of triumph as they pulled him down with salvation not only in sight but almost at hand—

"Kitty-kitty," Dussander called. "Milk. Nice milk."

The cat came at last. It crossed half of the back yard and then sat again, but lightly, its tail twitching with worry. It didn't trust him; no. But Dussander knew the cat could smell the milk and so he was sanguine. Sooner or later it would come.

At Patin there had never been a contraband problem. Some of the prisoners came in with their valuables poked far up their asses in small chamois bags (and how often their valuables turned out not to be valuable at all—photographs, locks of hair, fake jewelry), often pushed up with sticks until they were past the point where even the long fingers of the trusty they had called Stinky-Thumbs could reach. One woman, he remembered, had had a small diamond, flawed, it turned out, really not valuable at all—but it had been in her family for six generations, passed from mother to eldest daughter (or so she said, but of course she was a Jew and all of them lied). She swallowed it before entering Patin. When it came out in her waste, she swallowed it again. She kept doing this, although eventually the diamond began to cut her insides and she bled.

There had been other ruses, although most only involved petty items such as a hoard of tobacco or a hair-ribbon or two. It didn't matter. In the room Dussander used for prisoner interrogations there was a hot plate and a homely kitchen table covered with a red checked cloth much like the one in his own kitchen. There was always a pot of lamb stew bubbling mellowly away on that hotplate. When contraband was suspected (and when was it not?) a member of the suspected clique would be brought to that room. Dussander would stand them by the hotplate, where the rich fumes from the stew wafted. Gently, he would ask them *Who.* Who is hiding gold? Who is hiding jewelry? Who has tobacco? Who gave the Givenet woman the pill for her baby? Who? The stew was never specifically promised; but always the aroma eventually loosened their tongues. Of course, a truncheon would have done the same, or a gun-barrel jammed into their filthy crotches, but the stew was . . . was *elegant.* Yes.

"Kitty-kitty," Dussander called. The cat's ears cocked forward. It half-rose, then half-remembered some long-ago kick, or perhaps a match that had burned its whiskers, and it settled back on its haunches. But soon it would move.

He had found a way of propitiating his nightmare. It was, in a way, no more than wearing the SS uniform . . . but raised to a greater power. Dussander was pleased with himself, only sorry that he had never thought of it before. He supposed he had the boy to thank for this new method of quieting himself, for showing him that the key to the past's terrors was not in rejection but in contemplation and even something like a friend's embrace. It was true that before the boy's unexpected arrival last summer he hadn't had any bad dreams for a long time, but he believed now that he had come to a coward's terms with his past. He had been forced to give up a part of himself. Now he had reclaimed it.

"Kitty-kitty," called Dussander, and a smile broke on his face, a kindly smile, a reassuring smile, the smile of all old men who have somehow come through the cruel courses of life to a safe place, still relatively intact, and with at least some wisdom.

The tom rose from its haunches, hesitated only a moment

longer, and then trotted across the remainder of the back yard with lithe grace. It mounted the steps, gave Dussander a final mistrustful look, laying back its chewed and scabby ears; then it began to drink the milk.

"*Nice* milk," Dussander said, pulling on the Playtex rubber gloves that had lain in his lap all the while. "*Nice* milk for a *nice* kitty." He had bought these gloves in the supermarket. He had stood in the express lane, and older women had looked at him approvingly, even speculatively. The gloves were advertised on TV. They had cuffs. They were so flexible you could pick up a dime while you were wearing them.

He stroked the cat's back with one green finger and talked to it soothingly. Its back began to arch with the rhythm of his strokes.

Just before the bowl was empty, he seized the cat.

It came electrically alive in his clenching hands, twisting and jerking, clawing at the rubber. Its body lashed limberly back and forth, and Dussander had no doubt that if its teeth or claws got into him, it would come off the winner. It was an old campaigner. It takes one to know one, Dussander thought, grinning.

Holding the cat prudently away from his body, the painful grin stamped on his face, Dussander pushed the back door open with his foot and went into the kitchen. The cat yowled and twisted and ripped at the rubber gloves. Its feral, triangular head flashed down and fastened on one green thumb.

"Nasty kitty," Dussander said reproachfully.

The oven door stood open. Dussander threw the cat inside. Its claws made a ripping, prickly sound as they disengaged from the gloves. Dussander slammed the oven door shut with one knee, provoking a painful twinge from his arthritis. Yet he continued to grin. Breathing hard, nearly panting, he propped himself against the stove for a moment, his head hanging down. It was a gas stove. He rarely used it for anything fancier than TV dinners and killing stray cats.

Faintly, rising up through the gas burners, he could hear the cat scratching and yowling to be let out.

Dussander twisted the oven dial over to 500°. There was an audible *pop!* as the oven pilot-light lit two double rows of hissing gas. The cat stopped yowling and began to scream. It sounded . . . yes . . . almost like a young boy. A young boy in terrible pain. The thought made Dussander smile even more broadly. His heart thundered in his chest. The cat scratched and whirled madly in the oven, still screaming. Soon, a hot, furry, burning smell began to seep out of the oven and into the room.

He scraped the remains of the cat out of the oven half an hour later, using a barbecue fork he had acquired for two dollars and ninety-eight cents at the Grant's in the shopping center a mile away.

The cat's roasted carcass went into an empty flour sack. He took the sack down cellar. The cellar floor had never been cemented. Shortly, Dussander came back up. He sprayed the kitchen with Glade until it reeked of artificial pine scent. He opened all the windows. He washed the barbecue fork and hung it up on the pegboard. Then he sat down to wait and see if the boy would come. He smiled and smiled.

Todd did come, about five minutes after Dussander had given up on him for the afternoon. He was wearing a warm-up jacket with his school colors on it; he was also wearing a San Diego Padres baseball cap. He carried his schoolbooks under his arm.

"Yucka-ducka," he said, coming into the kitchen and wrinkling his nose. "What's that smell? It's awful."

"I tried the oven," Dussander said, lighting a cigarette. "I'm afraid I burned my supper. I had to throw it out."

One day later that month the boy came much earlier than usual, long before school usually let out. Dussander was sitting in the kitchen, drinking Ancient Age bourbon from a chipped and discolored cup that had the words HERE'S YER CAWFEE MAW, HAW! HAW! HAW! written around the rim. He had his rocker out in the kitchen now and he was just drinking and rocking, rocking and drinking, bumping his slippers on the faded linoleum. He was pleasantly high. There had been no more bad dreams at all until just last night. Not since the tomcat with the chewed ears. Last night's had been particularly horrible, though. That could not be denied. *They* had dragged him down after he had gotten halfway up the hill, and *they* had begun to do unspeakable things to him before he was able to wake himself up. Yet, after his initial thrashing return to the world of real things, he had been confident. He could end the dreams whenever he wished. Perhaps a cat would not be enough this time. But there was always the dog pound. Yes. Always the pound.

Todd came abruptly into the kitchen, his face pale and shiny and strained. He had lost weight, all right, Dussander thought. And there was a queer white look in his eyes that Dussander did not like at all.

"You're going to help me," Todd said suddenly and defiantly.

"Really?" Dussander said mildly, but sudden apprehension leaped inside of him. He didn't let his face change as Todd slammed his books down on the table with a sudden, vicious overhand stroke. One of them spun-skated across the oilcloth and landed in a tent on the floor by Dussander's foot.

"Yes, you're fucking-A right!" Todd said shrilly. "You better believe it! Because this is your fault! All your fault!" Hectic spots of red mounted into his cheeks. "But you're going to have to help me get out of it, because I've got the goods on you! *I've got you right where I want you!*"

"I'll help you in any way I can," Dussander said quietly. He saw that he had folded his hands neatly in front of himself without even thinking about it—just as he had once done.

He leaned forward in the rocker until his chin was directly over his folded hands—as he had once done. His face was calm and friendly and enquiring; none of his growing apprehension showed. Sitting just so, he could almost imagine a pot of lamb stew simmering on the stove behind him. 'Tell me what the trouble is."

"This is the fucking *trouble*," Todd said viciously, and threw a folder at Dussander. It bounced off his chest and landed in his lap, and he was momentarily surprised by the heat of the anger which leaped up in him; the urge to rise and backhand the boy smartly. Instead, he kept the mild expression on his face. It was the boy's school-card, he saw, although the school seemed to be at ridiculous pains to hide the fact. Instead of a school-card, or a Grade Report, it was called a "Quarterly Progress Report." He grunted at that, and opened the card.

A typed half-sheet of paper fell out. Dussander put it aside for later examination and turned his attention to the boy's grades first.

"You seem to have fallen on the rocks, my boy," Dussander said, not without some pleasure. The boy had passed only English and American History. Every other grade was an F.

"It's not my fault," Todd hissed venomously. "It's *your* fault. All those *stories*. I have nightmares about them, do you know that? I sit down and open my books and I start thinking about whatever you told me that day and the next thing I know, my mother's telling me it's time to go to bed. Well, that's not my fault! *It isn't! You hear me? It isn't!*"

"I hear you very well," Dussander said, and read the typed note that had been tucked into Todd's card.

Dear Mr. and Mrs. Bowden,

This note is to suggest that we have a group confer-ence concerning Todd's second- and third-quarter grades. In light of Todd's previous good work in this school, his current grades suggest a specific problem which may be affecting his academic performance in a deleterious way. Such a problem can often be solved by a frank and open discussion.

I should point out that although Todd has passed the half-year, his final grades may be failing in some cases unless his work improves radically in the fourth quarter. Failing grades would entail summer school to avoid being kept back and causing a major scheduling problem.

I must also note that Todd is in the college division, and that his work so far this year is far below college acceptance levels. It is also below the level of academic ability assumed by the SAT tests.

Please be assured that I am ready to work out a mutually convenient time for us to meet. In a case such as this, earlier is usually better.

Sincerely yours,
Edward French

"Who is this Edward French?" Dussander asked, slipping the note back inside the card (part of him still marvelled at the American love of jargon; such a rolling missive to inform the parents that their son was flunking out!) and then refolding his hands. His premonition of disaster was stronger than ever, but he refused to give in to it. A year before, he would have done; a year ago he had been ready for disaster. Now he was not, but it seemed that the cursed boy had brought it to him anyway. "Is he your headmaster?"

"Rubber Ed? Hell, no. He's the guidance counsellor."

"*Guidance* counsellor? What is that?"

"You can figure it out," Todd said. He was nearly hysterical. "You read the goddam note!" He walked rapidly around the room, shooting sharp, quick glances at Dussander. "Well, I'm not going to let any of this shit go down. I'm just not. I'm not going to any summer school. My dad and mom are going to

Hawaii this summer and I'm going with them." He pointed at the card on the table. "Do you know what my dad will do if he sees that?"

Dussander shook his head.

"He'll get everything out of me. *Everything.* He'll know it was you. It couldn't be anything else, because nothing else has changed. He'll poke and pry and he'll get it all out of me. And then . . . then I'll . . . I'll be in dutch."

He stared at Dussander resentfully.

"They'll watch me. Hell, they might make me see a doctor, I don't know. How should *I* know? But I'm not getting in dutch. And I'm not going to any fucking summer school."

"Or to the reformatory," Dussander said. He said it very quietly.

Todd stopped circling the room. His face became very still. His cheeks and forehead, already pale, became even whiter. He stared at Dussander, and had to try twice before he could speak. "*What? What* did you just say?"

"My dear boy," Dussander said, assuming an air of great patience, "for the last five minutes I have listened to you pule and whine, and what all your puling and whining comes down to is this. *You* are in trouble. *You* might be found out. *You* might find yourself in adverse circumstances." Seeing that he had the boy's complete attention—at last—Dussander sipped reflectively from his cup.

"My boy," he went on, "that is a very dangerous attitude for you to have. And dangerous for me. The potential harm is much greater for me. You worry about your school-card. Pah! *This* for your school-card."

He flicked it off the table and onto the floor with one yellow finger.

"I am worried about my *life.*"

Todd did not reply; he simply went on looking at Dussander with that white-eyed, slightly crazed stare.

"The Israelis will not scruple at the fact that I am seventy-six. The death-penalty is still very much in favor over there, you know, especially when the man in the dock is a Nazi war criminal associated with the camps."

"You're a U.S. citizen," Todd said. "America wouldn't let them take you. I read up on that. I—"

"You read, but you don't *listen*! I am *not* a U.S. citizen! My papers came from *la cosa nostra*. I would be deported, and Mossad agents would be waiting for me wherever I deplaned."

"I wish they *would* hang you," Todd muttered, curling his hands into fists and staring down at them. "I was crazy to get mixed up with you in the first place."

"No doubt," Dussander said, and smiled thinly. "But you *are* mixed up with me. We must live in the present, boy, not in the past of 'I-should-have-nevers.' You must realize that your fate and my own are now inextricably entwined. If you 'blow the horn on me,' as your saying goes, do you think I will hesitate to blow the horn on you? Seven hundred thousand died at Patin. To the world at large I am a criminal, a monster, even the butcher your scandal-rags would have me. You are an accessory to all of that, my boy. You have criminal knowledge of an illegal alien, but you have not reported it. And if I am caught, I will tell the world all about you. When the reporters put their microphones in my face, it will be your name I'll repeat over and over again. 'Todd Bowden, yes, that is his name . . . how long? Almost a year. He wanted to know everything . . . all the gooshy parts. That's how he put it, yes: "All the gooshy parts." ' "

Todd's breath had stopped. His skin appeared transparent. Dussander smiled at him. He sipped bourbon.

"I think they will put you in jail. They may call it a reformatory, or a correctional facility—there may be a fancy name for it, like this 'Quarterly Progress Report' "—his lip curled—"but no matter what they call it, there will be bars on the windows."

Todd wet his lips. "I'd call you a liar. I'd tell them I just found out. They'd believe me, not you. You just better remember that."

Dussander's thin smile remained. "I thought you told me your father would get it all out of you."

Todd spoke slowly, as a person speaks when realization and verbalization occur simultaneously. "Maybe not. Maybe not this time. This isn't just breaking a window with a rock."

Dussander winced inwardly. He suspected that the boy's judgment was right—with so much at stake, he might indeed be able to convince his father. After all, when faced with such an unpleasant truth, what parent would not want to be convinced?

"Perhaps. Perhaps not. But how are you going to explain all those books you had to read to me because poor Mr. Denker is half-blind? My eyes are not what they were, but I can still read fine print with my spectacles. I can prove it."

"I'd say you fooled me!"

"Will you? And what reason will you be able to give for my fooling?"

"For . . . for friendship. Because you were lonely."

That, Dussander reflected, was just close enough to the truth to be believable. And once, in the beginning, the boy might have been able to bring it off. But now he was ragged; now he was coming apart in strings like a coat that has reached the end of its useful service. If a child shot off his cap pistol across the street, this boy would jump into the air and scream like a girl.

"Your school-card will also support my side of it," Dussander said. "It was not *Robinson Crusoe* that caused your grades to fall down so badly, my boy, was it?"

"Shut up, why don't you? Just shut up about it!"

"No," Dussander said. "I won't shut up about it." He lit a cigarette, scratching the wooden match alight on the gas oven door. "Not until I make you see the simple truth. We are in this together, sink or swim." He looked at Todd through the raftering smoke, not smiling, his old, lined face reptilian. "I will drag you down, boy. I promise you that. If anything comes out, *everything* will come out. That is my promise to you."

Todd stared at him sullenly and didn't reply.

"Now," Dussander said briskly, with the air of a man who has put a necessary unpleasantness behind him, "the question is, what are we going to do about this situation? Have you any ideas?"

"This will fix the report card," Todd said, and took a new bottle of ink eradicator from his jacket pocket. "About that fucking letter, I don't know."

Dussander looked at the ink eradicator approvingly. He had falsified a few reports of his own in his time. When the quotas had gone up to the point of fantasy . . . and far, far beyond. And . . . more like the situation they were now in—there had been the matter of the invoices . . . those which enumerated the spoils of war. Each week he would check the boxes of valuables, all of them to be sent back to Berlin in special train-cars that were like big safes on wheels. On the side of each box was a manila envelope, and inside the envelope there had been a verified invoice of that box's contents. So many rings, necklaces, chokers, so many grams of gold. Dussander, however, had had his own box of valuables—not very valuable valuables, but not insignificant, either. Jades. Tourmalines. Opals. A few flawed pearls. Industrial diamonds. And when he saw an item invoiced for Berlin that caught his eye or seemed a good investment, he would remove it, replace it with an item from his own box, and use ink eradicator on the invoice, changing their item for his. He had developed into a fairly expert forger . . . a talent that had come in handy more than once after the war was over.

"Good," he told Todd. "As for this other matter . . ."

Dussander began to rock again, sipping from his cup. Todd pulled a chair up to the table and began to go to work on his report card, which he had picked up from the floor without a word. Dussander's outward calm had had its effect on him and now he worked silently, his head bent studiously over the card, like any American boy who has set out to do the best by God job he can, whether that job be planting corn, pitching a no-hitter in the Little League World Series, or forging grades on his report card.

Dussander looked at the nape of his neck, lightly tanned and cleanly exposed between the fall of his hair and the round neck of his tee-shirt. His eyes drifted from there to the top counter drawer where he kept the butcher knives. One quick thrust—he knew where to put it—and the boy's spinal cord would be severed. His lips would be sealed forever. Dussander smiled regretfully. There would be questions asked if the boy disappeared. Too many of them. Some directed at him. Even if there was no letter with a friend, close scrutiny was something he could not afford. Too bad.

"This man French," he said, tapping the letter. "Does he know your parents in a social way?"

"Him?" Todd edged the word with contempt. "My mom and dad don't go anywhere that he could even get in."

"Has he ever met them in his professional capacity? Has he ever had conferences with them before?"

"No. I've always been near the top of my classes. Until now."

"So what does he know about them?" Dussander said, looking dreamily into his cup, which was now nearly empty. "Oh, he knows about *you*. He no doubt has all the records on you that he can use. Back to the fights you had in the kindergarten play yard. But what does he know about *them*?"

Todd put his pen and the small bottle of ink eradicator away. "Well, he knows their names. Of course. And their ages. He knows we're all Methodists. You don't have to fill that line out, but my folks always do. We don't go much, but he'd know that's what we are. He must know what my dad does for a living; that's on the forms, too. All that stuff they have to fill out every year. And I'm pretty sure that's all."

"Would he know if your parents were having troubles at home?"

"What's that supposed to mean?"

Dussander tossed off the last of the bourbon in his cup. "Squabbles. Fights. Your father sleeping on the couch. Your mother drinking too much." His eyes gleamed. "A divorce brewing."

Indignantly, Todd said: "There's nothing like that going on! No way!"

"I never said there was. But just think, boy. Suppose that things at your house were 'going to hell in a streetcar,' as the saying is."

Todd only looked at him, frowning.

"You would be worried about them," Dussander said. "Very worried. You would lose your appetite. You would sleep poorly. Saddest of all, your schoolwork would suffer. True? Very sad for the children, when there are troubles in the home."

Understanding dawned in the boy's eyes—understanding and something like dumb gratitude. Dussander was gratified.

"Yes, it is an unhappy situation when a family totters on the edge of destruction," Dussander said grandly, pouring more bourbon. He was getting quite drunk. "The daytime television dramas, they make this absolutely clear. There is acrimony. Backbiting and lies. Most of all, there is pain. Pain, my boy. You have no idea of the hell your parents are going through. They are so swallowed up by their own troubles that they have little time for the problems of their own son. His problems seem minor compared to theirs, *hein*? Someday, when the scars have begun to heal, they will no doubt take a fuller interest in him once again. But now the only concession they can make is to send the boy's kindly grandfather to Mr. French."

Todd's eyes had been gradually brightening to a glow that was nearly fervid. "Might work," he was muttering. "Might, yeah, might work, might—" He broke off suddenly. His eyes darkened again. "No, it won't. You don't look like me, not even a little bit. Rubber Ed will never believe it."

"Himmel! Gott im Himmel!" Dussander cried, getting to his feet, crossing the kitchen (a bit unsteadily), opening the cellar door, and pulling out a fresh bottle of Ancient Age. He spun off the cap and poured liberally. "For a smart boy, you are such a *Dummkopf.* When do grandfathers ever look like their grandsons? Huh? I got white hair. Do you have white hair?"

Approaching the table again, he reached out with surprising quickness, snatched an abundant handful of Todd's blonde hair, and pulled briskly.

"Cut it out!" Todd snapped, but he smiled a little.

"Besides," Dussander said, settling back into his rocker, "you have yellow hair and blue eyes. My eyes are blue, and before my hair turned white, it was yellow. You can tell me your whole family history. Your aunts and uncles. The people your father works with. Your mother's little hobbies. I will remember. I will study and remember. Two days later it will all be forgotten again—these days my memory is like a cloth bag filled with water—but I will remember for long enough." He smiled grimly. "In my time I have stayed ahead of Wiesenthal and pulled the wool over the eyes of Himmler himself. If I cannot fool one American public school teacher, I will pull my winding-shroud around me and crawl down into my grave."

"Maybe," Todd said slowly, and Dussander could see he had already accepted it. His eyes were luminous with relief.

"No—*surely!*" Dussander cried.

He began to cackle with laughter, the rocking chair squeaking back and forth. Todd looked at him, puzzled and a little frightened, but after a bit he began to laugh, too. In Dussander's kitchen they laughed and laughed, Dussander by the open window where the warm California breeze wafted in, and Todd rocked back on the rear legs of his kitchen chair, so that its back rested against the oven door, the white enamel of which was crisscrossed by the dark, charred-looking streaks made by Dussander's wooden matches as he struck them alight.

• • •

Rubber Ed French (his nickname, Todd had explained to Dussander, referred to the rubbers he always wore over his sneakers during wet weather) was a slight man who made an affectation of always wearing Keds to school. It was a touch of informality which he thought would endear him to the one hundred and six children between the ages of twelve and fourteen who made up his counselling load. He had five pairs of Keds, ranging in color from Fast Track Blue to Screaming Yellow Zonkers, totally unaware that behind his back he was known not only as Rubber Ed but as Sneaker Pete and The Ked Man, as in The Ked Man Cometh. He had been known as Pucker in college, and he would have been most humiliated of all to learn that even that shameful fact had somehow gotten out.

He rarely wore ties, preferring turtleneck sweaters. He had been wearing these ever since the mid-sixties, when David McCallum had popularized them in *The Man from U.N.C.L.E.* In his college days his classmates had been known to spy him crossing the quad and remark, "Here comes Pucker in his U.N.C.L.E. sweater." He had majored in Educational Psychology, and he privately considered himself to be the only good guidance counsellor he had ever met. He had real *rapport* with his kids. He could *get right down to it* with them; he could *rap* with them and be silently sympathetic if they had to do some shouting and *kick out the jams.* He could *get into their hangups* because he understood what a *bummer* it was to be thirteen when someone was *doing a number on your head* and you couldn't *get your shit together.*

The thing was, he had a damned hard time remembering what it had been like to be thirteen himself. He supposed that was the ultimate price you had to pay for growing up in the fifties. That, and travelling into the brave new world of the sixties nicknamed Pucker.

Now, as Todd Bowden's grandfather came into his office, closing the pebbled-glass door firmly behind him, Rubber Ed stood up respectfully but was careful not to come around his desk to greet the old man. He was aware of his sneakers. Sometimes the old-timers didn't understand that the sneakers were a psychological aid with kids who had teacher hangups—which was to say that some of the older folks couldn't *get behind* a guidance counsellor in Keds.

This is one fine-looking dude, Rubber Ed thought. His white hair was carefully brushed back. His three-piece suit was spotlessly clean. His dove-gray tie was impeccably knotted. In his left hand he held a furled black umbrella (outside, a light drizzle had been falling since the weekend) in a manner that was almost military. A few years ago Rubber Ed and his wife had gone on a Dorothy Sayers jag, reading everything by that estimable lady that they could lay their hands upon. It occurred to him now that this was her brainchild, Lord Peter Wimsey, to the life. It was Wimsey at seventy-five, years after both Bunter and Harriet Vane had passed on to their rewards. He made a mental note to tell Sondra about this when he got home.

"Mr. Bowden," he said respectfully, and offered his hand.

"A pleasure," Bowden said, and shook it. Rubber Ed was careful not to put on the firm and uncompromising pressure he applied to the hands of the fathers he saw; it was obvious from the gingerly way the old boy offered it that he had arthritis.

"A pleasure, Mr. French," Bowden repeated, and took a seat, carefully pulling up the knees of his trousers. He propped the umbrella between his feet and leaned on it, looking like an elderly, extremely urbane vulture that had come in to roost in Rubber Ed French's office. He had the slightest touch of an accent, Rubber Ed thought, but it wasn't the clipped intonation of the British upper class, as Wimsey's would have been; it was broader, more European. Anyway, the resemblance to Todd was quite striking. Especially through the nose and eyes.

"I'm glad you could come," Rubber Ed told him, resuming his own seat, "although in these cases the student's mother or father—"

This was the opening gambit, of course. Almost ten years

of experience in the counselling business had convinced him that when an aunt or an uncle or a grandparent showed up for a conference, it usually meant trouble at home—the sort of trouble that invariably turned out to be the root of the problem. To Rubber Ed, this came as a relief. Domestic problems were bad, but for a boy of Todd's intelligence, *a heavy drug trip* would have been much, much worse.

"Yes, of course," Bowden said, managing to look both sorrowful and angry at the same time. "My son and his wife asked me if I could come and talk this sorry business over with you, Mr. French. Todd is a good boy, believe me. This trouble with his school marks is only temporary."

"Well, we all hope so, don't we, Mr. Bowden? Smoke if you like. It's supposed to be off-limits on school property, but I'll never tell."

"Thank you."

Mr. Bowden took a half-crushed package of Camel cigarettes from his inner pocket, put one of the last two zigzagging smokes in his mouth, found a Diamond Blue-Tip match, scratched it on the heel of one black shoe, and lit up. He coughed an old man's dank cough over the first drag, shook the match out, and put the blackened stump into the ashtray Rubber Ed had produced. Rubber Ed watched this ritual, which seemed almost as formal as the old man's shoes, with frank fascination.

"Where to begin," Bowden said, his distressed face looking at Rubber Ed through a swirling raft of cigarette smoke.

"Well," Rubber Ed said kindly, "the very fact that you're here instead of Todd's parents tells me something, you know."

"Yes, I suppose it does. Very well." He folded his hands. The Camel protruded from between the second and third fingers of his right. He straightened his back and lifted his chin. There was something almost Prussian in his mental coming to terms, Rubber Ed thought, something that made him think of all those war movies he'd seen as a kid.

"My son and my daughter-in-law are having troubles in their home," Bowden said, biting off each word precisely. "Rather bad troubles, I should think." His eyes, old but amazingly bright, watched as Rubber Ed opened the folder centered in front of him on the desk blotter. There were sheets of paper inside, but not many.

"And you feel that these troubles are affecting Todd's academic performance?"

Bowden leaned forward perhaps six inches. His blue eyes never left Rubber Ed's brown ones. There was a heavily charged pause, and then Bowden said: "The mother drinks."

He resumed his former ramrod-straight position.

"Oh," Rubber Ed said.

"Yes," Bowden replied, nodding grimly. "The boy has told me that he has come home on two occasions and has found her sprawled out on the kitchen table. He knows how my son feels about her drinking problem, and so the boy has put dinner in the oven himself on these occasions, and has gotten her to drink enough black coffee so she will at least be awake when Richard comes home."

"That's bad," Rubber Ed said, although he had heard worse—mothers with heroin habits, fathers who had abruptly taken it into their heads to start banging their daughters . . . or their sons. "Has Mrs. Bowden thought about getting professional help for her problem?"

"The boy has tried to persuade her that would be the best course. She is much ashamed, I think. If she was given a little time . . ." He made a gesture with his cigarette that left a dissolving smoke-ring in the air. "You understand?"

"Yes, of course." Rubber Ed nodded, privately admiring the gesture that had produced the smoke-ring. "Your son . . . Todd's father . . ."

"He is not without blame," Bowden said harshly. "The hours he works, the meals he has missed, the nights when he must leave suddenly . . . I tell you, Mr. French, he is more married to his job than he is to Monica. I was raised to believe that a man's family came before everything. Was it not the same for you?"

"It sure was," Rubber Ed responded heartily. His father had been a night watchman for a large Los Angeles department store and he had really only seen his pop on weekends and vacations.

"That is another side of the problem," Bowden said.

Rubber Ed nodded and thought for a moment. "What about your other son, Mr. Bowden? Uh . . ." He looked down at the folder. "Harold. Todd's uncle."

"Harry and Deborah are in Minnesota now," Bowden said, quite truthfully. "He has a position there at the University medical school. It would be quite difficult for him to leave, and very unfair to ask him." His face took on a righteous cast. "Harry and his wife are quite happily married."

"I see." Rubber Ed looked at the file again for a moment and then closed it. "Mr. Bowden, I appreciate your frankness. I'll be just as frank with you."

"Thank you," Bowden said stiffly.

"We can't do as much for our students in the counselling area as we would like. There are six counsellors here, and we're each carrying a load of over a hundred students. My newest colleague, Hepburn, has a hundred and fifteen. At this age, in our society, all children need help."

"Of course." Bowden mashed his cigarette brutally into the ashtray and folded his hands once more.

"Sometimes bad problems get by us. Home environment and drugs are the two most common. At least Todd isn't mixed up with speed or mescaline or PCP."

"God forbid."

"Sometimes," Rubber Ed went on, "there's simply nothing we can do. It's depressing, but it's a fact of life. Usually the ones that are first to get spit out of the machine we're running here are the class troublemakers, the sullen, uncommunicative kids, the ones who refuse to even try. They are simply warm bodies waiting for the system to buck them up through the grades or waiting to get old enough so they can quit without their parents' permission and join the Army or get a job at the Speedy-Boy Carwash or marry their boyfriends. You understand? I'm being blunt. Our system is, as they say, not all it's cracked up to be."

"I appreciate your frankness."

"But it hurts when you see the machine starting to mash up someone like Todd. He ran out a ninety-two average for last year's work, and that puts him in the ninety-fifth percentile. His English averages are even better. He shows a flair for writing, and that's something special in a generation of kids that think culture begins in front of the TV and ends in the neighborhood movie theater. I was talking to the woman who had Todd in Comp last year. She said Todd passed in the finest term-paper she'd seen in twenty years of teaching. It was on the German death-camps during World War Two. She gave him the only A-plus she's ever given a composition student."

"I have read it," Bowden said. "It is very fine."

"He has also demonstrated above-average ability in the life sciences and social sciences, and while he's not going to be one of the great math whizzes of the century, all the notes I have indicate that he's given it the good old college try . . . until this year. Until this year. That's the whole story, in a nutshell."

"Yes."

"I hate like *hell* to see Todd go down the tubes this way, Mr. Bowden. And summer school . . . well, I said I'd be frank. Summer school often does a boy like Todd more harm than good. Your usual junior high school summer session is a zoo. All the monkeys and the laughing hyenas are in attendance, plus a full complement of dodo birds. Bad company for a boy like Todd."

"Certainly."

"So let's get to the bottom line, shall we? I suggest a series of appointments for Mr. and Mrs. Bowden at the Counselling Center downtown. Everything in confidence, of course. The man in charge down there, Harry Ackerman, is a good friend of mine. And I don't think Todd should go to them with the idea; I think you should." Rubber Ed smiled widely. "Maybe we can get everybody back on track by June. It's not impossible."

But Bowden looked positively alarmed by this idea.

"I believe they might resent the boy if I took that proposal to them now," he said. 'Things are very delicate. They could go either way. The boy has promised me he will work harder in his studies. He is very alarmed at this drop in his marks." He smiled thinly, a smile Ed French could not quite interpret. "More alarmed than you know."

"But—"

"And they would resent *me,*" Bowden pressed on quickly. "God knows they would. Monica already regards me as something of a meddler. I try not to be, but you see the situation. I feel that things are best left alone . . . for now."

"I've had a great deal of experience in these matters," Rubber Ed told Bowden. He folded his hands on Todd's file and looked at the old man earnestly. "I really think counselling is in order here. You'll understand that my interest in the marital problems your son and daughter-in-law are having begins and ends with the effect they're having on Todd . . . and right now, they're having quite an effect."

"Let me make a counter-proposal," Bowden said. "You have, I believe, a system of warning parents of poor grades?"

"Yes," Rubber Ed agreed cautiously. "Interpretation of Progress cards—IOP cards. The kids, of course, call them Flunk Cards. They only get them if their grade in a given course falls below seventy-eight. In other words, we give out IOP cards to kids who are pulling a D or an F in a given course."

"Very good," Bowden said. "Then what I suggest is this: if the boy gets one of those cards . . . even *one*"—he held up one gnarled finger—"I will approach my son and his wife about

your counselling. I will go further." He pronounced it *furdah.*
"If the boy receives one of your Flunk Cards in April—"

"We give them out in May, actually."

"Yes? If he receives one then, I guarantee that they will
accept the counselling proposal. They are worried about their
son, Mr. French. But now they are so wrapped up in their own
problem that . . ." He shrugged.

"I understand."

"So let us give them that long to solve their own problems.
Pulling one's self up by one's own shoelaces . . . that is the
American way, is it not?"

"Yes, I guess it is," Rubber Ed told him after a moment's
thought . . . and after a quick glance at the clock, which told him
he had another appointment in five minutes. "I'll accept that."

He stood, and Bowden stood with him. They shook hands
again, Rubber Ed being carefully mindful of the old party's
arthritis.

"But in all fairness, I ought to tell you that very few students can pull out of an eighteen-week tailspin in just four
weeks of classes. There's a huge amount of ground to be made
up—a *huge* amount. I suspect you'll have to come through on
your guarantee, Mr. Bowden."

Bowden offered his thin, disconcerting smile again. "Do
you?" was all he said.

Something had troubled Rubber Ed through the entire
interview, and he put his finger on it during lunch in the caf-
eteria, more than an hour after "Lord Peter" had left, umbrella
once again neatly tucked under his arm.

He and Todd's grandfather had talked for fifteen minutes at
least, probably closer to twenty, and Ed didn't think the old
man had once referred to his grandson by name.

Todd pedaled breathlessly up Dussander's walk and parked his
bike on its kickstand. School had let out only fifteen minutes
before. He took the front steps at one jump, used his doorkey,

and hurried down the hall to the sunlit kitchen. His face was a mixture of hopeful sunshine and gloomy clouds. He stood in the kitchen doorway for a moment, his stomach and his vocal cords knotted, watching Dussander as he rocked with his cupful of bourbon in his lap. He was still dressed in his best, although he had pulled his tie down two inches and loosened the top button of his shirt. He looked at Todd expressionlessly, his lizardlike eyes at half-mast.

"Well?" Todd finally managed.

Dussander left him hanging a moment longer, a moment that seemed at least ten years long to Todd. Then, deliberately, Dussander set his cup on the table next to his bottle of Ancient Age and said:

"The fool believed everything."

Todd let out his pent-up breath in a whooping gust of relief.

Before he could draw another breath in, Dussander added: "He wanted your poor, troubled parents to attend counselling sessions downtown with a friend of his. He was really quite insistent."

"Jesus! Did you . . . what did you . . . how did you handle it?"

"I thought quickly," Dussander replied. "Like the little girl in the Saki story, invention on short notice is one of my strong points. I promised him your parents would go in for such counselling if you received even one Flunk Card when they are given in May."

The blood fell out of Todd's face.

"You did *what?*" he nearly screamed. "I've already flunked two algebra quizzes and a history test since the marking period started!" He advanced into the room, his pale face now growing shiny with breaking sweat. "There was a French quiz this afternoon and I flunked that, too . . . I know I did. All I could think about was that goddamned Rubber Ed and whether or not you were taking care of him. You took care of him, all right," he finished bitterly. "Not get one Flunk Card? I'll probably get five or six."

"It was the best I could do without arousing suspicions," Dussander said. "This French, fool that he is, is only doing his job. Now you will do yours."

"What's that supposed to mean?" Todd's face was ugly and thunderous, his voice truculent.

"You will work. In the next four weeks you will work harder than you have ever worked in your life. Furthermore, on Monday you will go to each of your instructors and apologize to them for your poor showing thus far. You will—"

"It's impossible," Todd said. "You don't get it, man. It's *impossible.* I'm at least five weeks behind in science and history. In algebra it's more like ten."

"Nevertheless," Dussander said. He poured more bourbon.

"You think you're pretty smart, don't you?" Todd shouted at him. "Well, I don't take orders from you. The days when you gave orders are long over. *Do you get it?*" He lowered his voice abruptly. "The most lethal thing you've got around the house these days is a Shell No-Pest Strip. You're nothing but a broken-down old man who farts rotten eggs if he eats a taco. I bet you even pee in your bed."

"Listen to me, snotnose," Dussander said quietly.

Todd's head jerked angrily around at that.

"Before today," Dussander said carefully, "it was possible, *just barely* possible, that you could have denounced me and come out clean yourself. I don't believe you would have been up to the job with your nerves in their present state, but never mind that. It would have been technically possible. But now things have changed. Today I impersonated your grandfather, one Victor Bowden. No one can have the slightest doubt that I did it with . . . how is the word? . . . your connivance. If it comes out now, boy, you will look blacker than ever. And you will have no defense. I took care of that today."

"I wish—"

"You *wish!* You *wish!*" Dussander roared. "Never mind your wishes, your wishes make me *sick,* your wishes are no more than little piles of dogshit in the gutter! *All I want from you is to know if you understand the situation we are in!*"

"I understand it," Todd muttered. His fists had been tightly clenched while Dussander shouted at him—he was not used to being shouted at. Now he opened his hands and dully observed that he had dug bleeding half-moons into his palms. The cuts would have been worse, he supposed, but in the last four months or so he had taken up biting his nails.

"Good. Then you will make your sweet apologies, and you will study. In your free time at school you will study. During your lunch hours you will study. After school you will come here and study, and on your weekends you will come here and do more of the same."

"Not here," Todd said quickly. "At home."

"No. At home you will dawdle and daydream as you have all along. If you are here I can stand over you if I have to and watch you. I can protect my own interests in this matter. I can quiz you. I can listen to your lessons."

"If I don't want to come here, you can't make me."

Dussander drank. "That is true. Things will then go on as they have. You will fail. This guidance person, French, will expect me to make good on my promise. When I don't, he will call your parents. They will find out that kindly Mr. Denker impersonated your grandfather at your request. They will find out about the altered grades. They—"

"Oh, shut up. I'll come."

"You're already here. Begin with algebra."

"No *way*! It's Friday afternoon!"

"You study *every* afternoon now," Dussander said softly. "Begin with algebra."

Todd stared at him—only for a moment before dropping his eyes and fumbling his algebra text out of his bookbag—and Dussander saw murder in the boy's eyes. Not figurative murder; literal murder. It had been years since he had seen that dark, burning, speculative glance, but one never forgot it. He supposed he would have seen it in his own eyes if there had been a mirror at hand on the day he had looked at the white and defenseless nape of the boy's neck.

I must protect myself, he thought with some amazement. *One underestimates at one's own risk.*

He drank his bourbon and rocked and watched the boy study.

It was nearly five o'clock when Todd biked home. He felt washed out, hot-eyed, drained, impotently angry. Every time his eyes had wandered from the printed page—from the maddening, incomprehensible, fucking *stupid* world of sets, subsets, ordered pairs, and Cartesian co-ordinates—Dussander's sharp old man's voice had spoken. Otherwise he had remained completely silent . . . except for the maddening bump of his slippers on the floor and the squeak of the rocker. He sat there like a vulture waiting for its prey to expire. Why had he ever gotten into this? *How* had he gotten into it? This was a mess, a terrible mess. He had picked up some ground this afternoon—some of the set theory that had stumped him so badly just before the Christmas break had fallen into place with an almost audible click—but it was impossible to think he could pick up enough to scrape through next week's algebra test with even a D.

It was four weeks until the end of the world.

On the corner he saw a bluejay lying on the sidewalk, its beak slowly opening and closing. It was trying vainly to get onto its birdy-feet and hop away. One of its wings had been crushed, and Todd supposed a passing car had hit it and flipped it up onto the sidewalk like a tiddlywink. One of its beady eyes stared up at him.

Todd looked at it for a long time, holding the grips of his bike's apehanger handlebars lightly. Some of the warmth had gone out of the day and the air felt almost chilly. He supposed his friends had spent the afternoon goofing off down at the

Babe Ruth diamond on Walnut Street, maybe playing a little scrub, more likely playing pepper or three-flies-six-grounders or rolly-bat. It was the time of year when you started working your way up to baseball. There was some talk about getting up their own sandlot team this year to compete in the informal city league; there were dads enough willing to shlepp them around to games. Todd, of course, would pitch. He had been a Little League pitching star until he had grown out of the Senior Little League division last year. *Would have pitched.*

So what? He'd just have to tell them no. He'd just have to tell them: *Guys, I got mixed up with this war criminal. I got him right by the balls, and then—ha-ha, this'll killya, guys—then I found out he was holding my balls as tight as I was holding his. I started having funny dreams and the cold sweats. My grades went to hell and I changed them on my report card so my folks wouldn't find out and now I've got to hit the books really hard for the first time in my life. I'm not afraid of getting grounded, though. I'm afraid of going to the reformatory. And that's why I can't play any sandlot with you guys this year. You see how it is, guys.*

A thin smile, much like Dussander's and not at all like his former broad grin, touched his lips. There was no sunshine in it; it was a shady smile. There was no fun in it; no confidence. It merely said: *You see how it is, guys.*

He rolled his bike forward over the jay with exquisite slowness, hearing the newspaper crackle of its feathers and the crunch of its small hollow bones as they fractured inside it. He reversed, rolling over it again. It was still twitching. He rolled over it again, a single bloody feather stuck to his front tire, revolving up and down, up and down. By then the bird had stopped moving, the bird had kicked the bucket, the bird had punched out, the bird had gone to that great aviary in the sky, but Todd kept going forwards and backwards across its mashed body just the same. He did it for almost five minutes, and that thin smile never left his face. You see how it is, guys.

10

April, 1975.

The old man stood halfway down the compound's aisle, smiling broadly, as Dave Klingerman walked up to meet him. The frenzied barking that filled the air didn't seem to bother him in the slightest, or the smells of fur and urine, or the hundred different strays yapping and howling in their cages, dashing back and forth, leaping against the mesh. Klingerman pegged the old guy as a dog-lover right off the bat. His smile was sweet and pleasant. He offered Dave a swollen, arthritis-bunched hand carefully, and Klingerman shook it in the same spirit.

"Hello, sir!" he said, speaking up. "Noisy as hell, isn't it?"

"I don't mind," the old man said. "Not at all. My name is Arthur Denker."

"Klingerman. Dave Klingerman."

"I am pleased to meet you, sir. I read in the paper—I could not believe it—that you *give* dogs away here. Perhaps I misunderstood. In fact, I think I must have misunderstood."

"No, we give em away, all right," Dave said. "If we can't, we have to destroy em. Sixty days, that's what the State gives us. Shame. Come on in the office here. Quieter. Smells better, too."

In the office, Dave heard a story that was familiar (but nonetheless affecting): Arthur Denker was in his seventies. He had come to California when his wife died. He was not rich, but he tended what he did have with great care. He was lonely. His only friend was the boy who sometimes came to his house and read to him. In Germany he had owned a beautiful Saint Bernard. Now, in Santo Donato, he had a house with a good-sized back yard. The yard was fenced. And he had read in the paper . . . would it be possible that he could . . .

"Well, we don't have any Bernards," Dave said. "They go fast because they're so good with kids—"

"Oh, I understand. I didn't mean that—"

"—but I do have a half-grown shepherd pup. How would that be?"

Mr. Denker's eyes grew bright, as if he might be on the verge of tears. "Perfect," he said. "That would be perfect."

"The dog itself is free, but there are a few other charges. Distemper and rabies shots. A city dog license. All of it goes about twenty-five bucks for most people, but the State pays half if you're over sixty-five—part of the California Golden Ager program."

"Golden Ager . . . is that what I am?" Mr. Denker said, and laughed. For just a moment—it was silly—Dave felt a kind of chill.

"Uh . . . I guess so, sir."

"It is very reasonable."

"Sure, we think so. The same dog would cost you a hundred and twenty-five dollars in a pet shop. But people go to those places instead of here. They are paying for a set of papers, of course, not the dog." Dave shook his head. "If they only understood how many fine animals are abandoned every year."

"And if you can't find a suitable home for them within sixty days, they are destroyed?"

"We put them to sleep, yes."

"Put them to . . . ? I'm sorry, my English—"

"It's a city ordinance," Dave said. "Can't have dog-packs running the streets."

"You shoot them."

"No, we give them gas. It's very humane. They don't feel a thing."

"No," Mr. Denker said. "I am sure they don't."

Todd's seat in Beginning Algebra was four desks down in the second row. He sat there, trying to keep his face expressionless, as Mr. Storrman passed back the exams. But his ragged fingernails were digging into his palms again, and his entire body seemed to be running with a slow and caustic sweat.

Don't get your hopes up. Don't be such a goddam chump. There's no way you could have passed. You know *you didn't pass.*

Nevertheless, he could not completely squash the foolish hope. It had been the first algebra exam in weeks that looked as if it had been written in something other than Greek. He was sure that in his nervousness (nervousness? no, call it what it had really been: outright terror) he had not done that well, but maybe . . . well, if it had been anyone else but Storrman, who had a Yale padlock for a heart . . .

STOP IT! he commanded himself, and for a moment, a coldly horrible moment, he was positive he had screamed those two words aloud in the classroom. *You flunked, you know you did, not a thing in the world is going to change it.*

Storrman handed him his paper expressionlessly and moved on. Todd laid it face down on his initial-scarred desk. For a moment he didn't think he possessed sufficient will to even turn it over and know. At last he flipped it with such convulsive suddenness that the exam sheet tore. His tongue stuck to the roof of his mouth as he stared at it. His heart seemed to stop for a moment.

The number 83 was written in a circle at the top of the sheet. Below it was a letter-grade: C+. Below the letter-grade was a brief notation: *Good improvement! I think I'm twice as relieved as you should be. Check errors carefully. At least three of them are arithmetical rather than conceptual.*

His heartbeat began again, at triple-time. Relief washed over him, but it was not cool—it was hot and complicated and strange. He closed his eyes, not hearing the class as it buzzed over the exam and began the pre-ordained fight for an extra point here or there. Todd saw redness behind his eyes. It pulsed like flowing blood with the rhythm of his heartbeat. In that instant he hated Dussander more than he ever had before. His hands snapped shut into fists and he only wished, wished, wished, that Dussander's scrawny chicken neck could have been between them.

• • •

Dick and Monica Bowden had twin beds, separated by a night-stand with a pretty imitation Tiffany lamp standing on it. Their room was done in genuine redwood, and the walls were comfortably lined with books. Across the room, nestled between two ivory bookends (bull elephants on their hind legs), was a round Sony TV. Dick was watching Johnny Carson with the earplug in while Monica read the new Michael Crichton that had come from the book club that day.

"Dick?" She put a bookmark (THIS IS WHERE I FELL ASLEEP, it said) into the Crichton and closed it.

On the TV, Buddy Hackett had just broken everyone up. Dick smiled.

"Dick?" she said more loudly.

He pulled the earplug out. "What?"

"Do you think Todd's all right?"

He looked at her for a moment, frowning, then shook his head a little. *"Je ne comprends pas, chérie."* His limping French was a joke between them. His father had sent him an extra two hundred dollars to hire a tutor when he was flunking French. He had gotten Monica Darrow, picking her name at random from the cards tacked up on the Union bulletin board. By Christmas she had been wearing his pin . . . and he had managed a C in French.

"Well . . . he's lost weight."

"He looks a little scrawny, sure," Dick said. He put the TV earplug in his lap, where it emitted tiny squawking sounds. "He's growing up, Monica."

"So soon?" she asked uneasily.

He laughed. "So soon. I shot up seven inches as a teenager—from a five-foot-six shrimp at twelve to the beautiful six-foot-one mass of muscle you see before you today. My mother said that when I was fourteen you could hear me growing in the night."

"Good thing not all of you grew that much."

"It's all in how you use it."

"Want to use it tonight?"

"The wench grows bold," Dick Bowden said, and threw the earplug across the room.

After, as he was drifting off to sleep:

"Dick, he's having bad dreams, too."

"Nightmares?" he muttered.

"Nightmares. I've heard him moaning in his sleep two or three times when I've gone down to use the bathroom in the night. I didn't want to wake him up. It's silly, but my grand-mother used to say you could drive a person insane if you woke them up in the middle of a bad dream."

"She was the Polack, wasn't she?"

"The Polack, yeah, the Polack. Nice talk!"

"You know what I mean. Why don't you just use the upstairs john?" He had put it in himself two years ago.

"You know the flush always wakes you up," she said.

"So don't flush it."

"Dick, that's nasty."

He sighed.

"Sometimes when I go in, he's sweating. And the sheets are damp."

He grinned in the dark. "I bet."

"What's *that* . . . oh." She slapped him lightly. "That's nasty, too. Besides, he's only thirteen."

"Fourteen next month. He's not too young. A little preco-cious, maybe, but not too young."

"How old were you?"

"Fourteen or fifteen. I don't remember exactly. But I remem-ber I woke up thinking I'd died and gone to heaven."

"But you were older than Todd is now."

"All that stuff's happening younger. It must be the milk . . . or the fluoride. Do you know they have sanitary napkin dis-pensers in all the girls' rooms of the school we built in Jackson

Park last year? And that's a *grammar school.* Now your average sixth-grader is only eleven. How old were you when you started?"

"I don't remember," she said. "All I know is Todd's dreams don't sound like . . . like he died and went to heaven."

"Have you asked him about them?"

"Once. About six weeks ago. You were off playing golf with that horrible Ernie Jacobs."

"That horrible Ernie Jacobs is going to make me a full partner by 1977, if he doesn't screw himself to death with that high-yellow secretary of his before then. Besides, he always pays the greens fees. What did Todd say?"

"That he didn't remember. But a sort of . . . shadow crossed his face. I think he *did* remember."

"Monica, I don't remember everything from my dear dead youth, but one thing I do remember is that wet dreams are not always pleasant. In fact, they can be downright unpleasant."

"How can that be?"

"Guilt. All kinds of guilt. Some of it maybe all the way from babyhood, when it was made very clear to him that wetting the bed was wrong. Then there's the sex thing. Who knows what brings a wet dream on? Copping a feel on the bus? Looking up a girl's skirt in study hall? I don't know. The only one I can really remember was going off the high board at the YMCA pool on co-ed day and losing my trunks when I hit the water."

"You got off on that?" she asked, giggling a little.

"Yeah. So if the kid doesn't want to talk to you about his John Thomas problems, don't force him."

"We did our damn best to raise him without all those needless guilts."

"You can't escape them. He brings them home from school like the colds he used to pick up in the first grade. From his friends, or the way his teachers mince around certain subjects. He probably got it from my dad, too. 'Don't touch it in the night, Todd, or your hands'll grow hair and you'll go blind and you'll start to lose your memory, and after awhile your thing will turn black and rot off. So be careful, Todd.'"

"Dick Bowden! Your dad would never—"

"He wouldn't. Hell, he *did.* Just like your Polack grandmother told you that waking somebody up in the middle of a nightmare might drive them nuts. He also told me to always wipe off the ring of a public toilet before I sat on it so I wouldn't get 'other people's germs.' I guess that was his way of saying syphilis. I bet your grandmother laid that one on you, too."

"No, my mother," she said absently. "And she told me to always flush. Which is why I go downstairs."

"It still wakes me up," Dick mumbled.

"What?"

"Nothing."

This time he had actually drifted halfway over the threshold of sleep when she spoke his name again.

"What?" he asked, a little impatiently.

"You don't suppose . . . oh, never mind. Go back to sleep."

"No, go on, finish. I'm awake again. I don't suppose what?"

"That old man. Mr. Denker. You don't think Todd's seeing too much of him, do you? Maybe he's . . . oh, I don't know . . . filling Todd up with a lot of stories."

"The real heavy horrors," Dick said. "The day the Essen Motor Works dropped below quota." He snickered.

"It was just an idea," she said, a little stiffly. The covers rustled as she turned over on her side. "Sorry I bothered you."

He put a hand on her bare shoulder. "I'll tell you something, babe," he said, and stopped for a moment, thinking carefully, choosing his words. "I've been worried about Todd, too, sometimes. Not the same things you've been worried about, but worried is worried, right?"

She turned back to him. "About what?"

"Well, I grew up a lot different than he's growing up. My dad had the store. Vic the Grocer, everyone called him. He had a book where he kept the names of the people who owed him, and how much they owed. You know what he called it?"

"No." Dick rarely talked about his boyhood; she had always thought it was because he hadn't enjoyed it. She listened carefully now.

"He called it the Left Hand Book. He said the right hand was business, but the right hand should never know what the left hand was doing. He said if the right hand *did* know, it would probably grab a meat-cleaver and chop the left hand right off."

"You never told me that."

"Well, I didn't like the old man very much when we first got married, and the truth is I still spend a lot of time not liking him. I couldn't understand why I had to wear pants from the Goodwill box while Mrs. Mazursky could get a ham on credit with that same old story about how her husband was going back to work next week. The only work that fucking wino Bill Mazursky ever had was holding onto a twelve-cent bottle of musky so it wouldn't fly away.

"All I ever wanted in those days was to get out of the neighborhood and away from my old man's life. So I made grades and played sports I didn't really like and got a scholarship at UCLA. And I made damn sure I stayed in the top ten per cent of my classes because the only Left Hand Book the colleges kept in those days was for the GIs that fought the war. My dad sent me money for my textbooks, but the only other money I ever took from him was the time I wrote home in a panic because I was flunking funnybook French. I met you. And I found out later from Mr. Halleck down the block that my dad put a lien on his car to scare up that two hundred bucks.

"And now I've got you, and we've got Todd. I've always thought he was a damned fine boy, and I've tried to make sure he's always had everything he ever needed . . . anything that would help him grow into a fine man. I used to laugh at that old wheeze about a man wanting his son to be better than he was, but as I get older it seems less funny and more true. I never want Todd to have to wear pants from a Goodwill box because some wino's wife got a ham on credit. You understand?"

"Yes, of course I do," she said quietly.

"Then, about ten years ago, just before my old man finally got tired of fighting off the urban renewal guys and retired, he had a minor stroke. He was in the hospital for ten days. And the people from the neighborhood, the guineas and the krauts, even some of the jigs that started to move in around 1955 or so . . . they paid his bill. Every fucking cent. I couldn't believe it. They kept the store open, too. Fiona Castellano got four or five of her friends who were out of work to come in on shifts. When my old man got back, the books balanced out to the cent."

"Wow," she said, very softly.

"You know what he said to me? My old man? That he'd always been afraid of getting old—of being scared and hurting and all by himself. Of having to go into the hospital and not being able to make ends meet anymore. Of dying. He said that after the stroke he wasn't scared anymore. He said he thought he could die well. 'You mean die happy, Pap?' I asked him. 'No,' he said. 'I don't think anyone dies happy, Dickie.' He always called me Dickie, still does, and that's another thing I guess I'll never be able to like. He said he didn't think anyone died happy, but you could die well. That impressed me."

He was silent for a long, thoughtful time.

"The last five or six years I've been able to get some perspective on my old man. Maybe because he's down there in San Remo and out of my hair. I started thinking that maybe the Left Hand Book wasn't such a bad idea. That was when I started to worry about Todd. I kept wanting to tell him about how there was maybe something more to life than me being able to take all of you to Hawaii for a month or being able to buy Todd pants that don't smell like the mothballs they used to put in the Goodwill box. I could never figure out how to tell him those things. But I think maybe he knows. And it takes a load off my mind."

"Reading to Mr. Denker, you mean?"

"Yes. He's not getting anything for that. Denker can't pay him. Here's this old guy, thousands of miles from any friends or relatives that might still be living, here's this guy that's everything my father was afraid of. And there's Todd."

"I never thought of it just like that."

"Have you noticed the way Todd gets when you talk to him about that old man?"

"He gets very quiet."

"Sure. He gets tongue-tied and embarrassed, like he was doing something nasty. Just like my pop used to when someone tried to thank him for laying some credit on them. We're Todd's right hand, that's all. You and me and all the rest—the house, the ski-trips to Tahoe, the Thunderbird in the garage, his color TV. All his right hand. And he doesn't want us to see what his left hand is up to."

"You don't think he's seeing too much of Denker, then?"

"Honey, look at his grades! If *they* were falling off, I'd be the first one to say Hey, enough is enough, already, don't go overboard. His grades are the first place trouble would show up. And how have they been?"

"As good as ever, after that first slip."

"So what are we talking about? Listen, I've got a conference at nine, babe. If I don't get some sleep, I'm going to be sloppy."

"Sure, go to sleep," she said indulgently, and as he turned over, she kissed him lightly on one shoulderblade. "I love you."

"Love you too," he said comfortably, and closed his eyes. "Everything's fine, Monica. You worry too much."

"I know I do. Goodnight."

They slept.

"Stop looking out the window," Dussander said. "There is nothing out there to interest you."

Todd looked at him sullenly. His history text was open on

the table, showing a color plate of Teddy Roosevelt cresting San Juan Hill. Helpless Cubans were falling away from the hooves of Teddy's horse. Teddy was grinning a wide American grin, the grin of a man who knew that God was in His heaven and everything was bully. Todd Bowden was not grinning.

"You like being a slave-driver, don't you?" he asked.

"I like being a free man," Dussander said. "Study."

"Suck my cock."

"As a boy," Dussander said, "I would have had my mouth washed out with lye soap for saying such a thing."

"Times change."

"Do they?" Dussander sipped his bourbon. "Study."

Todd stared at Dussander. "You're nothing but a goddamned rummy. You know that?"

"Study."

"*Shut up!*" Todd slammed his book shut. It made a riflecrack sound in Dussander's kitchen. "I can never catch up, anyway. Not in time for the test. There's fifty pages of this shit left, all the way up to World War One. I'll make a crib in Study Hall Two tomorrow."

Harshly, Dussander said: "You will do no such thing!"

"Why not? Who's going to stop me? You?"

"Boy, you are still having a hard time comprehending the stakes we play for. Do you think I enjoy keeping your snivelling brat nose in your books?" His voice rose, whipsawing, demanding, commanding. "Do you think I enjoy listening to your tantrums, your kindergarten swears? 'Suck my cock,'" Dussander mimicked savagely in a high, falsetto voice that made Todd flush darkly. "'Suck my cock, so what, who cares, I'll do it tomorrow, suck my cock'!"

"Well, you *like* it!" Todd shouted back. "Yeah, you *like* it! The only time you don't feel like a zombie is when you're on my back! So give me a fucking break!"

"If you are caught with one of these cribbing papers, what do you think will happen? Who will be told first?"

Todd looked at his hands with their ragged, bitten finger-nails and said nothing.

"Who?"

"Jesus, you know. Rubber Ed. Then my folks, I guess."

Dussander nodded. "Me, I guess that too. Study. Put your cribbing paper in your head, where it belongs."

"I hate you," Todd said dully. "I really do." But he opened his book again and Teddy Roosevelt grinned up at him, Teddy galloping into the twentieth century with his saber in his hand, Cubans falling back in disarray before him—possibly before the force of his fierce American grin.

Dussander began to rock again. He held his teacup of bour-bon in his hands. "That's a good boy," he said, almost tenderly.

Todd had his first wet dream on the last night of April, and he awoke to the sound of rain whispering secretly through the leaves and branches of the tree outside his window.

In the dream, he had been in one of the Patin laboratories. He was standing at the end of a long, low table. A lush young girl of amazing beauty had been secured to this table with clamps. Dussander was assisting him. Dussander wore a white butcher's apron and nothing else. When he pivoted to turn on the monitoring equipment, Todd could see Dussander's scrawny buttocks grinding at each other like misshapen white stones.

He handed something to Todd, something he recognized immediately, although he had never actually seen one. It was a dildo. The tip of it was polished metal, winking in the light of the overhead fluorescents like heartless chrome. The dildo was hollow. Snaking out of it was a black electrical cord that ended in a red rubber bulb.

"Go ahead," Dussander said. "The Fuehrer says it's all right. He says it's your reward for studying."

Todd looked down at himself and saw that he was naked. His small penis was fully erect, jutting plumply up at an angle from the thin peachdown of his pubic hair. He slipped the dildo on. The fit was tight but there was some sort of lubricant in there. The friction was pleasant. No; it was more than pleasant. It was delightful.

He looked down at the girl and felt a strange shift in his thoughts . . . as if they had slipped into a perfect groove. Suddenly all things seemed right. Doors had been opened. He would go through them. He took the red rubber bulb in his left hand, put his knees on the table, and paused for just a moment, gauging the angle while his Norseman's prick made its own angle up and out from his slight boy's body.

Dimly, far off, he could hear Dussander reciting: "Test run eighty-four. Electricity, sexual stimulus, metabolism. Based on the Thyssen theories of negative reinforcement. Subject is a young Jewish girl, approximately sixteen years of age, no scars, no identifying marks, no known disabilities—"

She cried out when the tip of the dildo touched her. Todd found the cry pleasant, as he did her fruitless struggles to free herself, or, lacking that, to at least bring her legs together.

This is what they can't show in those magazines about the war, he thought, *but it's there, just the same.*

He thrust forward suddenly, parting her with no grace. She shrieked like a fireball.

After her initial thrashings and efforts to expel him, she lay perfectly still, enduring. The lubricated interior of the dildo pulled and slid against Todd's engorgement. Delightful. Heavenly. His ringers toyed with the rubber bulb in his left hand.

Far away, Dussander recited pulse, blood pressure, respiration, alpha waves, beta waves, stroke count.

As the climax began to build inside him, Todd became perfectly still and squeezed the bulb. Her eyes, which had been closed, flew open, bulging. Her tongue fluttered in the pink cavity of her mouth. Her arms and legs thrummed. But the real action was in her torso, rising and falling, vibrating, every muscle

(oh every muscle every muscle moves tightens closes every)
every muscle and the sensation at climax was
(ecstasy)
oh it was, it was

(the end of the world thundering outside)

He woke to that sound and the sound of rain. He was huddled on his side in a dark ball, his heart beating at a sprinter's pace. His lower belly was covered with a warm, sticky liquid. There was an instant of panicky horror when he feared he might be bleeding to death . . . and then he realized what it *really* was, and he felt a fainting, nauseated revulsion. Semen. Come. Jizz. Jungle-juice. Words from fences and locker rooms and the walls of gas station bathrooms. There was nothing here he wanted.

His hands balled helplessly into fists. His dream-climax recurred to him, pallid now, senseless, frightening. But nerve-endings still tingled, retreating slowly from their spike-point. That final scene, fading now, was disgusting and yet somehow compulsive, like an unsuspecting bite into a piece of tropical fruit which, you realized (a second too late), had only tasted so amazingly sweet because it was rotten.

It came to him then. What he would have to do.

There was only one way he could get himself back again. He would have to kill Dussander. It was the only way. Games were done; storytime was over. This was survival.

"Kill him and it's all over," he whispered in the darkness, with the rain in the tree outside and semen drying on his belly. Whispering it made it seem real.

Dussander always kept three or four fifths of Ancient Age on a shelf over the steep cellar stairs. He would go to the door, open it (half-crocked already, more often than not), and go down two steps. Then he would lean out, put one hand on the shelf, and grip the fresh bottle by the neck with his other hand. The cellar floor was not paved, but the dirt was hard-packed and Dussander, with a machinelike efficiency that Todd now thought of as Prussian rather than German, oiled it once every two months to keep bugs from breeding in the dirt. Cement or no cement, old bones break easily. And old men have accidents. The post-mortem would show that "Mr. Denker" had had a skinful of booze when he "fell."

What happened, Todd?

He didn't answer the door so I used the key he gave me. Sometimes he falls asleep. I went into the kitchen and saw the cellar door was open. I went down the stairs and he . . . he . . .

Then, of course, tears.

It would work.

He would have himself back again.

For a long time Todd lay awake in the dark, listening to the thunder retreat westward, out over the Pacific, listening to the secret sound of the rain. He thought he would stay awake the rest of the night, going over it and over it. But he fell asleep only moments later and slept dreamlessly with one fist curled under his chin. He woke on the first of May fully rested for the first time in months.

11

May, 1975.

For Todd, that Friday was the longest of his life. He sat in class after class, hearing nothing, waiting only for the last five minutes, when the instructor would take out his or her small pile of Flunk Cards and distribute them. Each time an instructor approached Todd's desk with that pile of cards, he grew cold. Each time he or she passed him without stopping, he felt waves of dizziness and semi-hysteria.

Algebra was the worst. Storrman approached . . . hesitated . . . and just as Todd became convinced he was going to pass on, he laid a Flunk Card face down on Todd's desk. Todd looked at it coldly, with no feelings at all. Now that it had happened, he was only cold. *Well, that's it,* he thought. *Point, game, set, and match. Unless Dussander can think of something else. And I have my doubts.*

Without much interest, he turned the Flunk Card over to see by how much he had missed his C. It must have been close, but trust old Stony Storrman not to give anyone a break. He saw that the grade-spaces were utterly blank—both the letter-grade space and the numerical-grade space. Written in the comments section was this message: *I'm sure glad I don't have to give you one of these for* real! *Chas. Storrman.*

The dizziness came again, more savagely this time, roaring through his head, making it feel like a balloon filled with helium. He gripped the sides of his desk as hard as he could, holding one thought with total obsessive tightness: *You will not faint, not faint, not faint.* Little by little the waves of dizziness passed, and then he had to control an urge to run up the aisle after Storrman, turn him around, and poke his eyes out with the freshly sharpened pencil he held in his hand. And through it all his face remained carefully blank. The only sign that anything at all was going on inside was a mild tic in one eyelid.

School let out for the week fifteen minutes later. Todd walked slowly around the building to the bike-racks, his head down, his hands shoved into his pockets, his books tucked into the crook of his right arm, oblivious of the running, shouting students. He tossed the books into his bike-basket, unlocked the Schwinn, and pedaled away. Toward Dussander's house.

Today, he thought. *Today is your day, old man.*

"And so," Dussander said, pouring bourbon into his cup as Todd entered the kitchen, "the accused returns from the dock. How said they, prisoner?" He was wearing his bathrobe and a pair of hairy wool socks that climbed halfway up his shins. Socks like that, Todd thought, would be easy to slip in. He glanced at the bottle of Ancient Age Dussander was currently working. It was down to the last three fingers.

"No D's, no F's, no Flunk Cards," Todd said. "I'll still have to change some of my grades in June, but maybe just the averages. I'll be getting all A's and B's this quarter if I keep up my work."

"Oh, you'll keep it up, all right," Dussander said. "We will see to it." He drank and then tipped more bourbon into his cup. "This calls for a celebration." His speech was slightly blurred—hardly enough to be noticeable, but Todd knew the old fuck was as drunk as he ever got. Yes, today. It would have to be today.

But he was cool.

"Celebrate pigshit," he told Dussander.

"I'm afraid the delivery boy hasn't arrived with the beluga and the truffles yet," Dussander said, ignoring him. "Help is so unreliable these days. What about a few Ritz crackers and some Velveeta while we wait?"

"Okay," Todd said. "What the hell."

Dussander stood up (one knee banged the table, making him wince) and crossed to the refrigerator. He got out the cheese, took a knife from the drawer and a plate from the cupboard, and a box of Ritz crackers from the breadbox.

"All carefully injected with prussic acid," he told Todd as he set the cheese and crackers down on the table. He grinned, and Todd saw that he had left out his false teeth again today. Nevertheless, Todd smiled back.

"So quiet today!" Dussander exclaimed. "I would have expected you to turn handsprings all the way up the hall." He emptied the last of the bourbon into his cup, sipped, smacked his lips.

"I guess I'm still numb," Todd said. He bit into a cracker. He had stopped refusing Dussander's food a long time ago. Dussander thought there was a letter with one of Todd's friends—there was not, of course; he had friends, but none he trusted *that* much. He supposed Dussander had guessed that long ago, but he knew Dussander didn't quite dare put his guess to such an extreme test as murder.

"What shall we talk about today?" Dussander enquired, tossing off the last shot. "I give you the day off from studying, how's that? Uh? Uh?" When he drank, his accent became thicker. It was an accent Todd had come to hate. Now he felt okay about the accent; he felt okay about everything. He felt very cool all over. He looked at his hands, the hands which would give the push, and they looked just as they always did. They were not trembling; they were cool.

"I don't care," he said. "Anything you want."

"Shall I tell you about the special soap we made? Our experiments with enforced homosexuality? Or perhaps you would like to hear how I escaped Berlin after I had been foolish enough to go back. That was a close one, I can tell you." He pantomimed shaving one stubby cheek and laughed.

"Anything," Todd said. "Really." He watched Dussander examine the empty bottle and then get up with it in one hand. Dussander took it to the wastebasket and dropped it in.

"No, none of those, I think," Dussander said. "You don't seem to be in the mood." He stood reflectively by the wastebasket for a moment and then crossed the kitchen to the cellar door. His wool socks whispered on the hilly linoleum. "I think today I will instead tell you the story of an old man who was afraid."

Dussander opened the cellar door. His back was now to the table. Todd stood up quietly.

"He was afraid," Dussander went on, "of a certain young boy who was, in a queer way, his friend. A smart boy. His mother called this boy 'apt pupil,' and the old man had already discovered he *was* an apt pupil . . . although perhaps not in the way his mother thought."

Dussander fumbled with the old-fashioned electrical switch on the wall, trying to turn it with his bunched and clumsy fingers. Todd walked—almost glided—across the linoleum, not stepping on any of the places where it squeaked or creaked. He knew this kitchen as well as his own, now. Maybe better.

"At first, the boy was not the old man's friend," Dussander said. He managed to turn the switch at last. He descended the first step with a veteran drunk's care. "At first the old man disliked the boy a great deal. Then he grew to . . . to enjoy his company, although there was still a strong element of dislike there." He was looking at the shelf now but still holding the railing. Todd, cool—no, now he was *cold*—stepped behind him and calculated the chances of one strong push dislodging Dussander's hold on the railing. He decided to wait until Dussander leaned forward.

"Part of the old man's enjoyment came from a feeling of equality," Dussander went on thoughtfully. "You see, the boy and the old man had each other in mutual deathgrips. Each knew something the other wanted kept secret. And then . . . ah, then it became apparent to the old man that things were changing. Yes. He was losing his hold—some of it or all of it, depending on how desperate the boy might be, and how clever. It occurred to this old man on one long and sleepless night that it might be well for him to acquire a new hold on the boy. For his own safety."

Now Dussander let go of the railing and leaned out over the steep cellar stairs, but Todd remained perfectly still. The bone-deep cold was melting out of him, being replaced by a rosy flush of anger and confusion. As Dussander grasped his fresh bottle, Todd thought viciously that the old man had the stinkiest cellar in town, oil or no oil. It smelled as if something had died down there.

"So the old man got out of his bed right then. What is sleep to an old man? Very little. And he sat at his small desk, thinking about how cleverly he had enmeshed the boy in the very crimes the boy was holding over his own head. He sat thinking about how hard the boy had worked, how very hard, to bring his school marks back up. And how, when they *were* back up, he would have no further need for the old man alive. And if the old man were dead, the boy could be free."

He turned around now, holding the fresh bottle of Ancient Age by the neck.

"I heard you, you know," he said, almost gently. "From the moment you pushed your chair back and stood up. You are not as quiet as you imagine, boy. At least not yet."

Todd said nothing.

"So!" Dussander exclaimed, stepping back into the kitchen and closing the cellar door firmly behind him. "The old man wrote everything down, *nicht wahr*? From first word to last he wrote it down. When he was finally finished it was almost dawn and his hand was singing from the arthritis—the *verdammt* arthritis—but he felt good for the first times in weeks. He felt *safe*. He got back into his bed and slept until mid-afternoon. In fact, if he had slept any longer, he would have missed his favorite—*General Hospital*."

He had regained his rocker now. He sat down, produced a worn jackknife with a yellow ivory handle, and began to cut painstakingly around the seal covering the top of the bourbon bottle.

"On the following day the old man dressed in his best suit and went down to the bank where he kept his little checking and savings accounts. He spoke to one of the bank officers, who was able to answer all the old man's questions most satisfactorily. He rented a safety deposit box. The bank officer explained to the old man that he would have a key and the bank would have a key. To open the box, both keys would be needed. No one but the old man could use the old man's key without a signed, notarized letter of permission from the old man himself. With one exception."

Dussander smiled toothlessly into Todd Bowden's white, set face.

"That exception is made in the event of the box-holder's death," he said. Still looking at Todd, still smiling, Dussander put his jackknife back into the pocket of his robe, unscrewed the cap of the bourbon bottle, and poured a fresh jolt into his cup.

"What happens then?" Todd asked hoarsely.

"Then the box is opened in the presence of a bank official and a representative of the Internal Revenue Service. The contents of the box are inventoried. In this case they will find only a twelve-page document. Non-taxable . . . but highly interesting."

The fingers of Todd's hands crept toward each other and locked tightly. "You can't do that," he said in a stunned and unbelieving voice. It was the voice of a person who observes another person walking on the ceiling. "You can't. . . can't do that."

"My boy," Dussander said kindly, "I have."

"But . . . I . . . you . . ." His voice suddenly rose to an agonized howl. "You're *old*! Don't you know that you're *old*? You could die! *You could die anytime!*"

Dussander got up. He went to one of the kitchen cabinets and took down a small glass. This glass had once held jelly. Cartoon characters danced around the rim. Todd recognized them all—Fred and Wilma Flintstone, Barney and Betty Rubble, Pebbles and Bamm-Bamm. He had grown up with them. He watched as Dussander wiped this jelly-glass almost ceremonially with a dishtowel. He watched as Dussander set it in front of him. He watched as Dussander poured a finger of bourbon into it.

"What's that for?" Todd muttered. "I don't drink. Drinking's for cheap stewbums like you."

"Lift your glass, boy. It is a special occasion. Today you drink."

Todd looked at him for a long moment, then picked up the glass. Dussander clicked his cheap ceramic cup smartly against it.

"I make a toast, boy—long life! Long life to both of us! *Prosit!*" He tossed his bourbon off at a gulp and then began to laugh. He rocked back and forth, stockinged feet hitting the linoleum, laughing, and Todd thought he had never looked so much like a vulture, a vulture in a bathrobe, a noisome beast of carrion.

"I hate you," he whispered, and then Dussander began to choke on his own laughter. His face turned a dull brick color; it sounded as if he were coughing, laughing, and strangling, all at the same time. Todd, scared, got up quickly and clapped him on the back until the coughing fit had passed.

"Danke schön," he said. "Drink your drink. It will do you good."

Todd drank it. It tasted like very bad cold-medicine and lit a fire in his gut.

"I can't believe you drink this shit all day," he said, putting the glass back on the table and shuddering. "You ought to quit it. Quit drinking *and* smoking."

"Your concern for my health is touching," Dussander said. He produced a crumpled pack of cigarettes from the same bathrobe pocket into which the jackknife had disappeared. "And I am equally solicitous of your own welfare, boy. Almost every day I read in the paper where a cyclist has been killed at a busy intersection. You should give it up. You should walk. Or ride the bus, like me."

"Why don't you go fuck yourself?" Todd burst out.

"My boy," Dussander said, pouring more bourbon and beginning to laugh again, "we are fucking each other—didn't you know that?"

One day about a week later, Todd was sitting on a disused mail platform down in the old trainyard. He chucked cinders out across the rusty, weed-infested tracks one at a time.

Why shouldn't I kill him anyway?

Because he was a logical boy, the logical answer came first. No reason at all. Sooner or later Dussander was going to die, and given Dussander's habits, it would probably be sooner. Whether he killed the old man or whether Dussander died of a heart attack in his bathtub, it was all going to come out. At least he could have the pleasure of wringing the old vulture's neck.

Sooner or later—that phrase defied logic.

Maybe it'll be later, Todd thought. *Cigarettes or not, booze or not, he's a tough old bastard. He's lasted this long, so . . . so maybe it'll be later.*

From beneath him came a fuzzy snort.

Todd jumped to his feet, dropping a handful of cinders he had been holding. That snorting sound came again.

He paused, on the verge of running, but the snort didn't recur. Nine hundred yards away, an eight-lane freeway swept across the horizon above this weed- and junk-strewn cul-de-sac with its deserted buildings, rusty Cyclone fences, and splintery, warped platforms. The cars up on the freeway glistened in the sun like exotic hard-shelled beetles. Eight lanes of traffic up there, nothing down here but Todd, a few birds . . . and whatever had snorted.

Cautiously, he bent down with his hands on his knees and peered under the mail platform. There was a wino lying up in there among the yellow weeds and empty cans and dusty old bottles. It was impossible to tell his age; Todd put him at somewhere between thirty and four hundred. He was wearing a strappy tee-shirt that was caked with dried vomit, green pants that were far too big for him, and gray leather workshoes cracked in a hundred places. The cracks gaped like agonized mouths. Todd thought he smelled like Dussander's cellar.

The wino's red-laced eyes opened slowly and stared at Todd with a bleary lack of wonder. As they did, Todd thought of the Swiss Army knife in his pocket, the Angler model. He had purchased it at a sporting goods store in Redondo Beach almost a year ago. He could hear the clerk that had waited on him in his mind: *You couldn't pick a better knife than that one, son—a knife like that could save your life someday. We sell fifteen hundred Swiss knives every damn year.*

Fifteen hundred a year.

He put his hand in his pocket and gripped the knife. In his mind's eye he saw Dussander's jackknife working slowly around the neck of the bourbon bottle, slitting the seal. A moment later he became aware that he had an erection.

Cold terror stole into him.

The wino swiped a hand over his cracked lips and then licked them with a tongue which nicotine had turned a permanent dismal yellow. "Got a dime, kid?"

Todd looked at him expressionlessly.

"Gotta get to L.A. Need another dime for the bus. I got a pointment, me. Got a job offertunity. Nice kid like you must have a dime. Maybe you got a quarter."

Yessir, you could clean out a damn bluegill with a knife like that . . . hell, you could clean out a damn marlin with it if you had to. We sell fifteen hundred of those a year. Every sporting goods store and Army-Navy Surplus in America sells them, and if you decided to use this one to clean out some dirty, shitty old wino, nobody *could trace it back to you, absolutely NOBODY.*

The wino's voice dropped; it became a confidential, tenebrous whisper. "For a buck I'd do you a blowjob, you never had a better. You'd come your brains out, kid, you'd—"

Todd pulled his hand out of his pocket. He wasn't sure what was in it until he opened it. Two quarters. Two nickles. A dime. Some pennies. He threw them at the wino and fled.

12

June, 1975.

Todd Bowden, now fourteen, came biking up Dussander's walk and parked his bike on the kickstand. The L.A. *Times* was on the bottom step; he picked it up. He looked at the bell, below which the neat legends ARTHUR DENKER and NO SOLIC-ITORS, NO PEDDLERS, NO SALESMEN still kept their places. He didn't bother with the bell now, of course; he had his key.

Somewhere close by was the popping, burping sound of a Lawn-Boy. He looked at Dussander's grass and saw it could use a cutting; he would have to tell the old man to find a boy with a mower. Dussander forgot little things like that more often now. Maybe it was senility; maybe it was just the pickling influence of Ancient Age on his brains. That was an adult thought for a boy of fourteen to have, but such thoughts no longer struck Todd as singular. He had many adult thoughts these days. Most of them were not so great.

He let himself in.

He had his usual instant of cold terror as he entered the kitchen and saw Dussander slumped slightly sideways in his rocker, the cup on the table, a half-empty bottle of bourbon beside it. A cigarette had burned its entire length down to lacy gray ash in a mayonnaise cover where several other butts had been mashed out. Dussander's mouth hung open. His face was yellow. His big hands dangled limply over the rocker's arms. He didn't seem to be breathing.

"Dussander," he said, a little too harshly. "Rise and shine, Dussander."

He felt a wave of relief as the old man twitched, blinked, and finally sat up.

"Is it you? And so early?"

"They let us out early on the last day of school," Todd said. He pointed to the remains of the cigarette in the mayonnaise cover. "Someday you'll burn down the house doing that."

"Maybe," Dussander said indifferently. He fumbled out his cigarettes, shot one from the pack (it almost rolled off the edge of the table before Dussander was able to catch it), and at last got it going. A protracted fit of coughing followed, and Todd winced in disgust. When the old man really got going, Todd half-expected him to start spitting out grayish-black chunks of lung-tissue onto the table . . . and he'd probably grin as he did it.

At last the coughing eased enough for Dussander to say, "What have you got there?"

STEPHEN KING

"Report card."

Dussander took it, opened it, and held it away from him at arm's length so he could read it. "English . . . A. American History . . . A. Earth Science . . . B-plus. Your Community and You . . . A. Primary French . . . B-minus. Beginning Algebra . . . B." He put it down. "Very good. What is the slang? We have saved your bacon, boy. Will you have to change any of these averages in the last column?"

"French and algebra, but no more than eight or nine points in all. I don't think any of this is ever going to come out. And I guess I owe that to you. I'm not proud of it, but it's the truth. So, thanks."

"What a touching speech," Dussander said, and began to cough again.

"I guess I won't be seeing you around too much from now on," Todd said, and Dussander abruptly stopped coughing.

"No?" he said, politely enough.

"No," Todd said. "We're going to Hawaii for a month starting on June twenty-fifth. In September I'll be going to school across town. It's this bussing thing."

"Oh yes, the *Schwarzen,*" Dussander said, idly watching a fly as it trundled across the red and white check of the oilcloth. "For twenty years this country has worried and whined about the *Schwarzen.* But we know the solution . . . don't we, boy?" He smiled toothlessly at Todd and Todd looked down, feeling the old sickening lift and drop in his stomach. Terror, hate, and a desire to do something so awful it could only be fully contemplated in his dreams.

"Look, I plan to go to college, in case you didn't know," Todd said. "I know that's a long time off, but I think about it. I even know what I want to major in. History."

"Admirable. He who will not learn from the past is—"

"Oh, shut up," Todd said.

Dussander did so, amiably enough. He knew the boy wasn't done . . . not yet. He sat with his hands folded, watching him.

108

"I could get my letter back from my friend," Todd suddenly blurted. "You know that? I could let you read it, and then you could watch me burn it. If—"

"—if I would remove a certain document from my safety deposit box."

"Well . . . yeah."

Dussander uttered a long, windy, rueful sigh. "My boy," he said. "Still you do not understand the situation. You never have, right from the beginning. Partly because you are only a boy, but not entirely . . . even in the beginning, you were a very *old* boy. No, the real villain was and is your absurd American self-confidence that never allowed you to consider the possible consequences of what you were doing . . . which does not allow it even now."

Todd began to speak and Dussander raised his hand adamantly, suddenly the world's oldest traffic cop.

"No, don't contradict me. It's true. Go on if you like. Leave the house, get out of here, never come back. Can I stop you? No. Of course I can't. Enjoy yourself in Hawaii while I sit in this hot, grease-smelling kitchen and wait to see if the *Schwarzen* in Watts will decide to start killing policemen and burning their shitty tenements again this year. I can't stop you any more than I can stop getting older a day at a time."

He looked at Todd fixedly, so fixedly that Todd looked away.

"Down deep inside, I don't like you. Nothing could make me like you. You forced yourself on me. You are an unbidden guest in my house. You have made me open crypts perhaps better left shut, because I have discovered that some of the corpses were buried alive, and that a few of those *still* have some wind left in them.

"You yourself have become enmeshed, but do I pity you because of that? *Gott im Himmel!* You have made your bed; should I pity you if you sleep badly in it? No . . . I don't pity you, and I don't like you, but I have come to respect you a little bit. So don't try my patience by asking me to explain this

109

twice. We could obtain our documents and destroy them here in my kitchen. And still it would not be over. We would, in fact, be no better off than we are at this minute."

"I don't understand you."

"No, because you have never studied the consequences of what you have set in motion. But attend me, boy. If we burned our letters here, in this jar cover, how would I know you hadn't made a copy? Or two? Or three? Down at the library they have a Xerox machine, for a nickle anyone can make a photocopy. For a dollar, you could post a copy of my death-warrant on every streetcorner for twenty blocks. Two *miles* of death-warrants, boy! Think of it! Can you tell me how I would know you hadn't done such a thing?"

"I . . . well, I . . . I . . ." Todd realized he was floundering and forced himself to shut his mouth. All of a sudden his skin felt too warm, and for no reason at all he found himself remembering something that had happened when he was seven or eight. He and a friend of his had been crawling through a culvert which ran beneath the old Freight Bypass Road just out of town. The friend, skinnier than Todd, had had no problem . . . but Todd had gotten stuck. He had become suddenly aware of the feet of rock and earth over his head, all that dark *weight,* and when an L.A.-bound semi passed above, shaking the earth and making the corrugated pipe vibrate with a low, tuneless, and somehow sinister note, he had begun to cry and to struggle witlessly, throwing himself forward, pistoning with his legs, yelling for help. At last he had gotten moving again, and when he finally struggled out of the pipe, he had fainted.

Dussander had just outlined a piece of duplicity so fundamental that it had never even crossed his mind. He could feel his skin getting hotter, and he thought: *I won't cry.*

"And how would you know I hadn't made *two* copies for my safety deposit box . . . that I had burned one and left the other there?"

Trapped. I'm trapped just like in the pipe that time and who are you going to yell for now?

His heart speeded up in his chest. He felt sweat break on the backs of his hands and the nape of his neck. He remembered how it had been in that pipe, the smell of old water, the feel of the cool, ribbed metal, the way everything shook when the truck passed overhead. He remembered how hot and desperate the tears had been.

"Even if there were some impartial third party we could go to, always there would be doubts. The problem is insoluble, boy. Believe it."

Trapped. Trapped in the pipe. No way out of this one.

He felt the world go gray. *Won't cry. Won't faint.* He forced himself to come back.

Dussander took a deep drink from his cup and looked at Todd over the rim.

"Now I tell you two more things. First, that if your part in this matter came out, your punishment would be quite small. It is even possible—no, more than that, *likely*—that it would never come out in the papers at all. I frightened you with reform school once, when I was badly afraid you might crack and tell everything. But do I believe that? No—I used it the way a father will use the 'boogerman' to frighten a child into coming home before dark. I don't believe that they would send you there, not in this country where they spank killers on the wrist and send them out onto the streets to kill again after two years of watching color TV in a penitentiary.

"But it might well ruin your life all the same. There are records . . . and people talk. Always, they talk. Such a juicy scandal is not allowed to wither; it is bottled, like wine. And, of course, as the years pass, your culpability will grow with you. Your silence will grow more damning. If the truth came out today, people would say, 'But he is just a child!' . . . not knowing, as I do, what an *old* child you are. But what would they say, boy, if the truth about me, coupled with the fact that you knew about me as early as 1974 *but kept silent,* came out while you are in high school? That would be bad. For it to come out while you are in college would be disaster. As a young man just starting out in business . . . Armageddon. You understand this first thing?"

Todd was silent, but Dussander seemed satisfied. He nodded. Still nodding, he said: "Second, I don't believe you *have* a letter."

Todd strove to keep a poker face, but he was terribly afraid his eyes had widened in shock. Dussander was studying him avidly, and Todd was suddenly, nakedly aware that this old man had interrogated hundreds, perhaps *thousands* of people. He was an expert. Todd felt that his skull had turned to window-glass and all things were flashing inside in large letters.

"I asked myself whom you would trust so much. Who are your friends . . . whom do you run with? Whom does this boy, this self-sufficient, coldly controlled little *boy,* go to with his loyalty? The answer is, nobody."

Dussander's eyes gleamed yellowly.

"Many times I have studied you and calculated the odds. I know you, and I know much of your character—no, not all, because one human being can never know everything that is in another human being's heart—but I know so little about what you do and whom you see outside of this house. So I think, 'Dussander, there is a chance that you are wrong. After all these years, do you want to be captured and maybe killed because you misjudged a boy?' Maybe when I was younger I would have taken the chance—the odds are good odds, and the chance is a small chance. It is very strange to me, you know— the older one becomes, the less one has to lose in matters of life and death . . . and yet, one becomes more and more con-servative."

He looked hard into Todd's face.

"I have one more thing to say, and then you can go when you want. What I have to say is that, while I doubt the existence of your letter, never doubt the existence of mine. *The document I have described to you exists.* If I die today . . . tomorrow . . . everything will come out. *Everything.*"

"Then there's nothing for me," Todd said. He uttered a dazed little laugh. "Don't you see that?"

"But there is. Years will go by. As they pass, your hold on me will become worth less and less, because no matter how important my life and liberty remain to me, the Americans and—yes, even the Israelis—will have less and less interest in taking them away."

"Yeah? Then why don't they let that guy Hess go?"

"If the Americans had sole custody of him—the Americans who let killers out with a spank on the wrist—they *would* have let him go," Dussander said. "Are the Americans going to allow the Israelis to extradite an eighty-year-old man so they can hang him as they hanged Eichmann? I think not. Not in a country where they put photographs of firemen rescuing kittens from trees on the front pages of city newspapers.

"No, your hold over me will weaken even as mine over you grows stronger. No situation is static. And there will come a time—if I live long enough—when I will decide what you know no longer matters. Then I will destroy the document."

"But so many things could happen to you in between! Accidents, sickness, disease—"

Dussander shrugged. " 'There will be water if God wills it, and we will find it if God wills it, and we will drink it if God wills it.' What happens is not up to us."

Todd looked at the old man for a long time—for a very long time. There were flaws in Dussander's arguments—there had to be. A way out, an escape hatch either for both of them or for Todd alone. A way to cry it off—times, guys, I hurt my foot, allee-allee-in-free. A black knowledge of the years ahead trembled somewhere behind his eyes; he could feel it there, waiting to be born as conscious thought. Everywhere he went, everything he did—

He thought of a cartoon character with an anvil suspended over its head. By the time he graduated from high school, Dussander would be eighty-one, and that would not be the end; by the time he collected his B.A., Dussander would be eighty-five and he would still feel that he wasn't old enough, he would finish his master's thesis and graduate school the year Dussander turned eighty-seven . . . and Dussander still might not feel safe.

"No," Todd said thickly. "What you're saying . . . I can't face that."

"My boy," Dussander said gently, and Todd heard for the first time and with dawning horror the slight accent the old man had put on the first word. "My boy . . . you must."

Todd stared at him, his tongue swelling and thickening in his mouth until it seemed it must fill his throat and choke him. Then he wheeled and blundered out of the house.

Dussander watched all of this with no expression at all, and when the door had slammed shut and the boy's running footsteps stopped, meaning that he had mounted his bike, he lit a cigarette. There was, of course, no safe deposit box, no document. But the boy believed those things existed; he had believed utterly. He was safe. It was ended.

But it was not ended.

That night they both dreamed of murder, and both of them awoke in mingled terror and exhilaration.

Todd awoke with the now familiar stickiness of his lower belly. Dussander, too old for such things, put on the SS uniform and then lay down again, waiting for his racing heart to slow. The uniform was cheaply made and already beginning to fray.

In Dussander's dream he had finally reached the camp at the top of the hill. The wide gate slid open for him and then rumbled shut on its steel track once he was inside. Both the gate and the fence surrounding the camp were electrified. His scrawny, naked pursuers threw themselves against the fence in wave after wave; Dussander had laughed at them and he had strutted back and forth, his chest thrown out, his cap cocked at exactly the right angle. The high, winey smell of burning flesh filled the black air, and he had awakened in southern California thinking of jack-o'-lanterns and the night when vampires seek the blue flame.

Two days before the Bowdens were scheduled to fly to Hawaii, Todd went back to the abandoned trainyard where folks had once boarded trains for San Francisco, Seattle, and Las Vegas; where other, older folks had once boarded the trolley for Los Angeles.

It was nearly dusk when he got there. On the curve of freeway nine hundred yards away, most of the cars were now showing their parking lights. Although it was warm, Todd was wearing a light jacket. Tucked into his belt under it was a butcher knife wrapped in an old hand-towel. He had purchased the knife in a discount department store, one of the big ones surrounded by acres of parking lot.

He looked under the platform where the wino had been the month before. His mind turned and turned, but it turned on nothing; everything inside him at that moment was shades of black on black.

What he found was the same wino or possibly another; they all looked pretty much the same.

"Hey!" Todd said. "Hey! You want some money?"

The wino turned over, blinking. He saw Todd's wide, sunny grin and began to grin back. A moment later the butcher knife descended, all whicker-snicker and chrome-white, slicker-slicing through the stubbly right cheek. Blood sprayed. Todd could see the blade in the wino's opening mouth . . . and then its tip caught for a moment in the left corner of the wino's lips, pulling his mouth into an insanely cockeyed grin. Then it was the knife that was making the grin; he was carving the wino like a Halloween pumpkin.

He stabbed the wino thirty-seven times. He kept count. Thirty-seven, counting the first strike, which went through the wino's cheek and then turned his tentative smile into a great grisly grin. The wino stopped trying to scream after the fourth stroke. He stopped trying to scramble away from Todd after the sixth. Todd then crawled all the way under the platform and finished the job.

On his way home he threw the knife into the river. His pants were bloodstained. He tossed them into the washing machine and set it to wash cold. There were still faint stains on the pants when they came out, but they didn't concern Todd. They would fade in time. He found the next day that he could barely lift his right arm to the level of his shoulder. He told his father he must have strained it throwing pepper with some of the guys in the park.

"It'll get better in Hawaii," Dick Bowden said, ruffling Todd's hair, and it did; by the time they came home, it was as good as new.

13

It was July again.

Dussander, carefully dressed in one of his three suits (not his best), was standing at the bus stop and waiting for the last local of the day to take him home. It was 10:45 p.m. He had been to a film, a light and frothy comedy that he had enjoyed a great deal. He had been in a fine mood ever since the morning mail. There had been a postcard from the boy, a glossy color photo of Waikiki Beach with bone-white highrise hotels standing in the background. There was a brief message on the reverse.

Dear Mr. Denker,

   Boy this sure is some place. I've been swimming every
day. My dad caught a big fish and my mom is catching
up on her reading (joke). Tomorrow we're going to a vol-
cano. I'll try not to fall in! Hope you're okay.

Stay healthy,
Todd

He was still smiling faintly at the significance of that last
when a hand touched his elbow.

"Mister?"

"Yes?"

He turned, on his guard—even in Santo Donato, muggers
were not unknown—and then winced at the aroma. It seemed
to be a combination of beer, halitosis, dried sweat, and possibly Musterole. It was a bum in baggy pants. He—*it*—wore a
flannel shirt and very old loafers that were currently being held
together with dirty bands of adhesive tape. The face looming
above this motley costume looked like the death of God.

   "You got an extra dime, mister? I gotta get to L.A., me. Got
a job offertunity. I need just a dime more for the express bus. I
wudn't ask if it wadn't a big chance for me."

Dussander had begun to frown, but now his smile reasserted
itself.

   "Is it really a bus ride you wish?"

The wino smiled sickly, not understanding.

   "Suppose you ride the bus home with me," Dussander pro-
posed. "I can offer you a drink, a meal, a bath, and a bed. All
I ask in return is a little conversation. I am an old man. I live
alone. Company is sometimes very welcome."

   The drunk's smile abruptly grew more healthy as the situation clarified itself. Here was a well-to-do old faggot with a
taste for slumming.

   "All by yourself! Bitch, innit?"

Dussander answered the broad, insinuating grin with a polite smile. "I only ask that you sit away from me on the bus. You smell rather strongly."

"Maybe you don't want me stinking up your place, then," the drunk said with sudden, tipsy dignity.

"Come, the bus will be here in a minute. Get off one stop after I do and then walk back two blocks. I'll wait for you on the corner. In the morning I will see what I can spare. Perhaps two dollars."

"Maybe even five," the drunk said brightly. His dignity, tipsy or otherwise, had been forgotten.

"Perhaps, perhaps," Dussander said impatiently. He could now hear the low diesel drone of the approaching bus. He pressed a quarter, the correct bus fare, into the bum's grimy hand and strolled a few paces away without looking back.

The bum stood undecided as the headlights of the local swept over the rise. He was still standing and frowning down at the quarter when the old faggot got on the bus without looking back. The bum began to walk away and then—at the last second—he reversed direction and boarded the bus just before the doors folded closed. He put the quarter into the fare-box with the expression of a man putting a hundred dollars down on a long shot. He passed Dussander without doing more than glancing at him and sat at the back of the bus. He dozed off a little, and when he woke up, the rich old faggot was gone. He got off at the next stop, not knowing if it was the right one or not, and not really caring.

He walked back two blocks and saw a dim shape under the streetlight. It was the old faggot, all right. The faggot was watching him approach, and he was standing as if at attention.

For just a moment the bum felt a chill of apprehension, an urge to just turn away and forget the whole thing.

Then the old man was gripping him by the arm . . . and his grip was surprisingly firm.

"Good," the old man said. "I'm very glad you came. My house is down here. It's not far."

"Maybe even ten," the bum said, allowing himself to be led.

"Maybe even ten," the old faggot agreed, and then laughed. "Who knows?"

14

The Bi-Centennial year arrived.

Todd came by to see Dussander half a dozen times between his return from Hawaii in the summer of 1975 and the trip he and his parents took to Rome just as all the drum-thumping, flag-waving, and Tall Ships-watching was approaching its climax.

These visits to Dussander were low-key and in no way unpleasant; the two of them found they could pass the time civilly enough. They spoke more in silences than they did in words, and their actual conversations would have put an FBI agent to sleep. Todd told the old man that he had been seeing a girl named Angela Farrow off and on. He wasn't nuts about her, but she was the daughter of one of his mother's friends. The old man told Todd he had taken up braiding rugs because he had read such an activity was good for arthritis. He showed Todd several samples of his work, and Todd dutifully admired them.

The boy had grown quite a bit, had he not? (Well, two inches.) Had Dussander given up smoking? (No, but he had been forced to cut down; they made him cough too much now.) How had his schoolwork been? (Challenging but exciting; he had made all A's and B's, had gone to the state finals with his Science Fair project on solar power, and was now thinking of majoring in anthropology instead of history when he got to college.) Who was mowing Dussander's lawn this year?

(Randy Chambers from just down the street—a good boy, but rather fat and slow.)

During that year Dussander had put an end to three winos in his kitchen. He had been approached at the downtown bus stop some twenty times, had made the drink-dinner-bath-and-bed offer seven times. He had been turned down twice, and on two other occasions the winos had simply walked off with the quarters Dussander gave them for the fare-box. After some thought, he had worked out a way around this; he simply bought a book of coupons. They were two dollars and fifty cents, good for fifteen rides, and non-negotiable at the local liquor stores.

On very warm days just lately, Dussander had noticed an unpleasant smell drifting up from his cellar. He kept his doors and windows firmly shut on these days.

Todd Bowden had found a wino sleeping it off in an abandoned drainage culvert behind a vacant lot on Cienaga Way—this had been in December, during the Christmas vacation. He had stood there for some time, hands stuffed into his pockets, looking at the wino and trembling. He had returned to the lot six times over a period of five weeks, always wearing his light jacket, zipped halfway up to conceal the Craftsman hammer tucked into his belt. At last he had come upon the wino again—that one or some other, and who really gave a fuck—on the first day of March. He had begun with the hammer end of the tool, and then at some point (he didn't really remember when; everything had been swimming in a red haze) he had switched to the claw end, obliterating the wino's face.

For Kurt Dussander, the winos were a half-cynical propitiation of gods he had finally recognized . . . or re-recognized. And the winos were fun. They made him feel alive. He was beginning to feel that the years he had spent in Santo Donato—the years before the boy had turned up on his doorstep with his big blue eyes and his wide American grin—had been years spent being old before his time. He had been just past his mid-sixties when he came here. And he felt much younger than that now.

The idea of propitiating gods would have startled Todd at first—but it might have gained eventual acceptance. After stabbing the wino under the train platform, he had expected his nightmares to intensify—to perhaps even drive him crazy. He had expected waves of paralyzing guilt that might well end with a blurted confession or the taking of his own life.

Instead of any of those things, he had gone to Hawaii with his parents and enjoyed the best vacation of his life.

He had begun high school last September feeling oddly new and refreshed, as if a different person had jumped into his Todd Bowden skin. Things that had made no particular impression on him since earliest childhood—the sunlight just after dawn, the look of the ocean off the Fish Pier, the sight of people hurrying on a downtown street at just that moment of dusk when the streetlights come on—these things now imprinted themselves on his mind again in a series of bright cameos, in images so clear they seemed electroplated. He tasted life on his tongue like a draught of wine straight from the bottle.

After he had seen the stewbum in the culvert, but before he killed him, the nightmares had begun again.

The most common one involved the wino he had stabbed to death in the abandoned trainyard. Home from school, he burst into the house, a cheery *Hi, Monica-baby!* on his lips. It died there as he saw the dead wino in the raised breakfast nook. He was sitting slumped over their butcher-block table in his puke-smelling shirt and pants. Blood had streaked across the bright tiled floor; it was drying on the stainless steel counters. There were bloody handprints on the natural pine cupboards.

Clipped to the note-board by the fridge was a message from his mother: *Todd—Gone to the store. Back by 3:30.* The hands of the stylish sunburst clock over the Jenn-Air range stood at 3:20 and the drunk was sprawled dead up there in the nook like some horrid oozing relic from the subcellar of a junkshop and there was blood everywhere, and Todd began trying to clean it up, wiping every exposed surface, all the time screaming at the dead wino that he had to *go,* had to leave him *alone,* and the wino just lolled there and stayed dead, grinning up at the ceiling, and freshets of blood kept pouring from the stab-wounds in his dirty skin. Todd grabbed the O Cedar mop from the closet and began to slide it madly back and forth across the floor, aware that he was not really getting the blood up, only diluting it, spreading it around, but unable to stop. And just as he heard his mother's Town and Country wagon turn into the driveway, he realized the wino was Dussander. He woke from these dreams sweating and gasping, clutching double handfuls of the bedclothes.

But after he finally found the wino in the culvert again— that wino or some other—and used the hammer on him, these dreams went away. He supposed he might have to kill again, and maybe more than once. It was too bad, but of course their time of usefulness as human creatures was over. Except their usefulness to Todd, of course. And Todd, like everyone else he knew, was only tailoring his lifestyle to fit his own particular needs as he grew older. Really, he was no different than anybody. You had to make your own way in the world; if you were going to get along, you had to do it by yourself.

15

In the fall of his junior year, Todd played varsity tailback for the Santo Donato Cougars and was named All-Conference. And in the second quarter of that year, the quarter which ended in late January of 1977, he won the American Legion Patriotic Essay Contest. This contest was open to all city high school students who were taking American history courses. Todd's piece was called "An American's Responsibility." During the baseball season that year he was the school's star pitcher, winning four and losing none. His batting average was .361. At the awards assembly in June he was named Athlete of the Year and given a plaque by Coach Haines (Coach Haines, who had once taken him aside and told him to keep practicing his curve "because none of these niggers can hit a curve-ball, Bowden, not one of them"). Monica Bowden burst into tears when Todd called her from school and told her he was going to get the award. Dick Bowden strutted around his office for two weeks following the ceremony, trying not to boast. That summer they rented a cabin in Big Sur and stayed there for two weeks and Todd snorkled his brains out. During that same year Todd killed four derelicts. He stabbed two of them and bludgeoned two of them. He had taken to wearing two pairs of pants on what he now acknowledged to be hunting expeditions. Sometimes he rode the city busses, looking for likely spots. The best two, he found, were the Santo Donato Mission for the Indigent on Douglas Street, and around the corner from the Salvation Army on Euclid. He would walk slowly through both of these neighborhoods, waiting to be panhandled. When a wino approached him, Todd would tell him that he, Todd, wanted a bottle of whiskey, and if the wino would buy it, Todd would share the bottle. He knew a place, he said, where they could go. It was a different place every time, of course. He resisted a strong urge to go back either to the trainyard or to the culvert behind the vacant lot on Cienaga Way. Revisiting the scene of a previous crime would have been unwise.

During the same year Dussander smoked sparingly, drank Ancient Age bourbon, and watched TV. Todd came by once in awhile, but their conversations became increasingly arid. They were growing apart. Dussander celebrated his seventy-ninth birthday that year, which was also the year Todd turned sixteen. Dussander remarked that sixteen was the best year of a young man's life, forty-one the best year of a middle-aged man's, and seventy-nine the best of an old man's. Todd nodded politely. Dussander had been quite drunk, and cackled in a way that made Todd distinctly uneasy.

Dussander had dispatched two winos during Todd's academic year of 1976–77. The second had been livelier than he looked; even after Dussander had gotten the man soddenly drunk he had tottered around the kitchen with the haft of a steak-knife jutting from the base of his neck, gushing blood down the front of his shirt and onto the floor. The wino had re-discovered the front hall after two staggering circuits of the kitchen and had almost escaped the house.

Dussander had stood in the kitchen, eyes wide with shocked unbelief, watching the wino grunt and puff his way toward the door, rebounding from one side of the hall to the other and knocking cheap Currier & Ives reproductions to the floor. His paralysis had not broken until the wino was actually groping for the doorknob. Then Dussander had bolted across the room, jerked open the utility drawer, and pulled out his meat-fork. He ran down the hall with the meat-fork held out in front of him and drove it into the wino's back.

Dussander had stood over him, panting, his old heart racing in a frightening way . . . racing like that of a heart-attack victim on that Saturday night TV program he enjoyed, *Emergency!* But at last it had slowed back into a normal rhythm and he knew he was going to be all right.

There had been a great deal of blood to clean up.

That had been four months ago, and since then he had not made his offer at the downtown bus stop. He was frightened of the way he had almost bungled the last one . . . but when he remembered the way he had handled things at the last moment, pride rose in his heart. In the end the wino had never made it out the door, and that was the important thing.

16

In the fall of 1977, during the first quarter of his senior year, Todd joined the Rifle Club. By June of 1978 he had qualified as a marksman. He made All-Conference in football again, won five and lost one during the baseball season (the loss coming as the result of two errors and one unearned run), and made the third highest Merit Scholarship score in the school's history. He applied to Berkeley and was promptly accepted. By April he knew he would either be valedictorian or salutatorian on graduation night. He very badly wanted to be valedictorian.

During the latter half of his senior year, an odd impulse came on him—one which was as frightening to Todd as it was irrational. He seemed to be clearly and firmly in control of it, and *that* at least was comforting, but that such a thought should have occurred at all was scary. He had made an arrangement with life. He had worked things out. His life was much like his mother's bright and sunshiny kitchen, where all the surfaces were dressed in chrome, Formica, or stainless steel—a place where everything worked when you pressed the buttons. There were deep and dark cupboards in this kitchen, of course, but many things could be stored in them and their doors still be closed.

This new impulse reminded him of the dream in which he had come home to discover the dead and bleeding wino in his mother's clean, well-lighted place. It was as if, in the bright and careful arrangement he had made, in that a-place-for-everything-and-everything-in-its-place kitchen of his mind, a dark and bloody intruder now lurched and shambled, looking for a place to die conspicuously . . .

A quarter of a mile from the Bowden house was the freeway, running eight lanes wide. A steep and brushy bank led down to it. There was plenty of good cover on the bank. His father had given him a Winchester .30-.30 for Christmas, and it had a removable telescopic sight. During rush hour, when all eight lanes were jammed, he could pick a spot on that bank and . . . why, he could easily . . .

Do what?

Commit suicide?

Destroy everything he had worked for these last four years?
Say *what?*
No *sir,* no *ma'am,* no *way.*
It is, as they say, to laugh.
Sure it was . . . but the impulse remained.

One Saturday a few weeks before his high school graduation, Todd cased the .30-.30 after carefully emptying the magazine. He put the rifle in the back seat of his father's new toy—a used Porsche. He drove to the spot where the brushy slope dropped steeply down to the freeway. His mother and father had taken the station wagon and had driven to L.A. for the weekend. Dick, now a full partner, would be holding discussions with the Hyatt people about a new Reno hotel.

Todd's heart bumped in his chest and his mouth was full of sour, electric spit as he worked his way down the grade with the cased rifle in his arms. He came to a fallen tree and sat cross-legged behind it. He uncased the rifle and laid it on the dead tree's smooth trunk. A branch jutting off at an angle made a nice rest for the barrel. He snugged the buttplate into the hollow of his right shoulder and peered into the telescopic sight.

Stupid! his mind screamed at him. *Boy, this is really stupid! If someone sees you, it's not going to matter if the gun's loaded or not! You'll get in plenty of trouble, maybe even end up with some Chippie shooting at you!*

It was mid-morning and the Saturday traffic was light. He settled the crosshairs on a woman behind the wheel of a blue Toyota. The woman's window was half-open and the round collar of her sleeveless blouse was fluttering. Todd centered the crosshairs on her temple and dry-fired. It was bad for the firing-pin, but what the fuck.

"Pow," he whispered as the Toyota disappeared beneath the underpass half a mile up from the slope where Todd sat. He swallowed around a lump that tasted like a stuck-together mass of pennies.

Here came a man behind the wheel of a Subaru Brat pickup truck. This man had a scuzzy-looking gray beard and was wearing a San Diego Padres baseball hat.

"You're . . . you're a dirty rat . . . the dirty rat that shot my bruddah," Todd whispered, giggling a little, and dry-fired the .30-.30 again.

He shot at five others, the impotent snap of the hammer spoiling the illusion at the end of each "kill." Then he cased the rifle again. He carried it back up the slope, bending low to keep from being seen. He put it into the back of the Porsche. There was a dry hot pounding in his temples. He drove home. Went up to his room. Masturbated.

17

The stewbum was wearing a ragged, unravelling reindeer sweater that looked so startling it almost seemed surreal here in southern California. He also wore seaman's issue bluejeans which were out at the knees, showing white, hairy flesh and a number of peeling scabs. He raised the jelly-glass—Fred and Wilma, Barney and Betty dancing around the rim in what might have been some grotesque fertility rite—and tossed off the knock of Ancient Age at a gulp. He smacked his lips for the last time in this world.

"Mister, that hits the old spot. I don't mind saying so."

"I always enjoy a drink in the evening," Dussander agreed from behind him, and then rammed the butcher knife into the stewbum's neck. There was the sound of ripping gristle, a sound like a drumstick being torn enthusiastically from a freshly roasted chicken. The jelly-glass fell from the stewbum's hand and onto the table. It rolled toward the edge, its movement enhancing the illusion that the cartoon characters on it were dancing.

The stewbum threw his head back and tried to scream.

Nothing came out but a hideous whistling sound. His eyes widened, widened . . . and then his head thumped soggily onto the red and white oilcloth check that covered Dussander's kitchen table. The stewbum's upper plate slithered halfway out of his mouth like a semi-detachable grin.

Dussander yanked the knife free—he had to use both hands to do it—and crossed to the kitchen sink. It was filled with hot water, Lemon Fresh Joy, and dirty supper dishes. The knife disappeared into a billow of citrus-smelling suds like a very small fighter plane diving into a cloud.

He crossed to the table again and paused there, resting one hand on the dead stewbum's shoulder while a spasm of coughing rattled through him. He took his handkerchief from his back pocket and spat yellowish-brown phlegm into it. He had been smoking too much lately. He always did when he was making up his mind to do another one. But this one had gone smoothly; really very smoothly. He had been afraid after the mess he had made with the last one that he might be tempting fate sorely to try it again.

Now, if he hurried, he would still be able to watch the second half of *Lawrence Welk*.

He bustled across the kitchen, opened the cellar door, and turned on the light switch. He went back to the sink and got the package of green plastic garbage bags from the cupboard beneath. He shook one out as he walked back to the slumped wino. Blood had run across the oilcloth in all directions. It had puddled in the wino's lap and on the hilly, faded linoleum. It would be on the chair, too, but all of those things would clean up.

Dussander grabbed the stewbum by the hair and yanked his head up. It came with boneless ease, and a moment later the wino was lolling backwards, like a man about to get a pre-haircut shampoo. Dussander pulled the garbage bag down over the wino's head, over his shoulders, and down his arms to the elbows. That was as far as it would go. He unbuckled his late guest's belt and pulled it free of the fraying belt-loops. He wrapped the belt around the garbage bag two or three inches above the elbows and buckled it tight. Plastic rustled. Dussander began to hum under his breath.

The wino's feet were clad in scuffed and dirty Hush Puppies. They made a limp V on the floor as Dussander seized the belt and dragged the corpse toward the cellar door. Something white tumbled out of the plastic bag and clicked on the floor. It was the stewbum's upper plate, Dussander saw. He picked it up and stuffed it into one of the wino's front pockets.

He laid the wino down in the cellar doorway with his head now lolling backward onto the second stair-level. Dussander climbed around the body and gave it three healthy kicks. The body moved slightly on the first two, and the third sent it slithering bonelessly down the stairs. Halfway down, the feet flew up over the head and the body executed an acrobatic roll. It belly-whopped onto the packed dirt of the cellar floor with a solid thud. One Hush Puppy flew off, and Dussander made a mental note to pick it up.

He went down the stairs, skirted the body, and approached his toolbench. To the left of the bench a spade, a rake, and a hoe leaned against the wall in a neat rank. Dussander selected the spade. A little exercise was good for an old man. A little exercise could make you feel young.

The smell down here was not good, but it didn't bother him much. He limed the place once a month (once every three days after he had "done" one of his winos) and he had gotten a fan which he ran upstairs to keep the smell from permeating the house on very warm still days. Josef Kramer, he remembered, had been fond of saying that the dead speak, but we hear them with our noses.

Dussander picked a spot in the cellar's north corner and went to work. The dimensions of the grave were two and a half feet by six feet. He had gotten to a depth of two feet, half deep enough, when the first paralyzing pain struck him in the chest

129

like a shotgun blast. He straightened up, eyes flaring wide. Then the pain rolled down his arm . . . unbelievable pain, as if an invisible hand had seized all the blood-vessels in there and was now pulling them. He watched the spade tumble sideways and felt his knees buckle. For one horrible moment he felt sure that he was going to fall into the grave himself.

Somehow he staggered backwards three paces and sat down on his workbench with a plop. There was an expression of stupid surprise on his face—he could feel it—and he thought he must look like one of those silent movie comedians after he'd been hit by the swinging door or stepped in the cow patty. He put his head down between his knees and gasped.

Fifteen minutes crawled by. The pain had begun to abate somewhat, but he did not believe he would be able to stand. For the first time he understood all the truths of old age which he had been spared until now. He was terrified almost to the point of whimpering. Death had brushed by him in this dank, smelly cellar; it had touched Dussander with the hem of its robe. It might be back for him yet. But he would not die down here; not if he could help it.

He got up, hands crossed on his chest, as if to hold the fragile machinery together. He staggered across the open space between the workbench and the stairs. His left foot tripped over the dead wino's outstretched leg and he went to his knees with a small cry. There was a sullen flare of pain in his chest. He looked up the stairs—the steep, steep stairs. Twelve of them. The square of light at the top was mockingly distant.

"*Ein,*" Kurt Dussander said, and pulled himself grimly up onto the first stair-level. "*Zwei, Drei, Vier.*"

It took him twenty minutes to reach the linoleum floor of the kitchen. Twice, on the stairs, the pain had threatened to come back, and both times Dussander had waited with his eyes closed to see what would happen, perfectly aware that if it came back as strongly as it had come upon him down there, he would probably die. Both times the pain had faded away again.

He crawled across the kitchen floor to the table, avoiding the pools and streaks of blood, which were now congealing. He got the bottle of Ancient Age, took a swallow, and closed his eyes. Something that had been cinched tight in his chest seemed to loosen a little. The pain faded a bit more. After another five minutes he began to work his way slowly down the hall. His telephone sat on a small table halfway down.

It was quarter past nine when the phone rang in the Bowden house. Todd was sitting cross-legged on the couch, going over his notes for the trig final. Trig was a bitch for him, as all maths were and probably always would be. His father was seated across the room, going through the checkbook stubs with a portable calculator on his lap and a mildly disbelieving expression on his face. Monica, closest to the phone, was watching the James Bond movie Todd had taped off HBO two evenings before.

"Hello?" She listened. A faint frown touched her face and she held the handset out to Todd. "It's Mr. Denker. He sounds excited about something. Or upset."

Todd's heart leaped into his throat, but his expression hardly changed. "Really?" He went to the phone and took it from her. "Hi, Mr. Denker."

Dussander's voice was hoarse and short. "Come over right away, boy. I've had a heart attack. Quite a bad one, I think."

"Gee," Todd said, trying to collect his flying thoughts, to see around the fear that now bulked huge in his own mind. "That's interesting, all right, but it's pretty late and I was studying—"

"I understand that you cannot talk," Dussander said in that harsh, almost barking voice. "But you can listen. I cannot call an ambulance or dial two-two-two, boy . . . at least not yet. There is a mess here. I need help . . . and that means *you* need help."

"Well . . . if you put it that way . . ." Todd's heartbeat had reached a hundred and twenty beats a minute, but his face was calm, almost serene. Hadn't he known all along that a night like this would come? Yes, of course he had.

"Tell your parents I've had a letter," Dussander said. "An important letter. You understand?"

"Yeah, okay," Todd said.

"Now we see, boy. We see what you are made of."

"Sure," Todd said. He suddenly became aware that his mother was watching him instead of the movie, and he forced a stiff grin onto his face. "Bye."

Dussander was saying something else now, but Todd hung up on it.

"I'm going over to Mr. Denker's for awhile," he said, speaking to both of them but looking at his mother—that faint expression of concern was still on her face. "Can I pick up anything for either of you at the store?"

"Pipe cleaners for me and a small package of fiscal responsibility for your mother," Dick said.

"Very funny," Monica said. "Todd, is Mr. Denker—"

"What in the name of *God* did you get at Fielding's?" Dick interrupted.

"That knick-knack shelf in the closet. I told you that. There's nothing wrong with Mr. Denker, is there, Todd? He sounded a little strange."

"There really *are* such things as knick-knack shelves? I thought those crazy women who write British mysteries made them up so there would always be a place where the killer could find a blunt instrument."

"Dick, can I get a word in edgeways?"

"Sure. Be my guest. But for the *closet?*"

"He's okay, I guess," Todd said. He put on his letter jacket and zipped it up. "But he *was* excited. He got a letter from a nephew of his in Hamburg or Düsseldorf or someplace. He hasn't heard from any of his people in years, and now he's got this letter and his eyes aren't good enough for him to read it."

"Well isn't that a *bitch*," Dick said. "Go on, Todd. Get over there and ease the man's mind."

"I thought he had someone to read to him," Monica said. "A new boy."

"He does," Todd said, suddenly hating his mother, hating the half-informed intuition he saw swimming in her eyes. "Maybe he wasn't home, or maybe he couldn't come over this late."

"Oh. Well . . . go on, then. But be careful."

"I will. You don't need anything at the store?"

"No. How's your studying for that calculus final going?"

"It's trig," Todd said. "Okay, I guess. I was just getting ready to call it a night." This was a rather large lie.

"You want to take the Porsche?" Dick asked.

"No, I'll ride my bike." He wanted the extra five minutes to collect his thoughts and get his emotions under control—to try, at least. And in his present state, he would probably drive the Porsche into a telephone pole.

"Strap your reflector-patch on your knee," Monica said, "and tell Mr. Denker hello for us."

"Okay."

That doubt was still in his mother's eyes but it was less evident now. He blew her a kiss and then went out to the garage where his bike—a racing-style Italian bike rather than a Schwinn now—was parked. His heart was still racing in his chest, and he felt a mad urge to take the .30-.30 back into the house and shoot both of his parents and then go down to the slope overlooking the freeway. No more worrying about Dussander. No more bad dreams, no more winos. He would shoot and shoot and shoot, only saving one bullet back for the end.

Then reason came back to him and he rode away toward Dussander's, his reflector-patch revolving up and down just above his knee, his long blonde hair streaming back from his brow.

· · ·

"Holy *Christ*!" Todd nearly screamed.

He was standing in the kitchen door. Dussander was slumped on his elbows, his china cup between them. Large drops of sweat stood out on his forehead. But it was not Dussander Todd was looking at. It was the blood. There seemed to be blood everywhere—it was puddled on the table, on the empty kitchen chair, on the floor.

"Where are you bleeding?" Todd shouted, at last getting his frozen feet to move again—it seemed to him that he had been standing in the doorway for at least a thousand years. *This is the end,* he was thinking, *this is the absolute end of everything. The balloon is going up high, baby, all the way to the sky, baby, and it's toot-toot-tootsie, goodbye.* All the same, he was careful not to step in any of the blood. "I thought you said you had a fucking heart attack!"

"It's not my blood," Dussander muttered.

"What?" Todd stopped. "What did you say?"

"Go downstairs. You will see what has to be done."

"What the hell *is* this?" Todd asked. A sudden terrible idea had come into his head.

"Don't waste our time, boy. I think you will not be too surprised at what you find downstairs. I think you have had experience in such matters as the one in my cellar. First-hand experience."

Todd looked at him, unbelieving, for another moment, and then he plunged down the cellar stairs two by two. His first look in the feeble yellow glow of the basement's only light made him think that Dussander had pushed a bag of garbage down here. Then he saw the protruding legs, and the dirty hands held down at the sides by the cinched belt.

"Holy Christ," he repeated, but this time the words had no force at all—they emerged in a slight, skeletal whisper.

He pressed the back of his right hand against lips that were as dry as sandpaper. He closed his eyes for a moment . . . and when he opened them again, he felt in control of himself at last.

Todd started moving.

He saw the spade-handle protruding from a shallow hole in the far corner and understood at once what Dussander had been doing when his ticker had seized up. A moment later he became fully aware of the cellar's fetid aroma—a smell like rotting tomatoes. He had smelled it before, but upstairs it was much fainter—and, of course, he hadn't been here very often over the past couple of years. Now he understood *exactly* what that smell meant and for several moments he had to struggle with his gorge. A series of choked gagging sounds, muffled by the hand he had clapped over his mouth and nose, came from him.

Little by little he got control of himself again.

He seized the wino's legs and dragged him across to the edge of the hole. He dropped them, skidded sweat from his forehead with the heel of his left hand, and stood absolutely still for a moment, thinking harder than he ever had in his life.

Then he seized the spade and began to deepen the hole. When it was five feet deep, he got out and shoved the derelict's body in with his foot. Todd stood at the edge of the grave, looking down. Tattered bluejeans. Filthy, scab-encrusted hands. It was a stewbum, all right. The irony was almost funny. So funny a person could scream with laughter.

He ran back upstairs.

"How are you?" he asked Dussander.

"I'll be all right. Have you taken care of it?"

"I'm doing it, okay?"

"Be quick. There's still up here."

"I'd like to find some pigs and feed you to them," Todd said, and went back down cellar before Dussander could reply.

He had almost completely covered the wino when he began to think there was something wrong. He stared into the grave, grasping the spade's handle with one hand. The wino's legs stuck partway out of the mound of dirt, as did the tips of his feet—one old shoe, possibly a Hush Puppy, and one filthy athletic sock that might actually have been white around the time that Taft was President.

One Hush Puppy? *One?*

Todd half-ran back around the furnace to the foot of the stairs. He glanced around wildly. A headache was beginning to thud against his temples, dull drillbits trying to work their way out. He spotted the old shoe five feet away, overturned in the shadow of some abandoned shelving. Todd grabbed it, ran back to the grave with it, and threw it in. Then he started to shovel again. He covered the shoe, the legs, everything.

When all the dirt was back in the hole, he slammed the spade down repeatedly to tamp it. Then he grabbed the rake and ran it back and forth, trying to disguise the fact the earth here had been recently turned. Not much use; without good camouflage, a hole that has been recently dug and then filled in always looks like a hole that has been recently dug and then filled in. Still, no one would have any occasion to come down here, would they? He and Dussander would damn well have to hope not.

Todd ran back upstairs. He was starting to pant.

Dussander's elbows had spread wide and his head had sagged down to the table. His eyes were closed, the lids a shiny purple—the color of asters.

"Dussander!" Todd shouted. There was a hot, juicy taste in his mouth—the taste of fear mixed with adrenaline and pulsing hot blood. "Don't you *dare* die on me, you old fuck!"

"Keep your voice down," Dussander said without opening his eyes. "You'll have everyone on the block over here."

"Where's your cleaner? Lestoil . . . Top Job . . . something like that. And rags. I need rags."

"All that is under the sink."

A lot of the blood had now dried on. Dussander raised his head and watched as Todd crawled across the floor, scrubbing first at the puddle on the linoleum and then at the drips that had straggled down the legs of the chair the wino had been sitting in. The boy was biting compulsively at his lips, champing at them, almost, like a horse at a bit. At last the job was finished. The astringent smell of cleaner filled the room.

"There is a box of old rags under the stairs," Dussander said. "Put those bloody ones on the bottom. Don't forget to wash your hands."

"I don't need your advice. You got me into this."

"Did I? I must say you took hold well." For a moment the old mockery was in Dussander's voice, and then a bitter grimace pulled his face into a new shape. "Hurry."

Todd took care of the rags, then hurried up the cellar stairs for the last time. He looked nervously down the stairs for a moment, then snapped off the light and closed the door. He went to the sink, rolled up his sleeves, and washed in the hottest water he could stand. He plunged his hands into the suds . . . and came up holding the butcher knife Dussander had used.

"I'd like to cut your throat with this," Todd said grimly.

"Yes, and then feed me to the pigs. I have no doubt of it."

Todd rinsed the knife, dried it, and put it away. He did the rest of the dishes quickly, let the water out, and rinsed the sink. He looked at the clock as he dried his hands and saw it was twenty minutes after ten.

He went to the phone in the hallway, picked up the receiver, and looked at it thoughtfully. The idea that he had forgotten something—something as potentially damning as the wino's shoe—nagged unpleasantly at his mind. What? He didn't know. If not for the headache, he might be able to get it. The triple-damned headache. It wasn't like him to forget things, and it was scary.

He dialed 222 and after a single ring, a voice answered: "This is Santo Donato MED-Q. Do you have a medical problem?"

"My name is Todd Bowden. I'm at 963 Claremont Street. I need an ambulance."

"What's the problem, son?"

"It's my friend, Mr. D—" He bit down on his lip so hard that it squirted blood, and for a moment he was lost, drowning in the pulses of pain from his head. *Dussander.* He had almost given this anonymous MED-Q voice Dussander's real name.

"Calm down, son," the voice said. 'Take it slow and you'll be fine."

"My friend Mr. Denker," Todd said. "I think he's had a heart attack."

"His symptoms?"

Todd began to give them, but the voice had heard enough as soon as Todd described the chest pain that had migrated to the left arm. He told Todd the ambulance would arrive in ten to twenty minutes, depending on the traffic. Todd hung up and pressed the heels of his hands against his eyes.

"Did you get it?" Dussander called weakly.

"*Yes!*" Todd screamed. "*Yes, I got it! Yes goddammit yes! Yes yes yes! Just shut up!*"

He pressed his hands even harder against his eyes, creating first senseless starflashes of light and then a bright field of red. *Get hold of yourself, Todd-baby. Get down, get funky, get cool. Dig it.*

He opened his eyes and picked up the telephone again. Now the hard part. Now it was time to call home.

"Hello?" Monica's soft, cultured voice in his ear. For a moment—just a moment—he saw himself slamming the muzzle of the .30-.30 into her nose and pulling the trigger into the first flow of blood.

"It's Todd, Mommy. Let me talk to Dad, quick."

He didn't call her mommy anymore. He knew she would get that signal quicker than anything else, and she did. "What's the matter? Is something wrong, Todd?"

"Just let me talk to him!"

"But what—"

The phone rattled and clunked. He heard his mother saying something to his father. Todd got ready.

"It's Mr. Denker, Daddy. He . . . it's a heart attack, I think. I'm pretty sure it is."

"Jesus!" His father's voice lagged away for a moment and Todd heard him repeating the information to his wife. Then he was back. "He's still alive? As far as you can tell?"

"He's alive. Conscious."

"All right, thank God for that. Call an ambulance."

"I just did."

"Two-two-two?"

"Yes."

"Good boy. How bad is he, can you tell?"

"I don't know, Dad. They said the ambulance would be here soon, but . . . I'm sorta scared. Can you come over and wait with me?"

"You bet. Give me four minutes."

Todd could hear his mother saying something else as his father hung up, breaking the connection. Todd replaced the receiver on his end.

Four minutes.

Four minutes to do anything that had been left undone. Four minutes to remember whatever it was that had been forgotten. Or *had* he forgotten anything? Maybe it was just nerves. God, he wished he hadn't had to call his father. But it was the natural thing to do, wasn't it? Sure. Was there some natural thing that he *hadn't* done? Something—?

"Oh, you shit-for-brains!" he suddenly moaned, and bolted back into the kitchen. Dussander's head lay on the table, his eyes half-open, sluggish.

"Dussander!" Todd cried. He shook Dussander roughly, and the old man groaned. "Wake up! Wake up, you stinking old bastard!"

"What? Is it the ambulance?"

"The letter! My father is coming over, he'll be here in no time. *Where's the fucking letter?*"

"What . . . what letter?"

139

"You told me to tell them you got an important letter. I said . . ." His heart sank. "I said it came from overseas . . . from Germany. Christ!" Todd ran his hands through his hair.

"A letter." Dussander raised his head with slow difficulty. His seamed cheeks were an unhealthy yellowish-white, his lips blue. "From Willi, I think. Willi Frankel. Dear . . . dear Willi."

Todd looked at his watch and saw that already two minutes had passed since he had hung up the phone. His father would not, *could* not make it from their house to Dussander's in four minutes, but he could do it damn fast in the Porsche. Fast, that was it. Everything was moving too fast. And there was still something wrong here; he *felt* it. But there was no time to stop and hunt around for the loophole.

"Yes, okay, I was reading it to you, and you got excited and had this heart attack. Good. Where is it?"

Dussander looked at him blankly.

"The letter! Where is it?"

"What letter?" Dussander asked vacantly, and Todd's hands itched to throttle the drunken old monster.

"The one I was reading to you! The one from Willi What's-his-face! Where is it?"

They both looked at the table, as if expecting to see the letter materialize there.

"Upstairs," Dussander said finally. "Look in my dresser. The third drawer. There is a small wooden box in the bottom of that drawer. You will have to break it open. I lost the key a long time ago. There are some very old letters from a friend of mine. None signed. None dated. All in German. A page or two will serve for window-fittings, as you would say. If you hurry—"

"Are you *crazy*?" Todd raged. "I don't understand German! How could I read you a letter written in German, you numb fuck?"

"Why would Willi write me in English?" Dussander countered wearily. "If you read me the letter in German, *I* would understand it even if *you* did not. Of course your pronunciation would be butchery, but still, I could—"

Dussander was right—right again, and Todd didn't wait to hear more. Even after a heart attack the old man was a step ahead. Todd raced down the hall to the stairs, pausing just long enough by the front door to make sure his father's Porsche wasn't pulling up even now. It wasn't, but Todd's watch told him just how tight things were getting; it had been five minutes now.

He took the stairs two at a time and burst into Dussander's bedroom. He had never been up here before, hadn't even been curious, and for a moment he only looked wildly around at the unfamiliar territory. Then he saw the dresser, a cheap item done in the style his father called Discount Store Modern. He fell on his knees in front of it and yanked at the third drawer. It came halfway out, then jigged sideways in its slot and stuck firmly.

"Goddam you," he whispered at it. His face was dead pale except for the spots of dark, bloody color flaring at each cheek and his blue eyes, which looked as dark as Atlantic storm-clouds. "Goddam you fucking thing come *out!*"

He yanked so hard that the entire dresser tottered forward and almost fell on him before deciding to settle back. The drawer shot all the way out and landed in Todd's lap. Dussander's socks and underwear and handkerchiefs spilled out all around him. He pawed through the stuff that was still in the drawer and came out with a wooden box about nine inches long and three inches deep. He tried to pull up the lid. Nothing happened. It was locked, just as Dussander had said. Nothing was free tonight.

He stuffed the spilled clothes back into the drawer and then rammed the drawer back into its oblong slot. It stuck again. Todd worked to free it, wiggling it back and forth, sweat running freely down his face. At last he was able to slam it shut. He got up with the box. How much time had passed now?

Dussander's bed was the type with posts at the foot and Todd brought the lock side of the box down on one of these posts as hard as he could, grinning at the shock of pain that vibrated in his hands and travelled all the way up to his elbows. He looked at the lock. The lock looked a bit dented, but it was intact. He brought it down on the post again, even harder this time, heedless of the pain. This time a chunk of wood flew off the bedpost, but the lock still didn't give. Todd uttered a little shriek of laughter and took the box to the other end of the bed. He raised it high over his head this time and brought it down with all his strength. This time the lock splintered.

As he flipped the lid up, headlights splashed across Dussander's window.

He pawed wildly through the box. Postcards. A locket. A much-folded picture of a woman wearing frilly black garters and nothing else. An old billfold. Several sets of ID. An empty leather passport folder. At the bottom, letters.

The lights grew brighter, and now he heard the distinctive beat of the Porsche's engine. It grew louder . . . and then cut off.

Todd grabbed three sheets of airmail-type stationery, closely written in German on both sides of each sheet, and ran out of the room again. He had almost gotten to the stairs when he realized he had left the forced box lying on Dussander's bed. He ran back, grabbed it, and opened the third dresser drawer.

It stuck again, this time with a firm shriek of wood against wood.

Out front, he heard the ratchet of the Porsche's emergency brake, the opening of the driver's-side door, the slam shut.

Faintly, Todd could hear himself moaning. He put the box in the askew drawer, stood up, and lashed out at it with his foot. The drawer closed neatly. He stood blinking at it for a moment and then fled back down the hall. He raced down the stairs. Halfway down them, he heard the rapid rattle of his father's shoes on Dussander's walk. Todd vaulted over the bannister, landed lightly, and ran into the kitchen, the airmail pages fluttering from his hand.

A hammering on the door. "Todd? Todd, it's me!"

And he could hear an ambulance siren in the distance as well. Dussander had drifted away into semi-consciousness again.

"Coming, Dad!" Todd shouted.

He put the airmail pages on the table, fanning them a little as if they had been dropped in a hurry, and then he went back down the hall and let his father in.

"Where is he?" Dick Bowden asked, shouldering past Todd.

"In the kitchen."

"You did everything just right, Todd," his father said, and hugged him in a rough, embarrassed way.

"I just hope I remembered everything," Todd said modestly, and then followed his father down the hall and into the kitchen.

In the rush to get Dussander out of the house, the letter was almost completely ignored. Todd's father picked it up briefly, then put it down when the medics came in with the stretcher. Todd and his father followed the ambulance, and his explanation of what had happened was accepted without question by the doctor attending Dussander's case. "Mr. Denker" was, after all, eighty years old, and his habits were not the best. The doctor also offered Todd a brusque commendation for his quick thinking and action. Todd thanked him wanly and then asked his father if they could go home.

As they rode back, Dick told him again how proud of him he was. Todd barely heard him. He was thinking about his .30-.30 again.

18

That was the same day Morris Heisel broke his back.

Morris had never *intended* to break his back; all he had

intended to do was nail up the corner of the rain-gutter on the west side of his house. Breaking his back was the furthest thing from his mind, he had had enough grief in his life without that, thank you very much. His first wife had died at the age of twenty-five, and both of their daughters were also dead. His brother was dead, killed in a tragic car accident not far from Disneyland in 1971. Morris himself was nearing sixty, and had a case of arthritis that was worsening early and fast. He also had warts on both hands, warts that seemed to grow back as fast as the doctor could burn them off. He was *also* prone to migraine headaches, and in the last couple of years, that *potzer* Rogan next door had taken to calling him "Morris the Cat." Morris had wondered aloud to Lydia, his second wife, how Rogan would like it if Morris took up calling him "Rogan the hemorrhoid."

"Quit it, Morris," Lydia said on these occasions. "You can't take a joke, you never *could* take a joke, sometimes I wonder how I could marry a man with absolutely *no* sense of humor. We go to Las Vegas," Lydia had said, addressing the empty kitchen as if an invisible horde of spectators which only she could see were standing there, "we see Buddy Hackett, and Morris doesn't laugh *once*."

Besides arthritis, warts, and migraines, Morris also had Lydia, who, God love her, had developed into something of a nag over the last five years or so . . . ever since her hysterectomy. So he had plenty of sorrows and plenty of problems without adding a broken back.

"*Morris!*" Lydia cried, coming to the back door and wiping suds from her hands with a dishtowel. "Morris, you come down off that ladder right now!"

"What?" He twisted his head so he could see her. He was almost at the top of his aluminum stepladder. There was a bright yellow sticker on this step which said: DANGER! BALANCE MAY SHIFT WITHOUT WARNING ABOVE THIS STEP! Morris was wearing his carpenter's apron with the wide pockets, one of the pockets filled with nails and the other filled with heavy-duty staples. The ground under the stepladder's feet was slightly uneven and the ladder rocked a little when he moved. His neck ached with the unlovely prelude to one of his migraines. He was out of temper. *"What?"*

"Come down from there, I said, before you break your back."

"I'm almost finished."

"You're rocking on that ladder like you were on a boat, Morris. Come down."

"I'll come down when I'm done!" he said angrily. "Leave me alone!"

"You'll break your back," she reiterated dolefully, and went into the house again.

Ten minutes later, as he was hammering the last nail into the rain-gutter, tipped back nearly to the point of overbalancing, he heard a feline yowl followed by fierce barking.

"What in God's name—?"

He looked around and the stepladder rocked alarmingly. At that same moment, their cat—it was named Lover Boy, *not* Morris—tore around the corner of the garage, its fur bushed out into hackles and its green eyes flaring. The Rogans' collie pup was in hot pursuit, its tongue hanging out and its leash dragging behind it.

Lover Boy, apparently not superstitious, ran under the stepladder. The collie pup followed.

"Look out, look out, you dumb mutt!" Morris shouted.

The ladder rocked. The pup bunted it with the side of its body. The ladder tipped over and Morris tipped with it, uttering a howl of dismay. Nails and staples flew out of his carpenter's apron. He landed half on and half off the concrete driveway, and a gigantic agony flared in his back. He did not so much hear his spine snap as feel it happen. Then the world grayed out for awhile.

When things swam back into focus, he was still lying half on and half off the driveway in a litter of nails and staples.

145

Lydia was kneeling over him, weeping. Rogan from next door was there, too, his face as white as a shroud.

"I told you!" Lydia babbled. "I told you to come down off that ladder! Now look! Now look at this!"

Morris found he had absolutely no desire to look. A suffocating, throbbing band of pain had cinched itself around his middle like a belt, and that was bad, but there was something much worse: he could feel nothing below that belt of pain— nothing at all.

"Wail later," he said huskily. "Call the doctor now."

"I'll do it," Rogan said, and ran back to his own house.

"Lydia," Morris said. He wet his lips.

"What? What, Morris?" She bent over him and a tear splashed on his cheek. It was touching, he supposed, but it had made him flinch, and the flinch had made the pain worse.

"Lydia, I also have one of my migraines."

"Oh, poor darling! Poor Morris! But I *told* you—"

"I've got the headache because that *potzer* Rogan's dog barked all night and kept me awake. Today the dog chases my cat and knocks over my ladder and I think my back is broken."

Lydia shrieked. The sound made Morris's head vibrate.

"Lydia," he said, and wet his lips again.

"What, darling?"

"I have suspected something for many years. Now I am sure."

"My poor Morris! What?"

"There is no God," Morris said, and fainted.

They took him to Santo Donato and his doctor told him, at about the same time that he would have ordinarily been sitting down to one of Lydia's wretched suppers, that he would never walk again. By then they had put him in a body-cast. Blood and urine samples had been taken. Dr. Kemmelman had peered into his eyes and tapped his knees with a little rubber hammer—but no reflexive twitch of the leg answered the taps. And at every turn there was Lydia, the tears streaming from her eyes, as she used up one handkerchief after another. Lydia, a woman who would have been at home married to Job, went everywhere well-supplied with little lace snotrags, just in case reason for an extended crying spell should occur. She had called her mother, and her mother would be here soon ("That's nice, Lydia"—although if there was anyone on earth Morris honestly loathed, it was Lydia's mother). She had called the rabbi, he would be here soon, too ("That's nice, Lydia"— although he hadn't set foot inside the synagogue in five years and wasn't sure what the rabbi's name was). She had called his boss, and while he wouldn't be here soon, he sent his greatest sympathies and condolences ("That's nice, Lydia"—although if there was anyone in a class with Lydia's mother, it was that cigar-chewing *putz* Frank Haskell). At last they gave Morris a Valium and took Lydia away. Shortly afterward, Morris just drifted away—no worries, no migraines, no nothing. If they kept giving him little blue pills like that, went his last thought, he would go on up that stepladder and break his back again.

When he woke up—or regained consciousness, that was more like it—dawn was just breaking and the hospital was as quiet as Morris supposed it ever got. He felt very calm . . . almost serene. He had no pain; his body felt swaddled and weightless. His bed had been surrounded by some sort of contraption like a squirrel cage—a thing of stainless steel bars, guy wires, and pulleys. His legs were being held up by cables attached to this gadget. His back seemed to be bowed by something beneath, but it was hard to tell—he had only the angle of his vision to judge by.

Others have it worse, he thought. *All over the world, others have it worse. In Israel, the Palestinians kill busloads of farmers who were committing the political crime of going into town to see a movie. The Israelis cope with this injustice by dropping bombs on the Palestinians and killing children along with whatever terrorists may be there.*

Others have it worse than me . . . which is not to say this is good, don't get that idea, but others have it worse.

He lifted one hand with some effort—there was pain somewhere in his body, but it was very faint—and made a weak fist in front of his eyes. There. Nothing wrong with his hands. Nothing wrong with his arms, either. So he couldn't feel anything below the waist, so what? There were people all over the world paralyzed from the *neck* down. There were people with leprosy. There were people dying of syphilis. Somewhere in the world right now, there might be people walking down the jetway and onto a plane that was going to crash. No, this wasn't good, but there were worse things in the world.

And there had been, once upon a time, *much* worse things in the world.

He raised his left arm. It seemed to float, disembodied, before his eyes—a scrawny old man's arm with the muscles deteriorating. He was in a hospital johnny but it had short sleeves and he could still read the numbers on the forearm, tattooed there in faded blue ink. P499965214. Worse things, yes, worse things than falling off a suburban stepladder and breaking your back and being taken to a clean and sterile metropolitan hospital and being given a Valium that was guaranteed to bubble your troubles away.

There were the showers, they were worse. His first wife, Ruth, had died in one of their filthy showers. There were the trenches that became graves—he could close his eyes and still see the men lined up along the open maw of the trenches, could still hear the volley of rifle-fire, could still remember the way they flopped backwards into the earth like badly made puppets. There were the crematoriums, they were worse, too, the crematoriums that filled the air with the steady sweet smell of Jews burning like torches no one could see. The horror-struck faces of old friends and relatives . . . faces that melted away like guttering candles, faces that seemed to melt away *before your very eyes*—thin, thinner, thinnest. Then one day they were gone. Where? Where does a torch-flame go when the cold wind has blown it out? Heaven. Hell? Lights in the darkness, candles in the wind. When Job finally broke down and questioned, God asked him: *Where were you when I made the world?* If Morris Heisel had been Job, he would have responded: *Where were You when my Ruth was dying, You* potzer, *You? Watching the Yankees and the Senators? If You can't pay attention to Your business better than this, get out of my face.*

Yes, there were worse things than breaking your back, he had no doubt of it. But what sort of God would have allowed him to break his back and become paralyzed for life after watching his wife die, and his daughters, and his friends?

No God at all, that was Who.

A tear trickled from the corner of his eye and ran slowly down the side of his head to his ear. Outside the hospital room, a bell rang softly. A nurse squeaked by on white crepe-soled shoes. His door was ajar, and on the far wall of the corridor outside he could read the letters NSIVE CA and guessed that the whole sign must read INTENSIVE CARE.

There was movement in the room—a rustle of bedclothes.

Moving very carefully, Morris turned his head to the right, away from the door. He saw a night-table next to him with a pitcher of water on it. There were two call-buttons on the table. Beyond it was another bed, and in the bed was a man who looked even older and sicker than Morris felt. He was not hooked into a giant exercise-wheel for gerbils like Morris was, but an IV feed stood beside his bed and some sort of monitoring console stood at its foot. The man's skin was sunken and yellow. Lines around his mouth and eyes had driven deep. His hair was yellowish-white, dry and lifeless. His thin eyelids had a bruised and shiny look, and in his big nose Morris saw the burst capillaries of the life-long drinker.

Morris looked away . . . and then looked back. As the dawn-light grew stronger and the hospital began to wake up, he began to have the strangest feeling that he knew his roommate. Could that be? The man looked to be somewhere between seventy-five and eighty, and Morris didn't believe he knew anyone quite that old—except for Lydia's mother, a horror Morris sometimes believed to be older than the Sphinx, whom the woman closely resembled.

Maybe the guy was someone he had known in the past, maybe even before he, Morris, came to America. Maybe. Maybe not. And why all of a sudden did it seem to matter? For that matter, why had all his memories of the camp, of Patin, come flooding back tonight, when he always tried to—and most times succeeded in—keeping those things buried?

He broke out in a sudden rash of gooseflesh, as if he had stepped into some mental haunted house where old bodies were unquiet and old ghosts walked. Could that be, even here and now in this clean hospital, thirty years after those dark times had ended?

He looked away from the old man in the other bed, and soon he had begun to feel sleepy again.

It's a trick of your mind that this other man seems familiar. Only your mind, amusing you in the best way it can, amusing you the way it used to try to amuse you in—

But he would not think of that. He would not *allow* himself to think of that.

Drifting into sleep, he thought of a boast he had made to Ruth (but never to Lydia; it didn't pay to boast to Lydia; she was not like Ruth, who would always smile sweetly at his harmless puffing and crowing): *I never forget a face.* Here was his chance to find out if that was still so. If he had really known the man in the other bed at some time or other, perhaps he could remember when . . . and where.

Very close to sleep, drifting back and forth across its threshold, Morris thought: *Perhaps I knew him in the camp.*

That would be ironic indeed—what they called a "jest of God." What God? Morris Heisel asked himself again, and slept.

19

Todd graduated salutatorian of his class, just possibly because of his poor grade on the trig final he had been studying for the night Dussander had his heart attack. It dragged his final grade in the course down to 89, one point below an A-minus average.

A week after graduation, the Bowdens went to visit Mr. Denker at Santo Donato General. Todd fidgeted through fifteen minutes of banalities and thank-yous and how-do-you-feels and was grateful for the break when the man in the other bed asked him if he could come over for a minute.

"You'll pardon me," the other man said apologetically. He was in a huge body-cast and was for some reason attached to an overhead system of pulleys and wires. "My name is Morris Heisel. I broke my back."

"That's too bad," Todd said gravely.

"*Oy*, too bad, he says! This boy has the gift of understatement!"

Todd started to apologize, but Heisel raised his hand, smiling a little. His face was pale and tired, the face of any old man in the hospital facing a life full of sweeping changes just ahead—and surely few of them for the better. In that way, Todd thought, he and Dussander were alike.

"No need," Morris said. "No need to answer a rude comment. You are a stranger. Does a stranger need to be inflicted with my problems?"

" 'No man is an island, entire of itself—' " Todd began, and Morris laughed.

"Donne, he quotes at me! A smart kid! Your friend there, is he very bad off?"

"Well, the doctors say he's doing fine, considering his age. He's eighty."

"That old!" Morris exclaimed. "He doesn't talk to me much,

you know. But from what he does say, I'd guess he's natural-ized. Like me. I'm Polish, you know. Originally, I mean. From Radom."

"Oh?" Todd said politely.

"Yes. You know what they call an orange manhole cover in Radom?"

"No," Todd said, smiling.

"Howard Johnson's," Morris said, and laughed. Todd laughed, too. Dussander glanced over at them, startled by the sound and frowning a little. Then Monica said something and he looked back at her again.

"*Is* your friend naturalized?"

"Oh, yes," Todd said. "He's from Germany. Essen. Do you know that town?"

"No," Morris said, "but I was only in Germany once. I won-der if he was in the war."

"I really couldn't say." Todd's eyes had gone distant.

"No? Well, it doesn't matter. That was a long time ago, the war. In another three years there will be people in this country constitutionally eligible to become President—President!— who weren't even born until after the war was over. To them it must seem there is no difference between the Miracle of Dunkirk and Hannibal taking his elephants over the Alps."

"Were you in the war?" Todd asked.

"I suppose I was, in a manner of speaking. You're a good boy to visit such an old man . . . two old men, counting me."

Todd smiled modestly.

"I'm tired now," Morris said. "Perhaps I'll sleep."

"I hope you'll feel better very soon," Todd said.

Morris nodded, smiled, and closed his eyes. Todd went back to Dussander's bed, where his parents were just getting ready to leave—his dad kept glancing at his watch and exclaiming with bluff heartiness at how late it was getting.

• • •

Two days later, Todd came back to the hospital alone. This time, Morris Heisel, immured in his body-cast, was deeply asleep in the other bed.

"You did well," Dussander said quietly. "Did you go back to the house later?"

"Yes. I burned the damned letter. I don't think anyone was too interested in that letter, and I was afraid . . . I don't know." He shrugged, unable to tell Dussander he'd been almost superstitiously afraid about the letter—afraid that maybe someone would wander into the house who could read German, someone who would notice references in the letter that were ten, perhaps twenty years out of date.

"Next time you come, smuggle me in something to drink," Dussander said. "I find I don't miss the cigarettes, but—"

"I won't be back again," Todd said flatly. "Not ever. It's the end. We're quits."

"Quits." Dussander folded his hands on his chest and smiled. It was not a gentle smile . . . but it was perhaps as close as Dussander could come to such a thing. "I thought that was in the cards. They are going to let me out of this graveyard next week . . . or so they promise. The doctor says I may have a few years left in my skin yet. I ask him how many, and he just laughs. I suspect that means no more than three, and probably no more than two. Still, I may give him a surprise."

Todd said nothing.

"But between you and me, boy, I have almost given up my hopes of seeing the century turn."

"I want to ask you about something," Todd said, looking at Dussander steadily. "That's why I came in today. I want to ask you about something you said once."

Todd glanced over his shoulder at the man in the other bed and then drew his chair closer to Dussander's bed. He could smell Dussander's smell, as dry as the Egyptian room in the museum.

"So ask."

"That wino. You said something about me having experience. First-hand experience. What was that supposed to mean?"

Dussander's smile widened a bit. "I read the newspapers, boy. Old men always read the newspapers, but not in the same way younger people do. Buzzards are known to gather at the ends of certain airport runways in South America when the crosswinds are treacherous, did you know that? That is how an old man reads the newspaper. A month ago there was a story in the Sunday paper. Not a front-page story, no one cares enough about bums and alcoholics to put them on the front page, but it was the lead story in the feature section, IS SOMEONE STALKING SANTO DONATO'S DOWN-AND-OUT?—that's what it was called. Crude. Yellow journalism. You Americans are famous for it."

Todd's hands were clenched into fists, hiding the butchered nails. He never read the Sunday papers, he had better things to do with his time. He had of course checked the papers every day for at least a week following each of his little adventures, and none of his stewbums had ever gotten beyond page three. The idea that someone had been making connections behind his back infuriated him.

"The story mentioned several murders, extremely brutal murders. Stabbings, bludgeonings. 'Subhuman brutality' was how the writer put it, but you know reporters. The writer of this lamentable piece admitted that there is a high death-rate among these unfortunates, and that Santo Donato has had more than its share of the indigent over the years. In any given year, not all of these men die naturally, or of their own bad habits. There are frequent murders. But in most cases the murderer is usually one of the deceased degenerate's compatriots, the motive no more than an argument over a penny-ante card-game or a bottle of muscatel. The killer is usually happy to confess. He is filled with remorse.

"But these recent killings have not been solved. Even more

ominous, to this yellow journalist's mind—or whatever passes for his mind—is the high disappearance rate over the last few years. Of course, he admits again, these men are not much more than modern-day hoboes. They come and go. But some of these left without picking up welfare checks or day-labor checks from Spell O' Work, which only pays on Fridays. Could some of these have been victims of this yellow journalist's Wino Killer, he asks? Victims who haven't been found? *Pah!*"

Dussander waved his hand in the air as if to dismiss such arrant irresponsibility.

"Only titillation, of course. Give people a comfortable little scare on Sunday morning. He calls up old bogies, threadbare but still useful—the Cleveland Torso Murderer, Zodiac, the mysterious Mr. X who killed the Black Dahlia, Springheel Jack. Such drivel. But it makes me think. What does an old man have to do but think when old friends don't come to visit anymore?"

Todd shrugged.

"I thought: 'If I wished to help this odious yellow-dog journalist, which I certainly do not, I could explain some of the disappearances. Not the corpses found stabbed or bludgeoned, not *them,* God rest their besotted souls, but some of the disappearances. Because at least some of the bums who disappeared are in my cellar.'"

"How many down there?" Todd asked in a low voice.

"Six," Dussander said calmly. "Counting the one you helped me dispose of, six."

"You're really nutso," Todd said. The skin below his eyes had gone white and shiny. "At some point you just blew all your fucking wheels."

" 'Blew my wheels.' What a charming idiom! Perhaps you're right! But then I said to myself: 'This newspaper jackal would love to pin the murders and the disappearances on the same somebody—his hypothetical Wino Killer.' But I think maybe that's not what happened at all.

155

"Then I say to myself: 'Do I know anybody who might be doing such things? Somebody who has been under as much strain as I have during the last few years? Someone who has also been listening to old ghosts rattle their chains?' And the answer is yes. I know *you,* boy."

"I've never killed anyone."

The image that came was not of the winos; they weren't people, not really people at all. The image that came was of himself crouched behind the dead tree, peering through the telescopic sight of his .30-.30, the crosshairs fixed on the temple of the man with the scuzzy beard, the man driving the Brat pickup.

"Perhaps not," Dussander agreed, amicably enough. "Yet you took hold so well that night. Your surprise was mostly anger at having been put in such a dangerous position by an old man's infirmity, I think. Am I wrong?"

"No, you're not wrong," Todd said. "I was pissed off at you and I still am. I covered it up for you because you've got something in a safety deposit box that could destroy my life."

"No. I do not."

"What? What are you talking about?"

"It was as much a bluff as your 'letter left with a friend.' You never wrote such a letter, there never was such a friend, and I have never written a single word about our . . . association, shall I call it? Now I lay my cards on the table. You saved my life. Never mind that you acted only to protect yourself; that does not change how speedily and efficiently you acted. I cannot hurt you, boy. I tell you that freely. I have looked death in the face and it frightens me, but not as badly as I thought it would. There is no document. It is as you say: we are quits."

Todd smiled: a weird upward corkscrewing of the lips. A strange, sardonic light danced and fluttered in his eyes.

"Herr Dussander," he said, "if only I could believe that."

In the evening Todd walked down to the slope overlooking the freeway, climbed down to the dead tree, and sat on it. It was just past twilight. The evening was warm. Car headlights cut through the dusk in long yellow daisy chains.

There is no document.

He hadn't realized how completely irretrievable the entire situation was until the discussion that had followed. Dussander suggested Todd search the house for a safety deposit key, and when he didn't find one, that would prove there was no safety deposit box and hence no document. But a key could be hidden anywhere—it could be put in a Crisco can and then buried, it could be put in a Sucrets tin and slid behind a board that had been loosened and then replaced; he might even have ridden the bus to San Diego and put it behind one of the rocks in the decorative stone wall which surrounded the bears' environmental area. For that matter, Todd went on, Dussander could even have thrown the key away. Why not? He had only needed it once, to put his written documents in. If he died, someone else would take it out.

Dussander nodded reluctantly at this, but after a moment's thought he made another suggestion. When he got well enough to go home, he would have the boy call every single bank in Santo Donato. He would tell each bank official he was calling for his grandfather. Poor grandfather, he would say, had grown lamentably senile over the last two years, and now he had misplaced the key to his safety deposit box. Even worse, he could no longer remember which bank the box was in. Could they just check their files for an Arthur Denker, no middle initial? And when Todd drew a blank at every bank in town—

Todd was already shaking his head again. First, a story like that was almost guaranteed to raise suspicions. It was too pat. They would probably suspect a con-game and get in touch with the police. Even if every one of them bought the story, it would do no good. If none of the almost nine dozen banks in Santo Donato had a box in the Denker name, it didn't mean that Dussander hadn't rented one in San Diego, L.A., or any town in between.

At last Dussander gave up.

"You have all the answers, boy. All, at least, but one. What would I stand to gain by lying to you? I invented this story to protect myself from you—that is a motive. Now I am trying to uninvent it. What possible gain do you see in that?"

Dussander got laboriously up on one elbow.

"For that matter, why would I need a document at all, at this point? I could destroy your life from this hospital bed, if that was what I wanted. I could open my mouth to the first passing doctor, they are all Jews, they would all know who I am, or at least who I was. But why would I do this? You are a fine student. You have a fine career ahead of you . . . unless you get careless with those winos of yours."

Todd's face froze. "I told you—"

"I know. You never heard of them, you never touched so much as a hair on their scaly, tick-ridden heads, all right, good, fine. I say no more about it. Only tell me, boy: why should I lie about this? We are quits, you say. But I tell you we can only be quits if we can trust each other."

Now, sitting behind the dead tree on the slope which ran down to the freeway, looking at all the anonymous headlights disappearing endlessly like slow tracer bullets, he knew well enough what he was afraid of.

Dussander talking about trust. That made him afraid.

The idea that Dussander might be tending a small but perfect flame of hatred deep in his heart, that made him afraid, too.

A hatred of Todd Bowden, who was young, clean-featured, unwrinkled; Todd Bowden, who was an apt pupil with a whole bright life stretching ahead of him.

But what he feared most was Dussander's refusal to use his name.

Todd. What was so hard about that, even for an old kraut whose teeth were mostly false? *Todd.* One syllable. Easy to say.

Put your tongue against the roof of your mouth, drop your teeth a little, replace your tongue, and it was out. Yet Dussander had always called him "boy." Only that. Contemptuous. *Anonymous.* Yes, that was it, anonymous. As anonymous as a concentration camp serial number.

Perhaps Dussander *was* telling the truth. No, not just perhaps; *probably.* But there were those fears . . . the worst of them being Dussander's refusal to use his name.

And at the root of it all was his own inability to make a hard and final decision. At the root of it all was a rueful truth: even after four years of visiting Dussander, he still didn't know what went on in the old man's head. Perhaps he wasn't such an apt pupil after all.

Cars and cars and cars. His fingers itched to hold his rifle. How many could he get? Three? Six? An even baker's dozen? And how many miles to Babylon?

He stirred restlessly, uneasily.

Only Dussander's death would tell the final truth, he supposed. Sometime during the next five years, maybe even sooner. Three to five . . . it sounded like a prison sentence. *Todd Bowden, this court hereby sentences you to three to five for associating with a known war criminal. Three to five at bad dreams and cold sweats.*

Sooner or later Dussander would simply drop dead. Then the waiting would begin. The knot in the stomach every time the phone or the doorbell rang.

He wasn't sure he could stand that.

His fingers itched to hold the gun and Todd curled them into fists and drove both fists into his crotch. Sick pain swallowed his belly and he lay for some time afterwards in a writhing ball on the ground, his lips pulled back in a silent shriek. The pain was dreadful, but it blotted out the endless parade of thoughts.

At least for awhile.

20

For Morris Heisel, that Sunday was a day of miracles.

The Atlanta Braves, his favorite baseball team, swept a double-header from the high and mighty Cincinnati Reds by scores of 7-1 and 8-0. Lydia, who boasted smugly of always taking care of herself and whose favorite saying was "An ounce of prevention is worth a pound of cure," slipped on her friend Janet's wet kitchen floor and sprained her hip. She was at home in bed. It wasn't serious, not at all, and thank God (what God) for that, but it meant she wouldn't be able to visit him for at least two days, maybe as long as four.

Four days without Lydia! Four days that he wouldn't have to hear about how she had warned him that the stepladder was wobbly and how he was up too high on it in the bargain. Four days when he wouldn't have to listen to her tell him how she'd always said the Rogans' pup was going to cause them grief, always chasing Lover Boy that way. Four days without Lydia asking him if he wasn't glad now that she had kept after him about sending in that insurance application, for if she had not, they would surely be on their way to the poorhouse now. Four days without having Lydia tell him that many people lived perfectly normal lives—almost, anyway—paralyzed from the waist down; why, every museum and gallery in the city had wheelchair ramps as well as stairs, and there were even special busses. After the observation, Lydia would smile bravely and then inevitably burst into tears.

Morris drifted off into a contented late afternoon nap.

When he woke up it was half-past five in the afternoon. His roommate was asleep. He still hadn't placed Denker, but all the same he felt sure that he had known the man at some time or other. He had begun to ask Denker about himself once or twice, but then something kept him from making more than the most banal conversation with the man—the weather, the last earthquake, the next earthquake, and yeah, the *Guide* says Myron Floren is going to come back for a special guest appearance this weekend on the Welk show.

Morris told himself he was holding back because it gave him a mental game to play, and when you were in a bodycast from your shoulders to your hips, mental games can come in handy. If you had a little mental contest going on, you didn't have to spend quite so much time wondering how it was going to be, pissing through a catheter for the rest of your life.

If he came right out and asked Denker, the mental game would probably come to a swift and unsatisfying conclusion. They would narrow their pasts down to some common experience—a train trip, a boat ride, possibly even the camp. Denker might have been in Patin; there had been plenty of German Jews there.

On the other hand, one of the nurses had told him Denker would probably be going home in a week or two. If Morris couldn't figure it out by then, he would mentally declare the game lost and ask the man straight out: *Say, I've had the feeling I know you—*

But there was more to it than just that, he admitted to himself. There was something in his feelings, a nasty sort of undertow, that made him think of that story "The Monkey's Paw," where every wish had been granted as the result of some evil turn of fate. The old couple who came into possession of the paw wished for a hundred dollars and received it as a gift of condolence when their only son was killed in a nasty mill accident. Then the mother had wished for the son to return to them. They had heard footsteps dragging up their walk shortly afterward; then pounding on the door. The mother, mad with joy, had gone rushing down the stairs to let in her only child. The father, mad with fear, scrabbled through the darkness for the dried paw, found it at last, and wished his son dead again. The mother threw the door open a moment later and found nothing on the stoop but an eddy of night wind.

In some way Morris felt that perhaps he *did* know where he and Denker had been acquainted, but that his knowledge was like the son of the old couple in the story—returned from the grave, but not as he was in his mother's memory; returned, instead, horribly crushed and mangled from his fall into the gnashing, whirling machinery. He felt that his knowledge of Denker might be a subconscious thing, pounding on the door between that area of his mind and that of rational under-standing and recognition, demanding admittance . . . and that another part of him was searching frantically for the monkey's paw, or its psychological equivalent; for the talisman that would wish away the knowledge forever.

Now he looked at Denker, frowning.

Denker, Denker, Where have I known you, Denker? Was it Patin? Is that why I don't want to know? But surely, two survivors of a com-mon horror do not have to be afraid of each other. Unless, of course . . .

He frowned. He felt very close to it, suddenly, but his feet were tingling, breaking his concentration, annoying him. They were tingling in just the way a limb tingles when you've slept on it and it's returning to normal circulation. If it wasn't for the damned body-cast, he could sit up and rub his feet until that tingle went away. He could—

Morris's eyes widened.

For a long time he lay perfectly still, Lydia forgotten, Denker forgotten, Patin forgotten, *everything* forgotten except that tingly feeling in his feet. Yes, *both* feet, but it was stronger in the right one. When you felt that tingle, you said *My foot went to sleep.*

But what you really meant, of course, was *My foot is waking up.*

Morris fumbled for a call-button. He pressed it again and again until the nurse came.

The nurse tried to dismiss it—she had had hopeful patients before. His doctor wasn't in the building, and the nurse didn't want to call him at home. Dr. Kemmelman had a vast reputa-tion for evil temper . . . especially when he was called at home.

Morris wouldn't let her dismiss it. He was a mild man, but now he was prepared to make more than a fuss; he was prepared to make an uproar if that's what it took. The Braves had taken two. Lydia had sprained her hip. But good things came in threes, everyone knew that.

At last the nurse came back with an intern, a young man named Dr. Timpnell whose hair looked as if it had been cut by a Lawn Boy with very dull blades. Dr. Timpnell pulled a Swiss Army knife from the pocket of his white pants, folded out the Phillips screwdriver attachment, and ran it from the toes of Morris's right foot down to the heel. The foot did not curl, but his toes twitched—it was an obvious twitch, too definite to miss. Morris burst into tears.

Timpnell, looking rather dazed, sat beside him on the bed and patted his hand.

"This sort of thing happens from time to time," he said (possibly from his wealth of practical experience, which stretched back perhaps as far as six months). "No doctor predicts it, but it *does* happen. And apparently it's happened to you."

Morris nodded through his tears.

"Obviously, you're not totally paralyzed." Timpnell was still patting his hand. "But I wouldn't try to predict if your recovery will be slight, partial, or total. I doubt if Dr. Kemmelman will, either. I suspect you'll have to undergo a lot of physical therapy, and not all of it will be pleasant. But it will be more pleasant than . . . you know."

"Yes," Morris said through his tears. "I know. Thank God!" He remembered telling Lydia there was no God and felt his face fill up with hot blood.

"I'll see that Dr. Kemmelman is informed," Timpnell said, giving Morris's hand a final pat and rising.

"Could you call my wife?" Morris asked. Because, doom-crying and hand-wringing aside, he felt *something* for her. Maybe it was even love, an emotion which seemed to have little to do with sometimes feeling like you could wring a person's neck.

"Yes, I'll see that it's done. Nurse, would you—?"

"Of course, doctor," the nurse said, and Timpnell could barely stifle his grin.

"Thank you," Morris said, wiping his eyes with a Kleenex from the box on the nightstand. "Thank you very much."

Timpnell went out. At some point during the discussion, Mr. Denker had awakened. Morris considered apologizing for all the noise, or perhaps for his tears, and then decided no apology was necessary.

"You are to be congratulated, I take it," Mr. Denker said.

"We'll see," Morris said, but like Timpnell, he was barely able to stifle his grin. "We'll see."

"Things have a way of working out," Denker replied vaguely, and then turned on the TV with the remote control device. It was now quarter to six, and they watched the last of *Hee Haw*. It was followed by the evening news. Unemployment was worse. Inflation was not so bad. Billy Carter was thinking about going into the beer business. A new Gallup poll showed that, if the election were to be held right then, there were four Republican candidates who could beat Billy's brother Jimmy. And there had been racial incidents following the murder of a black child in Miami. "A night of violence," the newscaster called it. Closer to home, an unidentified man had been found in an orchard near Highway 46, stabbed and bludgeoned.

Lydia called just before six-thirty. Dr. Kemmelman had called her and, based on the young intern's report, he had been cautiously optimistic. Lydia was cautiously joyous. She vowed to come in the following day even if it killed her. Morris told her he loved her. Tonight he loved everyone—Lydia, Dr. Timpnell with his Lawn Boy haircut, Mr. Denker, even the young girl who brought in the supper trays as Morris hung up.

Supper was hamburgers, mashed potatoes, a carrots-and-peas combination, and small dishes of ice cream for dessert. The candy striper who served it was Felice, a shy blonde girl of perhaps twenty. She had her own good news—her boyfriend had landed a job as a computer programmer with IBM and had formally asked her to marry him.

Mr. Denker, who exuded a certain courtly charm that all the young ladies responded to, expressed great pleasure. "Really, how wonderful. You must sit down and tell us all about it. Tell us everything. Omit nothing."

Felice blushed and smiled and said she couldn't do that. "We've still got the rest of the B Wing to do and C Wing after that. And look, here it is six-thirty!"

"Then tomorrow night, for sure. We insist . . . don't we, Mr. Heisel?"

"Yes, indeed," Morris murmured, but his mind was a million miles away.

(you must sit down and tell us all about it)

Words spoken in that exact-same bantering tone. He had heard them before; of that there could be no doubt. But had Denker been the one to speak them? *Had* he?

(tell us everything)

The voice of an urbane man. A cultured man. But there was a threat in the voice. A steel hand in a velvet glove. Yes.

Where?

(tell us everything, omit nothing.)

(? PATIN ?)

Morris Heisel looked at his supper. Mr. Denker had already fallen to with a will. The encounter with Felice had left him in the best of spirits—the way he had been after the young boy with the blonde hair came to visit him.

"A nice girl," Denker said, his words muffled by a mouthful of carrots and peas.

"Oh yes—

(you must sit down)

—Felice, you mean. She's

(and tell us all about it.)

very sweet."

(tell us everything, omit nothing.)

He looked down at his own supper, suddenly remembering how it got to be in the camps after awhile. At first you would have killed for a scrap of meat, no matter how maggoty or green with decay. But after awhile, that crazy hunger went away and your belly lay inside your middle like a small gray rock. You felt you would never be hungry again.

Until someone showed you food.

("tell us everything, my friend, omit nothing, you must sit down and tell us AAALLLLL about it.")

The main course on Morris's plastic hospital tray was hamburger. Why should it suddenly make him think of lamb? Not mutton, not chops—mutton was often stringy, chops often tough, and a person whose teeth had rotted out like old stumps would perhaps not be overly tempted by mutton or a chop. No, what he thought of now was a savory lamb stew, gravy-rich and full of vegetables. Soft tasty vegetables. Why think of lamp stew? Why, unless—

The door banged open. It was Lydia, her face rosy with smiles. An aluminum crutch was propped in her armpit and she was walking like Marshal Dillon's friend Chester. *"Morris!"* she trilled. Trailing her and looking just as tremulously happy was Emma Rogan from next door.

Mr. Denker, startled, dropped his fork. He cursed softly under his breath and picked it up off the floor with a wince.

"It's so *WONDERFUL!*" Lydia was almost baying with excitement. "I called Emma and asked her if we could come tonight instead of tomorrow, I had the crutch already, and I said, 'Em,' I said, 'if I can't bear this agony for Morris, what kind of wife am I to him?' Those were my very words, weren't they, Emma?"

Emma Rogan, perhaps remembering that her collie pup had caused at least some of the problem, nodded eagerly.

"So I called the hospital," Lydia said, shrugging her coat off and settling in for a good long visit, "and *they* said it was past visiting hours but in my case they would make an exception,

except we couldn't stay too long because we might bother Mr.
Denker. We aren't bothering you, are we, Mr. Denker?"

"No, dear lady," Mr. Denker said resignedly.

"Sit down, Emma, take Mr. Denker's chair, he's not using
it. Here, Morris, stop with the ice cream, you're slobbering it
all over yourself, just like a baby. Never mind, we'll have you
up and around in no time. I'll feed it to you. Goo-goo, ga-ga.
Open wide . . . over the teeth, over the gums . . . look out,
stomach, here it comes! . . . No, don't say a word, Mommy
knows best. Would you look at him, Emma, he hardly has any
hair left and I don't wonder, thinking he might never walk
again. It's God's mercy. I told him that stepladder was wobbly.
I said, 'Morris,' I said, 'come down off there before—' "

She fed him ice cream and chattered for the next hour and
by the time she left, hobbling ostentatiously on the crutch
while Emma held her other arm, thoughts of lamb stew and
voices echoing up through the years were the last things in
Morris Heisel's mind. He was exhausted. To say it had been a
busy day was putting it mildly. Morris fell deeply asleep.

He awoke sometime between 3:00 and 4:00 a.m. with a scream
locked behind his lips.

Now he knew. He knew exactly where and exactly when he
had been acquainted with the man in the other bed. Except his
name had not been Denker *then.* Oh no, not at all.

He had awakened from the most terrible nightmare of
his whole life. Someone had given him and Lydia a monkey's paw, and they had wished for money. Then, somehow,
a Western Union boy in a Hitler Youth uniform had been in
the room with them. He handed Morris a telegram which
read: REGRET TO INFORM YOU BOTH DAUGHTERS DEAD STOP
PATIN CONCENTRATION CAMP STOP GREATEST REGRETS AT
THIS FINAL SOLUTION STOP COMMANDANT'S LETTER FOL-
LOWS STOP WILL TELL YOU EVERYTHING AND OMIT NOTH-
ING STOP PLEASE ACCEPT OUR CHECK FOR 100 REICHMARKS

ON DEPOSIT YOUR BANK TOMORROW STOP SIGNED ADOLF
HITLER CHANCELLOR.

A great wail from Lydia, and although she had never even
seen Morris's daughters, she held the monkey's paw high and
wished for them to be returned to life. The room went dark.
And suddenly, from outside, came the sound of dragging,
lurching footfalls.

Morris was down on his hands and knees in a darkness that
suddenly stank of smoke and gas and death. He was searching
for the paw. One wish left. If he could find the paw he could
wish this dreadful dream away. He would spare himself the sight
of his daughters, thin as scarecrows, their eyes deep wounded
holes, their numbers burning on the scant flesh of their arms.

Hammering on the door.

In the nightmare, his search for the paw became ever more
frenzied, but it bore no fruit. It seemed to go on for years. And
then, behind him, the door crashed open. *No,* he thought. *I
won't look. I'll close my eyes. Rip them from my head if I have to, but
I won't look.*

But he did look. He had to look. In the dream it was as if
huge hands had grasped his head and wrenched it around.

It was not his daughters standing in the doorway; it was
Denker. A much younger Denker, a Denker who wore a Nazi
SS uniform, the cap with its death's-head insignia cocked rak-
ishly to one side. His buttons gleamed heartlessly, his boots
were polished to a killing gloss.

Clasped in his arms was a huge and slowly bubbling pot of
lamb stew.

And the dream-Denker, smiling his dark, suave smile, said:
*You must sit down and tell us all about it—as one friend to another,
hein? We have heard that gold has been hidden. That tobacco has
been hoarded. That it was not food-poisoning with Schneibel at all
but powdered glass in his supper two nights ago. You must not insult
our intelligence by pretending you know nothing. You knew EVERY-
THING. So tell it all. Omit nothing.*

And in the dark, smelling the maddening aroma of the stew, he told them everything. His stomach, which had been a small gray rock, was now a ravening tiger. Words spilled helplessly from his lips. They spewed from him in the senseless sermon of a lunatic, truth and falsehood all mixed together.

Brodin has his mother's wedding ring taped below his scrotum!

("you must sit down")

Laslo and Herman Dorksy have talked about rushing guard tower number three!

("and tell us everything!")

Rachel Tannenbaum's husband has tobacco, he gave the guard who comes on after Zeickert, the one they call Booger-Eater because he is always picking his nose and then putting his fingers in his mouth. Tannenbaum, some of it to Booger-Eater so he wouldn't take his wife's pearl earrings!

("oh that makes no sense no sense at all you've mixed up two different stories I think but that's all right quite all right we'd rather have you mix up two stories than omit one completely you must omit NOTHING!")

There is a man who has been calling out his dead son's name in order to get double rations!

("tell us his name")

I don't know it but I can point him out to you please yes I can show him to you I will I will I will I

("tell us everything you know")

will I will I will I will I will I will I will I

Until he swam up into consciousness with a scream in his throat like fire.

Trembling uncontrollably, he looked at the sleeping form in the other bed. He found himself staring particularly at the wrinkled, caved-in mouth. Old tiger with no teeth. Ancient and vicious rogue elephant with one tusk gone and the other rotted loose in its socket. Senile monster.

"Oh my *God,*" Morris Heisel whispered. His voice was high and faint, inaudible to anyone but himself. Tears trickled down his cheeks toward his ears. "Oh dear *God,* the man who murdered my wife and my daughters is sleeping in the same room with me, my *God,* oh dear dear *God,* he is here with me now in this room."

The tears began to flow faster now—tears of rage and horror, hot, scalding.

He trembled and waited for morning, and morning did not come for an age.

21

The next day, Monday, Todd was up at six o'clock in the morning and poking listlessly at a scrambled egg he had fixed for himself when his father came down still dressed in his monogrammed bathrobe and slippers.

"Mumph," he said to Todd, going past him to the refrigerator for orange juice.

Todd grunted back without looking up from his book, one of the 87th Squad mysteries. He had been lucky enough to land a summer job with a landscaping outfit that operated out of Pasadena. That would have been much too far to commute ordinarily, even if one of his parents had been willing to loan him a car for the summer (neither was), but his father was working on-site not far from there, and he was able to drop Todd off at a bus stop on his way and pick him up at the same place on his way back. Todd was less than wild about the arrangement; he didn't like riding home from work with his father and absolutely detested riding to work with him in the morning. It was in the mornings that he felt the most naked, when the wall between what he was and what he might be seemed the thinnest. It was worse after a night of bad dreams, but even if no dreams had come in the night, it was bad. One morning he realized with a fright so sudden it was almost terror that he had been seriously considering reaching across his father's briefcase, grabbing the wheel of the Porsche, and sending them corkscrewing into the two express lanes, cutting a swath of destruction through the morning commuters.

"You want another egg, Todd-O?"

"No thanks, Dad." Dick Bowden ate them fried. How could anyone stand to eat a fried egg? On the grill of the Jenn-Air for two minutes, then over easy. What you got on your plate at the end looked like a giant dead eye with a cataract over it, an eye that would bleed orange when you poked it with your fork.

He pushed his scrambled egg away. He had barely touched it.

Outside, the morning paper slapped the step.

His father finished cooking, turned off the grill, and came to the table. "Not hungry this morning, Todd-O?"

You call me that one more time and I'm going to stick my knife right up your fucking nose . . . Dad-O.

"Not much appetite, I guess."

Dick grinned affectionately at his son; there was still a tiny dab of shaving cream on the boy's right ear. "Betty Trask stole your appetite. That's my guess."

"Yeah, maybe that's it." He offered a wan smile that vanished as soon as his father went down the stairs from the breakfast nook to get the paper. *Would it wake you up if I told you what a cunt she is, Dad-O? How about if I said, "Oh, by the way, did you know your good friend Ray Trask's daughter is one of the biggest sluts in Santo Donato? She'd kiss her own twat if she was double-jointed, Dad-O. That's how much she thinks of it. Just a stinking little slut. Two lines of coke and she's yours for the night. And if you don't happen to have any coke, she's still yours for the night. She'd fuck a dog if she couldn't get a man." Think that'd wake you up, Dad-O? Get you a flying start on the day?*

He pushed the thoughts back away viciously, knowing they wouldn't stay gone.

His father came back with the paper. Todd glimpsed the headline: SPACE SHUTTLE WON'T FLY, EXPERT SAYS.

Dick sat down. "Betty's a fine-looking girl," he said. "She reminds me of your mother when I first met her."

"Is that so?"

"Pretty . . . young . . . fresh . . ." Dick Bowden's eyes had gone vague. Now they came back, focusing almost anxiously on his son. "Not that your mother isn't still a fine-looking woman. But at that age a girl has a certain . . . glow, I guess you'd say. It's there for awhile, and then it's gone." He shrugged and opened the paper. "*C'est la vie*, I guess."

She's a bitch in heat. Maybe that's what makes her glow.

"You're treating her right, aren't you, Todd-O?" His father was making his usual rapid trip through the paper toward the sports pages. "Not getting too fresh?"

"Everything's cool, Dad."

(*if he doesn't stop pretty soon I'll I'll do something, scream, throw his coffee in his face, something.*)

"Ray thinks you're a fine boy," Dick said absently. He had at last reached the sports. He became absorbed. There was blessed silence at the breakfast table.

Betty Trask had been all over him the very first time they went out. He had taken her to the local lovers' lane after the movie because he knew it would be expected of them; they could swap spits for half an hour or so and have all the right things to tell their respective friends the next day. She could roll her eyes and tell how she had fought off his advances— boys were so tiresome, really, and she never fucked on the first date, she wasn't that kind of girl. Her friends would agree and then all of them would troop into the girls' room and do whatever it was they did in there—put on fresh makeup, smoke Tampax, whatever.

And for a guy . . . well, you had to make out. You had to get at least to second base and try for third. Because there were reputations and reputations. Todd couldn't have cared less about having a stud reputation; he only wanted a reputation for being normal. And if you didn't at least *try,* word got around. People started to wonder if you were all right.

So he took them up on Jane's Hill, kissed them, felt their

tits, went a little further than that if they would allow it. And that was it. The girl would stop him, he would put up a little good-natured argument, and then take her home. No worries about what might be said in the girls' room the next day. No worries that anyone was going to think Todd Bowden was anything but normal. Except—

Except Betty Trask *was* the kind of girl who fucked on the first date. On every date. And in between dates.

The first time had been a month or so before the goddam Nazi's heart attack, and Todd thought he had done pretty well for a virgin . . . perhaps for the same reason a young pitcher will do well if he's tapped to throw the biggest game of the year with no forewarning. There had been no time to worry, to get all strung up about it.

Always before, Todd had been able to sense when a girl had made up her mind that on the next date she would just allow herself to be carried away. He was aware that he was personable and that both his looks and his prospects were good. The kind of boy their cunty mothers regarded as "a good catch." And when he sensed that physical capitulation about to happen, he would start dating some other girl. And whatever it said about his personality, Todd was able to admit to himself that if he ever started dating a truly frigid girl, he would probably be happy to date her for years to come. Maybe even marry her.

But the first time with Betty had gone fairly well—*she* was no virgin, even if he was. She had to help him get his cock into her, but she seemed to take that as a matter of course. And halfway through the act itself she had gurgled up from the blanket they were lying on: "I just *love* to fuck!" It was the tone of voice another girl might have used to express her love for strawberry whirl ice cream.

Later encounters—there had been five of them (five and a half, he supposed, if you wanted to count last night)—hadn't been so good. They had, in fact, gotten worse at what seemed an exponential rate . . . although he didn't believe even now that Betty had been aware of that (at least not until last night). In fact, quite the opposite. Betty apparently believed she had found the battering-ram of her dreams.

Todd hadn't felt any of the things he was supposed to feel at a time like that. Kissing her lips was like kissing warm but uncooked liver. Having her tongue in his mouth only made him wonder what kind of germs she was carrying, and sometimes he thought he could smell her fillings—an unpleasant metallic odor, like chrome. Her breasts were bags of meat. No more.

Todd had done it twice more with her before Dussander's heart attack. Each time he had more trouble getting erect. In both cases he had finally succeeded by using a fantasy. She was stripped naked in front of all their friends. Crying. Todd was forcing her to walk up and down before them while he cried out: *Show your tits! Let them see your snatch, you cheap slut! Spread your cheeks! That's right, bend over and SPREAD them!*

Betty's appreciation was not at all surprising. He was a good lover, not in spite of his problems but because of them. Getting hard was only the first step. Once you achieved erection, you had to have an orgasm. The fourth time they had done it—this was three days after Dussander's heart attack—he had pounded away at her for over ten minutes. Betty Trask thought she had died and gone to heaven; she had three orgasms and was trying for a fourth when Todd recalled an old fantasy . . . what was, in fact, the First Fantasy. The girl on the table, clamped and helpless. The huge dildo. The rubber squeeze-bulb. Only now, desperate and sweaty and almost insane with his desire to come and get this horror over with, the face of the girl on the table became Betty's face. That brought on a joyless, rubbery spasm that he supposed was, technically, at least, an orgasm. A moment later Betty was whispering in his ear, her breath warm and redolent of Juicy Fruit gum: "Lover, you do me any old time. Just call me."

Todd had nearly groaned aloud.

The nub of his dilemma was this: Wouldn't his reputation suffer if he broke off with a girl who obviously wanted to put out for him? Wouldn't people wonder why? Part of him said they would not. He remembered walking down the hall behind two senior boys during his freshman year and hearing one of them tell the other he had broken off with his girlfriend. The other wanted to know why. "Fucked 'er out," the first said, and both of them bellowed goatish laughter.

If someone asks me why I dropped her, I'll just say I fucked her out. But what if she says we only did it five times? Is that enough? What? . . . How much? . . . How many? . . . Who'll talk? . . . What'll they say?

So his mind ran on, as restless as a hungry rat in an insoluble maze. He was vaguely aware that he was turning a minor problem into a big problem, and that this very inability to solve the problem had something to say about how shaky he had gotten. But knowing it brought him no fresh ability to change his behavior, and he sank into a black depression.

College. College was the answer. College offered an excuse to break with Betty that no one could question. But September seemed so far away.

The fifth time it had taken him almost twenty minutes to get hard, but Betty had proclaimed the experience well worth the wait. And then, last night, he hadn't been able to perform at all.

"What are you, anyway?" Betty had asked petulantly. After twenty minutes of manipulating his lax penis, she was dishevelled and out of patience. "Are you one of those AC/DC guys?"

He very nearly strangled her on the spot. And if he'd had his .30-.30—

"Well, I'll be a son of a *gun!* Congratulations, son!"

"Huh?" He looked up and out of his black study.

"You made the Southern Cal High School All-Stars!" His father was grinning with pride and pleasure.

"Is that so?" For a moment he hardly knew what his father

175

was talking about; he had to grope for the meaning of the words. "Say, yeah, Coach Haines mentioned something to me about that at the end of the year. Said he was putting me and Billy DeLyons up. I never expected anything to happen."

"Well Jesus, you don't seem very excited about it!"

"I'm still trying

(who gives a ripe fuck?)

to get used to the idea." With a huge effort, he managed a grin. "Can I see the article?"

His father handed the paper across the table to Todd and got to his feet. "I'm going to wake Monica up. She's got to see this before we leave."

No, God—I can't face both of them this morning.

"Aw, don't do that. You know she won't be able to get back to sleep if you wake her up. We'll leave it for her on the table."

"Yes, I suppose we could do that. You're a damned thoughtful boy, Todd." He clapped Todd on the back, and Todd squeezed his eyes closed. At the same time he shrugged his shoulders in an aw-shucks gesture that made his father laugh. Todd opened his eyes again and looked at the paper.

4 BOYS NAMED TO SOUTHERN CAL ALL-STARS, the headline read. Beneath were pictures of them in their uniforms—the catcher and left-fielder from Fairview High, the harp southpaw from Mountford, and Todd to the far right, grinning openly out at the world from beneath the bill of his baseball cap. He read the story and saw that Billy DeLyons had made the second squad. That, at least, was something to feel happy about. DeLyons could claim he was a Methodist until his tongue fell out, if it made him feel good, but he wasn't fooling Todd. He knew perfectly well what Billy DeLyons was. Maybe he ought to introduce him to Betty Trask, she was another sheeny. He had wondered about that for a long time, and last night he had decided for sure. The Trasks were passing for white. One look at her nose and that olive complexion—her old man's was even worse—and you knew. That was probably why he hadn't been

able to get it up. It was simple: his cock had known the difference before his brain. Who did they think they were kidding,
calling themselves Trask?

"Congratulations again, son."

He looked up and first saw his father's hand stuck out, then
his father's foolishly grinning face.

Your buddy Trask is a yid! he heard himself yelling into his
father's face. *That's why I was impotent with his slut of a daughter last night! That's the reason!* Then, on the heels of that, the
cold voice that sometimes came at moments like this rose up
from deep inside him, shutting off the rising flood of irratio-
nality, as if

(GET HOLD OF YOURSELF RIGHT NOW)

behind steel gates.

He took his father's hand and shook it. Smiled guilelessly
into his father's proud face. Said: "Jeez, thanks, Dad."

They left that page of the newspaper folded back and a note
for Monica, which Dick insisted Todd write and sign *Your All-
Star Son, Todd.*

22

Ed French, aka "Pucker" French, aka Sneaker Pete and The
Ked Man, *also* aka Rubber Ed French, was in the small and
lovely seaside town of San Remo for a guidance counsellors'
convention. It was a waste of time if ever there had been one—
all guidance counsellors could ever agree on was not to agree
on anything—and he grew bored with the papers, seminars,
and discussion periods after a single day. Halfway through the
second day, he discovered he was also bored with San Remo,
and that of the adjectives small, lovely, and seaside, the *key*
adjective was probably *small.* Gorgeous views and redwood
trees aside, San Remo didn't have a movie theater or a bowling
alley, and Ed hadn't wanted to go in the place's only bar—it

had a dirt parking lot filled with pickup trucks, and most of the pickups had Reagan stickers on their rusty bumpers and tailgates. He wasn't afraid of being picked on, but he hadn't wanted to spend an evening looking at men in cowboy hats and listening to Loretta Lynn on the jukebox.

So here he was on the third day of a convention which stretched out over an incredible four days; here he was in room 217 of the Holiday Inn, his wife and daughter at home, the TV broken, an unpleasant smell hanging around in the bathroom. There was a swimming pool, but his eczema was so bad this summer that he wouldn't have been caught dead in a bathing suit. From the shins down he looked like a leper. He had an hour before the next workshop (Helping the Vocally Challenged Child—what they meant was doing something for kids who stuttered or who had cleft palates, but we wouldn't want to come right out and *say* that, Christ no, someone might lower our salaries), he had eaten lunch at San Remo's only restaurant, he didn't feel like a nap, and the TV's one station was showing a re-run of *Bewitched*.

So he sat down with the telephone book and began to flip through it aimlessly, hardly aware of what he was doing, wondering distantly if he knew anyone crazy enough about either small, lovely, or seaside to live in San Remo. He supposed this was what all the bored people in all the Holiday Inns all over the world ended up doing—looking for a forgotten friend or relative to call up on the phone. It was that, *Bewitched*, or the Gideon Bible. And if you did happen to get hold of somebody, what the hell did you say? "Frank! How the hell are you? And by the way, which was it—small, lovely, or seaside?" Sure. Right. Give that man a cigar and set him on fire.

Yet, as he lay on the bed flipping through the thin San Remo white pages and half-scanning the columns, it seemed to him that he *did* know somebody in San Remo. A book salesman? One of Sondra's nieces or nephews, of which there were marching battalions? A poker buddy from college? The relative of a student? That seemed to ring a bell, but he couldn't fine it down any more tightly.

He kept thumbing, and found he was sleepy after all. He had almost dozed off when it came to him and he sat up, wide-awake again.

Lord Peter!

They were re-running those Wimsey stories on PBS just lately—*Clouds of Witness, Murder Must Advertise, The Nine Tailors.* He and Sondra were hooked. A man named Ian Carmichael played Wimsey, and Sondra was nuts for him. So nuts, in fact, that Ed, who didn't think Carmichael looked like Lord Peter at all, actually became quite irritated.

"Sandy, the shape of his face is all wrong. And he's wearing false teeth, for heaven's sake!"

"Poo," Sondra had replied airily from the couch where she was curled up. "You're just jealous. He's so *handsome.*"

"Daddy's jealous, Daddy's jealous," little Norma sang, prancing around the living room in her duck pajamas.

"You should have been in bed an hour ago," Ed told her, gazing at his daughter with a jaundiced eye. "And if I keep noticing you're *here,* I'll probably remember that you aren't *there.*"

Little Norma was momentarily abashed. Ed turned back to Sondra.

"I remember back three or four years ago. I had a kid named Todd Bowden, and his grandfather came in for a conference. Now *that* guy looked like Wimsey. A very *old* Wimsey, but the shape of his face was right, and—"

"Wim-zee, Wim-zee, *Dim*-zee, *Jim*-zee," little Norma sang. "*Wim*-zee, *Bim*-zee, doodle-oodle-ooo-doo—"

"Shh, both of you," Sondra said. "I think he's the most *beautiful* man." Irritating woman!

But hadn't Todd Bowden's grandfather retired to San Remo? Sure. It had been on the forms. Todd had been one of the brightest boys in that year's class. Then, all at once, his grades had gone to hell. The old man had come in, told a familiar tale of marital difficulties, and had persuaded Ed to let the situation alone for awhile and see if things didn't straighten themselves out. Ed's view was that the old *laissez-faire* bit didn't work—if you told a teenage kid to root, hog, or die, he or she usually died. But the old man had been almost eerily persuasive (it was the resemblance to Wimsey, perhaps), and Ed had agreed to give Todd to the end of the next Flunk Card period. And damned if Todd hadn't pulled through. The old man must have gone right through the whole family and really kicked some ass, Ed thought. He looked like the type who not only could do it, but who might derive a certain dour pleasure from it. Then, just two days ago, he had seen Todd's picture in the paper—he had made the Southern Cal All-Stars in baseball. No mean feat when you consider that about five hundred boys were nominated each spring. He supposed he might never have come up with the grandfather's name if he hadn't seen the picture.

He flicked through the white pages more purposefully now, ran his finger down a column of fine type, and there it was. BOWDEN, VICTOR S. 403 Ridge Lane. Ed dialed the number and it rang several times at the other end. He was just about to hang up when an old man answered. "Hello?"

"Hello, Mr. Bowden. Ed French. From Santo Donato Junior High."

"Yes?" Politeness, but no more. Certainly no recognition. Well, the old guy was three years further along (weren't they all!) and things undoubtedly slipped his mind from time to time.

"Do you remember me, sir?"

"Should I?" Bowden's voice was cautious, and Ed smiled. The old man forgot things, but he didn't want anybody to know if he could help it. His own old man had been that way when his hearing started to go.

"I was your grandson Todd's guidance counsellor at S.D.J.H.S. I called to congratulate you. He sure tore up the pea-patch when he got to high school, didn't he? And now he's All-Conference to top it off. Wow!"

"*Todd!*" the old man said, his voice brightening immediately. "Yes, he certainly did a fine job, didn't he? Second in his class! And the girl who was ahead of him took the business courses." A sniff of disdain in the old man's voice. "My son called and offered to take me to Todd's commencement, but I'm in a wheelchair now. I broke my hip last January. I didn't want to go in a wheelchair. But I have his graduation picture right in the hall, you bet! Todd's made his parents very proud. And me, of course."

"Yes, I guess we got him over the hump," Ed said. He was smiling as he said it, but his smile was a trifle puzzled—somehow Todd's grandfather didn't sound the same. But it had been a long time ago, of course.

"Hump? What hump?"

"The little talk we had. When Todd was having problems with his course-work. Back in ninth."

"I'm not following you," the old man said slowly. "I would never presume to speak for Richard's son. It would cause trouble . . . ho-ho, you don't *know* how much trouble it would cause. You've made a mistake, young fellow."

"But—"

"Some sort of mistake. Got me confused with another student and another grandfather, I imagine."

Ed was moderately thunderstruck. For one of the few times in his life, he could not think of a single thing to say. If there was confusion, it sure wasn't on *his* part.

"Well," Bowden said doubtfully, "it was nice of you to call, Mr.—"

Ed found his tongue. "I'm right here in town, Mr. Bowden. It's a convention. Guidance counsellors. I'll be done around ten tomorrow morning, after the final paper is read. Could I come around to . . ." He consulted the phone book again. ". . . to Ridge Lane and see you for a few minutes?"

"What in the world for?"

"Just curiosity, I guess. It's all water over the dam now. But about three years ago, Todd got himself into a real crack with his grades. They were so bad I had to send a letter home with his report card requesting a conference with a parent, or, ideally, with both of his parents. What I got was his grandfather, a very pleasant man named Victor Bowden."

"But I've already told you—"

"Yes. I know. Just the same, I talked to *somebody* claiming to be Todd's grandfather. It doesn't matter much now, I suppose, but seeing is believing. I'd only take a few minutes of your time. It's all I *can* take, because I'm expected home by suppertime."

"Time is all I have," Bowden said, a bit ruefully. "I'll be here all day. You're welcome to stop in."

Ed thanked him, said goodbye, and hung up. He sat on the end of the bed, staring thoughtfully at the telephone. After awhile he got up and took a pack of Phillies Cheroots from the sport coat hanging on the back of the desk chair. He ought to go; there was a workshop, and if he wasn't there, he would be missed. He lit his Cheroot with a Holiday Inn match and dropped the burnt stub into a Holiday Inn ashtray. He went to the Holiday Inn window and looked blankly out into the Holiday Inn courtyard.

It doesn't matter much now, he had told Bowden, but it mattered to him. He wasn't used to being sold a bill of goods by one of his kids, and this unexpected news upset him. Technically he supposed it could still turn out to be a case of an old man's senility, but Victor Bowden hadn't sounded as if he was drooling in his beard yet. And, damn it, he didn't sound the *same.*

Had Todd Bowden jobbed him?

He decided it could have been done. Theoretically, at least. Especially by a bright boy like Todd. He could have jobbed *everyone,* not just Ed French. He could have forged his mother or father's name to the Flunk Cards he had been issued during his bad patch. Lots of kids discovered a latent forging ability when they got Flunk Cards. He could have used ink eradicator on his second- and third-quarter reports, changing the grades up for his parents and then back down again so that his home-room teacher wouldn't notice anything weird if he or she glanced at his card. The double application of eradicator would be visible to someone who was really looking, but home-room teachers carried an average of sixty students each. They were lucky if they could get the entire roll called before the first bell, let alone spot-checking returned cards for tampering.

As for Todd's final class standing, it would have dipped perhaps no more than three points overall—two bad marking periods out of a total of twelve. His other grades had been lopsidedly good enough to make up most of the difference. And how many parents drop by the school to look at the student records kept by the California Department of Education? Especially the parents of a bright student like Todd Bowden?

Frown lines appeared on Ed French's normally smooth forehead.

It doesn't matter much now. That was nothing but the truth. Todd's high school work had been exemplary; there was no way in the world you could fake a 94 percent. The boy was going on to Berkeley, the newspaper article had said, and Ed supposed his folks were damned proud—as they had every right to be. More and more it seemed to Ed that there was a vicious downside of American life, a greased skid of opportunism, cut corners, easy drugs, easy sex, a morality that grew cloudier each year. When your kid got through in standout style, parents had a right to be proud.

It doesn't matter much now—but who was his frigging grandfather?

That kept sticking into him. Who, indeed? Had Todd Bowden gone to the local branch of the Screen Actors' Guild and hung a notice on the bulletin board? YOUNG MAN IN

GRADES TROUBLE NEEDS OLDER MAN, PREF. 70-80 YRS., TO GIVE BOFFO PERFORMANCE AS GRANDFATHER, will pay union scale? Uh-uh. No way, José. And just what sort of adult would have fallen in with such a crazy conspiracy, and for what reason?

Ed French, aka Pucker, aka Rubber Ed, just didn't know. And because it didn't really matter, he stubbed out his Cheroot and went to his workshop. But his attention kept wandering.

The next day he drove out to Ridge Lane and had a long talk with Victor Bowden. They discussed grapes; they discussed the retail grocery business and how the big chain stores were pushing the little guys out; they discussed the political climate in southern California. Mr. Bowden offered Ed a glass of wine. Ed accepted with pleasure. He felt that he needed a glass of wine, even if it was only ten-forty in the morning. Victor Bowden looked as much like Peter Wimsey as a machine-gun looks like a shillelagh. Victor Bowden had no trace of the faint accent Ed remembered, and he was quite fat. The man who had purported to be Todd's grandfather had been whip-thin.

Before leaving, Ed told him: "I'd appreciate it if you wouldn't mention any of this to Mr. or Mrs. Bowden. There may be a perfectly reasonable explanation for all of it . . . and even if there isn't, it's all in the past."

"Sometimes," Bowden said, holding his glass of wine up to the sun and admiring its rich dark color, "the past don't rest so easy. Why else do people study history?"

Ed smiled uneasily and said nothing.

"But don't you worry. I never meddle in Richard's affairs. And Todd is a good boy. Salutatorian of his class . . . he must be a good boy. Am I right?"

"As rain," Ed French said heartily, and then asked for another glass of wine.

23

Dussander's sleep was uneasy; he lay in a trench of bad dreams.

They were breaking down the fence. Thousands, perhaps millions of them. They ran out of the jungle and threw themselves against the electrified barbed wire and now it was beginning to lean ominously inward. Some of the strands had given way and now coiled uneasily on the packed earth of the parade ground, squirting blue sparks. And still there was no end to them, no end. The Fuehrer was as mad as Rommel had claimed if he thought now—if he had ever thought— there could be a final solution to this problem. There were billions of them; they filled the universe; and they were all after him.

"Old man. Wake up, old man. Dussander. Wake up, old man, wake up."

At first he thought this was the voice of the dream.

Spoken in German; it had to be part of the dream. That was why the voice was so terrifying, of course. If he awoke he would escape it, so he swam upward . . .

The man was sitting by his bed on a chair that had been turned around backwards—a real man. "Wake up, old man," this visitor was saying. He was young—no more than thirty. His eyes were dark and studious behind plain steel-framed glasses. His brown hair was longish, collar-length, and for a confused moment Dussander thought it was the boy in a disguise. But this was not the boy, wearing a rather old-fashioned blue suit much too hot for the California climate. There was a small silver pin on the lapel of the suit. Silver, the metal you used to kill vampires and werewolves. It was a Jewish star.

"Are you speaking to me?" Dussander asked in German.

"Who else? Your roommate is gone."

"Heisel? Yes. He went home yesterday."

"Are you awake now?"

"Of course. But you've apparently mistaken me for someone

else. My name is Arthur Denker. Perhaps you have the wrong room."

"My name is Weiskopf. And yours is Kurt Dussander."

Dussander wanted to lick his lips but didn't. Just possibly this was still all part of the dream—a new phase, no more. *Bring me a wino and a steak-knife, Mr. Jewish Star in the Lapel, and I'll blow you away like smoke.*

"I know no Dussander," he told the young man. "I don't understand you. Shall I ring for the nurse?"

"You understand," Weiskopf said. He shifted position slightly and brushed a lock of hair from his forehead. The prosiness of this gesture dispelled Dussander's last hope.

"Heisel," Weiskopf said, and pointed at the empty bed.

"Heisel, Dussander, Weiskopf—none of these names mean anything to me."

"Heisel fell off a ladder while he was nailing a new gutter onto the side of his house," Weiskopf said. "He broke his back. He may never walk again. Unfortunate. But that was not the only tragedy of his life. He was an inmate of Patin, where he lost his wife and daughters. Patin, which you commanded."

"I think you are insane," Dussander said. "My name is Arthur Denker. I came to this country when my wife died. Before that I was—"

"Spare me your tale," Weiskopf said, raising a hand. "He had not forgotten your face. This face."

Weiskopf flicked a photograph into Dussander's face like a magician doing a trick. It was one of those the boy had shown him years ago. A young Dussander in a jauntily cocked SS cap, seated behind his desk.

Dussander spoke slowly, in English now, enunciating carefully.

"During the war I was a factory machinist. My job was to oversee the manufacture of drive-columns and power-trains for armored cars and trucks. Later I helped to build Tiger tanks. My reserve unit was called up during the battle of Berlin and

I fought honorably, if briefly. After the war I worked in Essen, at the Menschler Motor Works until—"

"—until it became necessary for you to run away to South America. With your gold that had been melted down from Jewish teeth and your silver melted down from Jewish jewelry and your numbered Swiss bank account. Mr. Heisel went home a happy man, you know. Oh, he had a bad moment when he woke up in the dark and realized with whom he was sharing a room. But he feels better now. He feels that God allowed him the sublime privilege of breaking his back so that he could be instrumental in the capture of one of the greatest butchers of human beings ever to live."

Dussander spoke slowly, enunciating carefully.

"During the war I was a factory machinist—"

"Oh, why not drop it? Your papers will not stand up to a serious examination. I know it and you know it. You are found out."

"My job was to oversee the manufacture of—"

"Of corpses! One way or another, you will be in Tel Aviv before the new year. The authorities are cooperating with us this time, Dussander. The Americans want to make us happy, and you are one of the things that will make us happy."

"—the manufacture of drive-columns and power-trains for armored cars and trucks. Later I helped to build Tiger tanks."

"Why be tiresome? Why drag it out?"

"My reserve unit was called up—"

"Very well then. You'll see me again. Soon."

Weiskopf rose. He left the room. For a moment his shadow bobbed on the wall and then that was gone, too. Dussander closed his eyes. He wondered if Weiskopf could be telling the truth about American cooperation. Three years ago, when oil was tight in America, he wouldn't have believed it. But the current upheaval in Iran might well harden American support for Israel. It was possible. And what did it matter? One way or the other, legal or illegal, Weiskopf and his colleagues would have him. On the subject of Nazis they were intransigent, and on the subject of the camps they were lunatics.

He was trembling all over. But he knew what he must do now.

24

The school records for the pupils who had passed through Santo Donato Junior High were kept in an old, rambling warehouse on the north side. It was not far from the abandoned trainyard. It was dark and echoing and it smelled of wax and polish and 999 Industrial Cleaner—it was also the school department's custodial warehouse.

Ed French got there around four in the afternoon with Norma in tow. A janitor let them in, told Ed what he wanted was on the fourth floor, and showed them to a creeping, clanking elevator that frightened Norma into an uncharacteristic silence.

She regained herself on the fourth floor, prancing and capering up and down the dim aisles of stacked boxes and files while Ed searched for and eventually found the files containing report cards from 1975. He pulled the second box and began to leaf through the B's. BORK. BOSTWICK. BOSWELL. BOWDEN, TODD. He pulled the card, shook his head impatiently over it in the dim light, and took it across to one of the high, dusty windows.

"Don't run around in here, honey," he called over his shoulder.

"Why, Daddy?"

"Because the trolls will get you," he said, and held Todd's card up to the light.

He saw it at once. This report card, in those files for three years now, had been carefully, almost professionally, doctored.

"Jesus Christ," Ed French muttered.

"Trolls, trolls, trolls!" Norma sang gleefully, as she continued to dance up and down the aisles.

25

Dussander walked carefully down the hospital corridor. He was still a bit unsteady on his legs. He was wearing his blue bathrobe over his white hospital johnny. It was night now, just after eight o'clock, and the nurses were changing shifts. The next half hour would be confused—he had observed that all the shift changes were confused. It was a time for exchanging notes, gossip, and drinking coffee at the nurses' station, which was just around the corner from the drinking fountain.

What he wanted was just across from the drinking fountain.

He was not noticed in the wide hallway, which at this hour reminded him of a long and echoing train station minutes before a passenger train departs. The walking wounded paraded slowly up and down, some dressed in robes as he was, others holding the backs of their johnnies together. Disconnected music came from half a dozen different transistor radios in half a dozen different rooms. Visitors came and went. A man laughed in one room and another man seemed to be weeping across the hall. A doctor walked by with his nose in a paperback novel.

Dussander went to the fountain, got a drink, wiped his mouth with his cupped hand, and looked at the closed door across the hall. This door was always locked—at least, that was the theory. In practice he had observed that it was sometimes both unlocked and unattended. Most often during the chaotic half hour when the shifts were changing and the nurses were gathered around the corner. Dussander had observed all of this with the trained and wary eye of a man who has been on the jump for a long, long time. He only wished he could observe the unmarked door for another week or so, looking for dangerous breaks in the pattern—he would only have the one chance. But he didn't have another week. His status as Werewolf in Residence might not become known for another two or three days, but it might happen tomorrow. He did not dare wait. When it came out, he would be watched constantly.

He took another small drink, wiped his mouth again, and looked both ways. Then, casually, with no effort at concealment, he stepped across the hall, turned the knob, and walked into the drug closet. If the woman in charge had happened to already be behind her desk, he was only nearsighted Mr. Denker. So sorry, dear lady, I thought it was the W.C. Stupid of me.

But the drug closet was empty.

He ran his eye over the top shelf at his left. Nothing but eyedrops and eardrops. Second shelf: laxatives, suppositories. On the third shelf he saw both Seconal and Veronal. He slipped a bottle of Seconals into the pocket of his robe. Then he went back to the door and stepped out without looking around, a puzzled smile on his face—that certainly wasn't the W.C., was it? *There* it was, right next to the drinking fountain. Stupid me!

He crossed to the door labelled men, went inside, and washed his hands. Then he went back down the hall to the semi-private room that was now completely private since the departure of the illustrious Mr. Heisel. On the table between the beds was a glass and a plastic pitcher filled with water. Pity there was no bourbon; really, it was a shame. But the pills would float him off just as nicely no matter how they were washed down.

"Morris Heisel, *salud,*" he said with a faint smile, and poured himself a glass of water. After all those years of jumping at shadows, of seeing faces that looked familiar on park benches or in restaurants or bus terminals, he had finally been recognized and turned in by a man he wouldn't have known from Adam. It was almost funny. He had barely spared Heisel two glances, Heisel and his broken back from God. On second thought, it wasn't *almost* funny; it was *very* funny.

He put three pills in his mouth, swallowed them with water, took three more, then three more. In the room across the hall he could see two old men hunched over a night-table, playing a grumpy game of cribbage. One of them had a hernia, Dussander knew. What was the other? Gallstones? Kidney stones? Tumor? Prostate? The horrors of old age. They were legion.

He refilled his water glass but didn't take any more pills right away. Too many could defeat his purpose. He might throw them up and they would pump the residue out of his stomach, saving him for whatever indignities the Americans and the Israelis could devise. He had no intention of trying to take his life stupidly, like a *Hausfrau* on a crying jag. When he began to get drowsy, he would take a few more. That would be fine.

The quavering voice of one of the cribbage players came to him, thin and triumphant: "A double run of three for eight . . . fifteens for twelve . . . and the right jack for thirteen. How do you like *those* apples?"

"Don't worry," the old man with the hernia said confidently. "I got first count. I'll peg out."

Peg out, Dussander thought, sleepy now. An apt enough phrase—but the Americans had a turn of idiom. *I don't give a tin shit, get hip or get out, stick it where the sun don't shine, money talks, nobody walks.* Wonderful idiom.

They thought they had him, but he was going to peg out before their very eyes.

He found himself wishing, of all absurd things, that he could leave a note for the boy. Wishing he could tell him to be very careful. To listen to an old man who had finally overstepped himself. He wished he could tell the boy that in the end he, Dussander, had come to respect him, even if he could never like him, and that talking to him had been better than listening to the run of his own thoughts. But any note, no matter how innocent, might cast suspicion on the boy, and Dussander did not want that. Oh, he would have a bad month or two, waiting for some government agent to show up and question him about a certain document that had been found in a safety deposit box rented to Kurt Dussander, aka Arthur Denker . . . but after a time, the boy would come to believe he had been telling the truth. There was no need for the boy to be touched by any of this, as long as he kept his head.

Dussander reached out with a hand that seemed to stretch for miles, got the glass of water, and took another three pills. He put the glass back, closed his eyes, and settled deeper into his soft, soft pillow. He had never felt so much like sleeping, and his sleep would be long. It would be restful.

Unless there were dreams.

The thought shocked him. *Dreams? Please God, no. Not those dreams. Not for eternity, not with all possibility of awakening gone. Not—*

In sudden terror, he tried to struggle awake. It seemed that hands were reaching eagerly up out of the bed to grab him, hands with hungry fingers.

(!NO!)

His thoughts broke up in a steepening spiral of darkness, and he rode down that spiral as if down a greased slide, down and down, to whatever dreams there are.

His overdose was discovered at 1:35 a.m., and he was pronounced dead fifteen minutes later. The nurse on duty was young and had been susceptible to elderly Mr. Denker's slightly ironic courtliness. She burst into tears. She was a Catholic, and she could not understand why such a sweet old man, who had been getting better, would want to do such a thing and damn his immortal soul to hell.

26

On Saturday morning in the Bowden household, nobody got up until at least nine. This morning at nine-thirty Todd and his father were reading at the table and Monica, who was a slow waker, served them scrambled eggs, juice, and coffee without speaking, still half in her dreams.

Todd was reading a paperback science fiction novel and Dick was absorbed in *Architectural Digest* when the paper slapped against the door.

"Want me to get it, Dad?"

"I will."

Dick brought it in, started to sip his coffee, and then choked on it as he got a look at the front page.

"Dick, what's wrong?" Monica asked, hurrying toward him.

Dick coughed out coffee that had gone down the wrong pipe, and while Todd looked at him over the top of the paperback in mild wonder, Monica started to pound him on the back. On the third stroke, her eyes fell to the paper's headline and she stopped in mid-stroke, as if playing statues. Her eyes widened until it seemed they might actually fall out onto the table.

"Holy God up in heaven!" Dick Bowden managed in a choked voice.

"Isn't that . . . I can't believe . . ." Monica began, and then stopped. She looked at Todd. "Oh, honey—"

His father was looking at him, too.

Alarmed now, Todd came around the table. "What's the matter?"

"Mr. Denker," Dick said—it was all he could manage.

Todd read the headline and understood everything. In dark letters it read: FUGITIVE NAZI COMMITS SUICIDE IN SANTO DONATO HOSPITAL. Below were two photos, side by side. Todd had seen both of them before. One showed Arthur Denker, six years younger and spryer. Todd knew it had been taken by a hippie street photographer, and that the old man had bought it only to make sure it didn't fall into the wrong hands by chance. The other photo showed an SS officer named Kurt Dussander behind his desk at Patin, his cap cocked to one side.

If they had the photograph the hippie had taken, they had been in his house.

Todd skimmed the article, his mind whizzing frantically. No mention of the winos. But the bodies would be found, and when they were, it would be a worldwide story, PATIN COMMANDANT NEVER LOST HIS TOUCH. HORROR IN NAZI'S BASEMENT. HE NEVER STOPPED KILLING.

Todd Bowden swayed on his feet.

Far away, echoing, he heard his mother cry sharply: "Catch him, Dick! He's fainting!"

The word

(*faintingfaintingfainting*)

repeated itself over and over. He dimly felt his father's arms grab him, and then for a little while Todd felt nothing, heard nothing at all.

27

Ed French was eating a danish when he unfolded the paper. He coughed, made a strange gagging sound, and spat dismembered pastry all over the table.

"Eddie!" Sondra French said with some alarm. "Are you okay?"

"Daddy's chokun, Daddy's chokun," little Norma proclaimed with nervous good humor, and then happily joined her mother in slamming Ed on the back. Ed barely felt the blows. He was still goggling down at the newspaper.

"What's wrong, Eddie?" Sondra asked again.

"Him! Him!" Ed shouted, stabbing his finger down at the paper so hard that his fingernail tore all the way through the A section.

"That man! Lord Peter!"

"What in God's name are you t—"

"*That's Todd Bowden's grandfather!*"

"What? That war criminal? Eddie, that's *crazy!*"

"But it's *him,*" Ed almost moaned. "Jesus Christ *Almighty,* that's *him!*"

Sondra French looked at the picture long and fixedly.

"He doesn't look like Peter Wimsey at all," she said finally.

28

Todd, pale as window-glass, sat on a couch between his mother and father.

Opposite them was a graying, polite police detective named Richler. Todd's father had offered to call the police, but Todd had done it himself, his voice cracking through the registers as it had done when he was fourteen.

He finished his recital. It hadn't taken long. He spoke with a mechanical colorlessness that scared the hell out of Monica. He was seventeen, true enough, but he was still a boy in so many ways. This was going to scar him forever.

"I read him . . . oh, I don't know. *Tom Jones. The Mill on the Floss.* That was a boring one. I didn't think we'd ever get through it. Some stories by Hawthorne—I remember he especially liked 'The Great Stone Face' and 'Young Goodman Brown.' We started *The Pickwick Papers,* but he didn't like it. He said Dickens could only be funny when he was being serious, and *Pickwick* was only kittenish. That was his word, kittenish. We got along the best with *Tom Jones.* We both liked that one."

"And that was three years ago," Richler said.

"Yes. I kept stopping in to see him when I got the chance, but in high school we were bussed across town . . . and some of the kids got up a scratch ballteam . . . there was more homework . . . you know . . . things just came up."

"You had less time."

"Less time, that's right. The work in high school was a lot harder . . . making the grades to get into college."

"But Todd is a very apt pupil," Monica said almost automatically. "He graduated salutatorian. We were so proud."

195

"I'll bet you were," Richler said with a warm smile. "I've got two boys in Fairview, down in the Valley, and they're just about able to keep their sports eligibility." He turned back to Todd. "You didn't read him any more books after you started high school?"

"No. Once in awhile I'd read him the paper. I'd come over and he'd ask me what the headlines were. He was interested in Watergate when that was going on. And he always wanted to know about the stock market, and the print on that page used to drive him batshit—sorry, Mom."

She patted his hand.

"I don't know why he was interested in the stocks, but he was."

"He had a few stocks," Richler said. "That's how he was getting by. He also had five different sets of ID salted around that house. He was a cagey one, all right."

"I suppose he kept the stocks in a safe deposit box somewhere," Todd remarked.

"Pardon me?" Richler raised his eyebrows.

"His stocks," Todd said. His father, who had also looked puzzled, now nodded at Richler.

"His stock certificates, the few that were left, were in a foot-locker under his bed," Richler said, "along with that photo of him as Denker. Did he have a safety deposit box, son? Did he ever say he did?"

Todd thought, and then shook his head. "I just thought that was where you kept your stocks. I don't know. This . . . this whole thing has just . . . you know . . . it blows my wheels." He shook his head in a dazed way that was perfectly real. He really *was* dazed. Yet, little by little, he felt his instinct of self-preservation surfacing. He felt a growing alertness, and the first stirrings of confidence. If Dussander had really taken a safety deposit box in which to store his insurance document, wouldn't he have transferred his remaining stock certificates there? And that photograph?

"We're working with the Israelis on this," Richler said. "In a very unofficial way. I'd be grateful if you didn't mention that if you decide to see any press people. They're real professionals. There's a man named Weiskopf who'd like to talk to you tomorrow, Todd. If that's okay by you and your folks."

"I guess so," Todd said, but he felt a touch of atavistic dread at the thought of being sniffed over by the same hounds that had chased Dussander for the last half of his life. Dussander had had a healthy respect for them, and Todd knew he would do well to keep that in mind.

"Mr. and Mrs. Bowden? Do you have any objections to Todd seeing Mr. Weiskopf?"

"Not if Todd doesn't," Dick Bowden said. "I'd like to be present, though. I've read about these Mossad characters—"

"Weiskopf isn't Mossad. He's what the Israelis call a special operative. In fact, he teaches Yiddish literature and English grammar. Also, he's written two novels." Richler smiled.

Dick raised a hand, dismissing it. "Whatever he is, I'm not going to let him badger Todd. From what I've read, these fellows can be a little *too* professional. Maybe he's okay. But I want you and this Weiskopf to remember that Todd tried to help that old man. He was flying under false colors, but Todd didn't know that."

"That's okay, Dad," Todd said with a wan smile.

"I just want you to help us all that you can," Richler said. "I appreciate your concern, Mr. Bowden. I think you're going to find that Weiskopf is a pleasant, low-pressure kind of guy. I've finished my own questions, but I'll break a little ground by telling you what the Israelis are most interested in. Todd was with Dussander when he had the heart attack that landed him in the hospital—"

"He asked me to come over and read him a letter," Todd said.

"We know." Richler leaned forward, elbows on his knees, tie swinging out to form a plumb-line to the floor. "The Israelis want to know about that letter. Dussander was a big fish, but he wasn't the last one in the lake—or so Sam Weiskopf says, and I believe him. They think Dussander might have known about a lot of other fish. Most of those still alive are probably in South America, but there may be others in a dozen countries . . . including the United States. Did you know they collared a man who had been an *Unterkommandant* at Buchenwald in the lobby of a Tel Aviv hotel?"

"Really!" Monica said, her eyes widening.

"Really." Richler nodded. "Two years ago. The point is just that the Israelis think the letter Dussander wanted Todd to read might have been from one of those other fish. Maybe they're right, maybe they're wrong. Either way, they want to know."

Todd, who had gone back to Dussander's house and burned the letter, said: "I'd help you—or this Weiskopf—if I could, Lieutenant Richler, but the letter was in German. It was really tough to read. I felt like a fool. Mr. Denker . . . Dussander . . . kept getting more excited and asking me to spell the words he couldn't understand because of my, you know, pronunciation. But I guess he was following all right. I remember once he laughed and said, 'Yes, yes, that is what you'd do, isn't it?' Then he said something in German. This was about two or three minutes before he had the heart attack. Something about *Dummkopf*. That means stupid in German, I think."

He was looking at Richler uncertainly, inwardly quite pleased with this lie.

Richler was nodding. "Yes, we understand that the letter was in German. The admitting doctor heard the story from you and corroborated it. But the letter *itself,* Todd . . . do you remember what happened to it?"

Here it is, Todd thought. *The crunch.*

"I guess it was still on the table when the ambulance came. When we all left. I couldn't testify to it in court, but—"

"I think there was a letter on the table," Dick said. "I picked something up and glanced at it. Airmail stationery, I think, but I didn't notice it was written in German."

"Then it should still be there," Richler said. "That's what we can't figure out."

"It's not?" Dick said. "I mean, it wasn't?"

"It wasn't, and it isn't."

"Maybe somebody broke in," Monica suggested.

"There would have been no need to *break* in," Richler said. "In the confusion of getting him out, the house was never locked. Dussander himself never thought to ask someone to lock up, apparently. His latchkey was still in the pocket of his pants when he died. His house was unlocked from the time the MED-Q attendants wheeled him out until we sealed it this morning at two-thirty a.m."

"Well, there you are," Dick said.

"No," Todd said. "I see what's bugging Lieutenant Richler." Oh yes, he saw it very well. You'd have to be blind to miss it. "Why would a burglar steal nothing but a letter? Especially one written in German? It doesn't listen. Mr. Denker didn't have much to steal, but a guy who broke in could find something better than that."

"You got it, all right," Richler said. "Not bad."

"Todd used to want to be a detective when he grew up," Monica said, and ruffled Todd's hair a bit. Since he had gotten big he seemed to object to that, but right now he didn't seem to mind. God, she hated to see him looking so pale. "I guess he's changed his mind to history these days."

"History is a good field," Richler said. "You can be an investigative historian. Have you ever read Josephine Tey?"

"No, sir."

"Doesn't matter. I just wish my boys had some ambition greater than seeing the Angels win the pennant this year."

Todd offered a wan smile and said nothing.

Richler turned serious again. "Anyway, I'll tell you the theory we're going on. We figure that someone, probably right here in Santo Donato, knew who and what Dussander was."

"Really?" Dick said.

"Oh yes. Someone who knew the truth. Maybe another fugitive Nazi. I know that sounds like Robert Ludlum stuff, but who would have thought there was even *one* fugitive Nazi in a quiet little suburb like this? And when Dussander was taken to the hospital, we think that Mr. X scooted over to the house and got that incriminating letter. And that by now it's so many decomposing ashes floating around in the sewer system."

"That doesn't make much sense either," Todd said.

"Why not, Todd?"

"Well, if Mr. Denk . . . if *Dussander* had an old buddy from the camps, or just an old Nazi buddy, why did he bother to have me come over and read him that letter? I mean, if you could have heard him correcting me, and stuff . . . at least this old Nazi buddy you're talking about would know how to speak German."

"A good point. Except maybe this other fellow is in a wheelchair, or blind. For all we know, it might be Bormann himself and he doesn't even dare go out and show his face."

"Guys that are blind or in wheelchairs aren't that good at scooting out to get letters," Todd said.

Richler looked admiring again. "True. But a blind man could steal a letter even if he couldn't read it, though. Or hire it done."

Todd thought this over, and nodded—but he shrugged at the same time to show how farfetched he thought the idea. Richler had progressed far beyond Robert Ludlum and into the land of Sax Rohmer. But how farfetched the idea was or wasn't didn't matter one fucking little bit, did it? No. What mattered was that Richler was still sniffing around . . . and that sheeny, Weiskopf, was also sniffing around. The letter, the goddam letter! Dussander's stupid goddam idea! And sud-

denly he was thinking of his .30-.30, cased and resting on its
shelf in the cool, dark garage. He pulled his mind away from
it quickly. The palms of his hands had gone damp.

"*Did* Dussander have any friends that you knew of?" Richler
was asking.

"Friends? No. There used to be a cleaning lady, but she
moved away and he didn't bother to get another one. In the
summer he hired a kid to mow his lawn, but I don't think he'd
gotten one this year. The grass is pretty long, isn't it?"

"Yes. We've knocked on a lot of doors, and it doesn't seem
as if he'd hired anyone. Did he get phone calls?"

"Sure," Todd said off-handedly . . . here was a gleam of light,
a possible escape-hatch that was relatively safe. Dussander's
phone had actually rung only half a dozen times or so in all the
time Todd had known him—salesmen, a polling organization
asking about breakfast foods, the rest wrong numbers. He only
had the phone in case he got sick . . . as he finally had, might
his soul rot in hell. "He used to get a call or two every week."

"Did he speak German on those occasions?" Richler asked
quickly. He seemed excited.

"No," Todd said, suddenly cautious. He didn't like Richler's
excitement—there was something wrong about it, something
dangerous. He felt sure of it, and suddenly Todd had to work
furiously to keep himself from breaking out in a sweat. "He
didn't talk much at all. I remember that a couple of times he
said things like, 'The boy who reads to me is here right now.
I'll call you back.'"

"I'll bet that's it!" Richler said, whacking his palms on his
thighs. "I'd bet two weeks' pay that was the guy!" He closed
his notebook with a snap (so far as Todd could see he had done
nothing but doodle in it) and stood up. "I want to thank all
three of you for your time. You in particular, Todd. I know
all of this has been a hell of a shock to you, but it will be over
soon. We're going to turn the house upside down this afternoon—cellar to attic and then back down to the cellar again.

We're bringing in all the special teams. We may find some trace of Dussander's phonemate yet."

"I hope so," Todd said.

Richler shook hands all around and left. Dick asked Todd if he felt like going out back and hitting the badminton birdie around until lunch. Todd said he didn't feel much like badminton *or* lunch, and went upstairs with his head down and his shoulders slumped. His parents exchanged sympathetic, troubled glances. Todd lay down on his bed, stared at the ceiling, and thought about his .30-.30. He could see it very clearly in his mind's eye. He thought about shoving the blued steel barrel right up Betty Trask's slimy Jewish cooze—just what she needed, a prick that never went soft. *How do you like it, Betty?* he heard himself asking her. *You just tell me if you get enough, okay?* He imagined her screams. And at last a terrible flat smile came to his face. *Sure, just tell me, you bitch . . . okay? Okay? Okay? . . .*

"So what do you think?" Weiskopf asked Richler when Richler picked him up at a luncheonette three blocks from the Bowden home.

"Oh, I think the kid was in on it somehow," Richler said. "Somehow, some way, to some degree. But is he cool? If you poured hot water into his mouth I think he'd spit out icecubes. I tripped him up a couple of times, but I've got nothing I could use in court. And if I'd gone much further, some smart lawyer might be able to get him off on entrapment a year or two down the road even if something *does* pull together. I mean, the courts are still going to look at him as a juvenile—the kid's only seventeen. In some ways, I'd guess he hasn't *really* been a juvenile since he was maybe eight. He's creepy, man." Richler stuck a cigarette in his mouth and laughed—the laugh had a shaky sound. "I mean, really fuckin creepy."

"What slips did he make?"

"The phone calls. That's the main thing. When I slipped

him the idea, I could see his eyes light up like a pinball machine." Richler turned left and wheeled the nondescript Chevy Nova down the freeway entrance ramp. Two hundred yards to their right was the slope and the dead tree where Todd had dry-fired his rifle at the freeway traffic one Saturday morning not long ago.

"He's saying to himself, 'This cop is off the wall if he thinks Dussander had a Nazi friend here in town, but if he *does* think that, it takes me off ground-zero.' So he says yeah, Dussander got one or two calls a week. Very mysterious. 'I can't talk now, Z-five, call later'—that type of thing. But Dussander's been getting a special 'quiet phone' rate for the last seven years. Almost no activity at all, and *no* long distance. He wasn't getting a call or two a week."

"What else?"

"He immediately jumped to the conclusion that the letter was gone and nothing else. He knew that was the only thing missing because he was the one who went back and took it."

Richler jammed his cigarette out in the ashtray.

"We *think* the letter was just a prop. We *think* that Dussander had the heart attack while he was trying to bury that body . . . the freshest body. There was dirt on his shoes and his cuffs, and so that's a pretty fair assumption. That means he called the kid *after* he had the heart attack, not before. He crawls upstairs and phones the kid. The kid flips out—as much as he ever flips out, anyway—and cooks up the letter story on the spur of the moment. It's not great, but not that bad, either . . . considering the circumstances. He goes over there and cleans up Dussander's mess for him. Now the kid is in fucking overdrive. MED-Q's coming, his father is coming, and he needs that letter for stage-dressing. He goes upstairs and breaks open that box—"

"You've got confirmation on that?" Weiskopf asked, lighting a cigarette of his own. It was an unfiltered Player, and to Richler it smelled like horseshit. No wonder the British

Empire fell, he thought, if they started smoking cigarettes like that.

"Yes, we've got confirmation right up the ying-yang," Richler said. "There are fingerprints on the box which match those in his school records. But his fingerprints are on almost *everything* in the goddam house!"

"Still, if you confront him with all of that, you can rattle him," Weiskopf said.

"Oh, listen, hey, you don't know this kid. When I said he was cool, I meant it. He'd say Dussander asked him to fetch the box once or twice so he could put something in it or take something out of it."

"His fingerprints are on the shovel."

"He'd say he used it to plant a rose-bush in the back yard." Richler took out his cigarettes but the pack was empty. Weiskopf offered him a Player. Richler took one puff and began coughing. "They taste as bad as they smell," he choked.

"Like those hamburgers we had for lunch yesterday," Weiskopf said, smiling. "Those Mac-Burgers."

"Big Macs," Richler said, and laughed. "Okay. So cross-cultural pollination doesn't always work." His smile faded. "He looks so clean-cut, you know?"

"Yes."

"This is no j.d. from Vasco with hair down to his asshole and chains on his motorcycle boots."

"No." Weiskopf stared at the traffic all around them and was very glad he wasn't driving. "He's just a boy. A white boy from a good home. And I find it difficult to believe that—"

"I thought you had them ready to handle rifles and grenades by the time they were eighteen. In Israel."

"Yes. But he was *fourteen* when all of this started. Why would a fourteen-year-old boy mix himself up with such a man as Dussander? I have tried and tried to understand that and still I can't."

"I'd settle for how," Richler said, and flicked the cigarette out the window. It was giving him a headache.

"Perhaps, if it did happen, it was just luck. A coincidence. Serendipity. I think there is black serendipity as well as white."

"I don't know what you're talking about," Richler said gloomily. "All I know is the kid is creepier than a bug under a rock."

"What I'm saying is simple. Any other boy would have been more than happy to tell his parents, or the police. To say, 'I have recognized a wanted man. He is living at this address. Yes, I am sure.' And then let the authorities take over. Or do you feel I am wrong?"

"No, I wouldn't say so. The kid would be in the limelight for a few days. Most kids would dig that. Picture in the paper, an interview on the evening news, probably a school assembly award for good citizenship." Richler laughed. "Hell, the kid would probably get a shot on *Real People*."

"What's that?"

"Never mind," Richler said. He had to raise his voice slightly because ten-wheelers were passing the Nova on either side. Weiskopf looked nervously from one to the other. "You don't want to know. But you're right about most kids. *Most* kids."

"But not *this* kid," Weiskopf said. "This boy, probably by dumb luck alone, penetrates Dussander's cover. Yet instead of going to his parents or the authorities . . . he goes to Dussander. Why? You say you don't care, but I think you do. I think it haunts you just as it does me."

"Not blackmail," Richler said. "That's for sure. That kid's got everything a kid could want. There was a dune-buggy in the garage, not to mention an elephant gun on the wall. And even if he wanted to squeeze Dussander just for the thrill of it, Dussander was practically unsqueezable. Except for those few stocks, he didn't have a pot to piss in."

"How sure are you that the boy doesn't know you've found the bodies?"

"I'm sure. Maybe I'll go back this afternoon and hit him with that. Right now it looks like our best shot." Richler struck the steering wheel lightly. "If all of this had come out even one day sooner, I think I would have tried for a search warrant."

"The clothes the boy was wearing that night?"

"Yeah. If we could have found soil samples on his clothes that matched the dirt in Dussander's cellar, I almost think we could break him. But the clothes he was wearing that night have probably been washed six times since then."

"What about the other dead winos? The ones your police department has been finding around the city?"

"Those belong to Dan Bozeman. I don't think there's any connection anyhow. Dussander just wasn't that strong . . . and more to the point, he had such a neat little racket already worked out. Promise them a drink and a meal, take them home on the city bus—the fucking city bus!—and waste them right in his kitchen."

Weiskopf said quietly: "It wasn't *Dussander* I was thinking of."

"What do you mean by th—" Richler began, and then his mouth snapped suddenly closed. There was a long, unbelieving moment of silence, broken only by the drone of the traffic all around them. Then Richler said softly: "Hey. Hey, come on now. Give me a fucking br—"

"As an agent of my government, I am only interested in Bowden because of what, if anything, he may know about Dussander's remaining contacts with the Nazi underground. But as a human being, I am becoming more and more interested in the boy himself. I'd like to know what makes him tick. I want to know *why*. And as I try to answer that question to my own satisfaction, I find that more and more I am asking myself *What else.*"

"But—"

"Do you suppose, I ask myself, that the very atrocities in which Dussander took part formed the basis of some attraction between them? That's an unholy idea, I tell myself. The things that happened in those camps still have power enough to make the stomach flutter with nausea. I feel that way myself, although the only close relative I ever had in the camps was my grandfather, and he died when I was three. But maybe there is something about what the Germans did that exercises a deadly fascination over us—something that opens the catacombs of the imagination. Maybe part of our dread and horror comes from a secret knowledge that under the right—or wrong—set of circumstances, we ourselves would be willing to build such places and staff them. Black serendipity. Maybe we know that under the right set of circumstances the things that live in the catacombs would be glad to crawl out. And what do you think they would look like? Like mad Fuehrers with forelocks and shoe-polish moustaches, *heil*-ing all over the place? Like red devils, or demons, or the dragon that floats on its stinking reptile wings?"

"I don't know," Richler said.

"I think most of them would look like ordinary accountants," Weiskopf said. "Little mind-men with graphs and flow-charts and electronic calculators, all ready to start maximizing the kill ratios so that *next* time they could perhaps kill twenty or thirty million instead of only six. And some of them might look like Todd Bowden."

"You're damn near as creepy as he is," Richler said.

Weiskopf nodded. "It's a creepy subject. Finding those dead men and animals in Dussander's cellar . . . *that* was creepy, *nu?* Have you ever thought that maybe this boy began with a simple interest in the camps? An interest not much different from the interests of boys who collect coins or stamps or who like to read about Wild West desperados? And that he went to Dussander to get his information straight from the horse's head?"

"Mouth," Richler said automatically. "Man, at this point I could believe anything."

"Maybe," Weiskopf muttered. It was almost lost in the roar of another ten-wheeler passing them, BUDWEISER was printed on the side in letters six feet tall. *What an amazing country,* Weiskopf thought, and lit a fresh cigarette. *They don't understand how we can live surrounded by half-mad Arabs, but if I lived here for two years I would have a nervous breakdown.* "Maybe. And maybe it isn't possible to stand close to murder piled on murder and not be touched by it."

29

The short guy who entered the squadroom brought stench after him like a wake. He smelled like rotten bananas and Wildroot Cream Oil and cockroach shit and the inside of a city garbage truck at the end of a busy morning. He was dressed in a pair of ageing herringbone pants, a ripped gray institutional shirt, and a faded blue warmup jacket from which most of the zipper hung loose like a string of pygmy teeth. The uppers of his shoes were bound to the lowers with Krazy Glue. A pestiferous hat sat on his head.

"Oh Christ, get out of here!" the duty sergeant cried. "You're not under arrest, Hap! I swear to God! I swear it on my mother's name! Get out of here! I want to breathe again."

"I want to talk to Lieutenant Bozeman."

"He died, Hap. It happened yesterday. We're all really fucked up over it. So get out and let us mourn in peace."

"I want to talk to Lieutenant Bozeman!" Hap said more loudly. His breath drifted fragrantly from his mouth: a juicy, fermenting mixture of pizza, Hall's Mentho-lyptus lozenges, and sweet red wine.

"He had to go to Siam on a case, Hap. So why don't you just get out of here? Go someplace and eat a lightbulb."

"I want to talk to Lieutenant Bozeman and I ain't leaving until I do!"

The duty sergeant fled the room. He returned about five minutes later with Bozeman, a thin, slightly stooped man of fifty.

"Take him into your office, okay, Dan?" the duty sergeant begged. "Won't that be all right?"

"Come on, Hap," Bozeman said, and a minute later they were in the three-sided stall that was Bozeman's office. Bozeman prudently opened his only window and turned on his fan before sitting down. "Do something for you, Hap?"

"You still on those murders, Lieutenant Bozeman?"

"The derelicts? Yeah, I guess that's still mine."

"Well, I know who greased 'em."

"Is that so, Hap?" Bozeman asked. He was busy lighting his pipe. He rarely smoked the pipe, but neither the fan nor the open window was quite enough to overwhelm Hap's smell. Soon, Bozeman thought, the paint would begin to blister and peel. He sighed.

"You remember I told you Poley was talkin to a guy just a day before they found him all cut up in that pipe? You member me tellin you that, Lieutenant Bozeman?"

"I remember." Several of the winos who hung around the Salvation Army and the soup kitchen a few blocks away had told a similar story about two of the murdered derelicts, Charles "Sonny" Brackett and Peter "Poley" Smith. They had seen a guy hanging around, a young guy, talking to Sonny and Poley. Nobody knew for sure if Poley had gone off with the guy, but Hap and two others claimed to have seen Poley Smith walk off with him. They had the idea that the "guy" was underage and willing to spring for a bottle of musky in exchange for some juice. Several other winos claimed to have seen a "guy" like that around. The description of this "guy" was superb, bound to stand up in court, coming as it did from such unimpeachable sources. Young, blond, and white. What else did you need to make a bust?

"Well, last night I was in the park," Hap said, "and I just happened to have this old bunch of newspapers—"

"There's a law against vagrancy in this city, Hap."

"I was just collectin em up," Hap said righteously. "It's so awful the way people litter. I was doon a public surface, Lieutenant. A friggin public surface. Some of those papers was a week old."

"Yes, Hap," Bozeman said. He remembered—vaguely—being quite hungry and looking forward keenly to his lunch. That time seemed long ago now.

"Well, when I woke up, one of those papers had blew onto my face and I was lookin right *at* the guy. Gave me a hell of a jump, I can tell you. Look. This is the guy. This guy right here."

Hap pulled a crumpled, yellowed, water-spotted sheet of newspaper from his warmup jacket and unfolded it. Bozeman leaned forward, now moderately interested. Hap put the paper on his desk so he could read the headline: 4 BOYS NAMED TO SOUTHERN CAL ALL-STARS. Below the head were four photos.

"Which one, Hap?"

Hap put a grimy finger on the picture to the far right. "Him. It says his name is Todd Bowden."

Bozeman looked from the picture to Hap, wondering how many of Hap's brain-cells were still unfried and in some kind of working order after twenty years of being sautéed in a bubbling sauce of cheap wine seasoned with an occasional shot of sterno.

"How can you be sure, Hap? He's wearing a baseball cap in the picture. I can't tell if he's got blonde hair or not."

"The grin," Hap said. "It's the way he's grinnin. He was grinnin at Poley in just that same ain't-life-grand way when they walked off together. I couldn't mistake that grin in a million years. That's him, that's the guy."

Bozeman barely heard the last; he was thinking, and thinking hard. *Todd Bowden.* There was something very familiar about that name. Something that bothered him even worse than the thought that a local high school hero might be going around and offing winos. He thought he had heard that name just this morning in conversation. He frowned, trying to remember where.

Hap was gone and Dan Bozeman was still trying to figure it out when Richler and Weiskopf came in . . . and it was the sound of their voices as they got coffee in the squadroom that finally brought it home to him.

"Holy God," said Lieutenant Bozeman, and got up in a hurry.

Both of his parents had offered to cancel their afternoon plans—Monica at the market and Dick golfing with some business people—and stay home with him, but Todd told them he would rather be alone. He thought he would clean his rifle and just sort of think the whole thing over. Try to get it straight in his mind.

'Todd," Dick said, and suddenly found he had nothing much to say. He supposed if he had been his own father, he would have at this point advised prayer. But the generations had turned, and the Bowdens weren't much into that these days. "Sometimes these things happen," he finished lamely, because Todd was still looking at him. 'Try not to brood about it."

"It'll be all right," Todd said.

After they were gone, he took some rags and a bottle of Alpaca gun oil out onto the bench beside the roses. He went back into the garage and got the .30-.30. He took it to the bench and broke it down, the dusty-sweet smell of the flowers lingering pleasantly in his nose. He cleaned the gun thoroughly, humming a tune as he did it, sometimes whistling a snatch between his teeth. Then he put the gun together again. He could have done it just as easily in the dark. His mind wandered free. When it came back some five minutes later, he observed that he had loaded the gun. The idea of target-shooting didn't much appeal, not today, but he had still loaded it. He told himself he didn't know why.

Sure you do, Todd-baby. The time, so to speak, has come.

And that was when the shiny yellow Saab turned into the driveway. The man who got out was vaguely familiar to Todd, but it wasn't until he slammed the car door and started to walk toward him that Todd saw the sneakers—low-topped Keds, light blue. Talk about Blasts from the Past; here, walking up the Bowden driveway, was Rubber Ed French, The Ked Man.

"Hi, Todd. Long time no see."

Todd leaned the rifle against the side of the bench and offered his wide and winsome grin. "Hi, Mr. French. What are you doing out here on the wild side of town?"

"Are your folks home?"

"Gee, no. Did you want them for something?"

"No," Ed French said after a long, thoughtful pause. "No, I guess not. I guess maybe it would be better if just you and I talked. For starters, anyway. You may be able to offer a perfectly reasonable explanation for all this. Although God knows I doubt it."

He reached into his hip pocket and brought out a newsclipping. Todd knew what it was even before Rubber Ed passed it to him, and for the second time that day he was looking at the side-by-side pictures of Dussander. The one the street photographer had taken had been circled in black ink. The meaning was clear enough to Todd; French had recognized Todd's "grandfather." And now he wanted to tell everyone in the world all about it. He wanted to midwife the good news. Good old Rubber Ed, with his jive talk and his motherfucking sneakers.

The police would be very interested—but, of course, they already were. He knew that now. The sinking feeling had begun about thirty minutes after Richler left. It was as if he had been riding high in a balloon filled with happy-gas. Then a cold steel arrow had ripped through the balloon's fabric, and now it was sinking steadily.

The phone calls, that was the biggie. Richler had trotted that out just as slick as warm owlshit. *Sure,* he had said, practically breaking his neck to rush into the trap. *He gets one or two calls a week.* Let them go ranting all over southern California looking for geriatric ex-Nazis. Fine. Except maybe they had gotten a different story from Ma Bell. Todd didn't know if the phone company could tell how much your phone got used . . . but there had been a look in Richler's eyes . . .

Then there was the letter. He had inadvertently told Richler that the house hadn't been burgled, and Richler had no doubt gone away thinking that the only way Todd could have known that was if he had been back . . . as he had been, not just once but three times, first to get the letter and twice more looking for anything incriminating. There had been nothing; even the SS uniform was gone, disposed of by Dussander sometime during the last four years.

And then there were the bodies. Richler had never mentioned the bodies.

At first Todd had thought that was good. Let them hunt a little longer while he got his own head—not to mention his story—straight. No fear about the dirt that had gotten on his clothes burying the body; they had all been cleaned later that same night. He ran them through the washer-dryer himself, perfectly aware that Dussander might die and then everything might come out. You can't be too careful, boy, as Dussander himself would have said.

Then, little by little, he had realized it was *not* good. The weather had been warm, and the warm weather always made the cellar smell worse; on his last trip to Dussander's house it had been a rank presence. Surely the police would have been interested in that smell, and would have tracked it to its source. So why had Richler withheld the information? Was he saving it for later? Saving it for a nasty little surprise? And if Richler was into planning nasty little surprises, it could only mean that he suspected.

Todd looked up from the clipping and saw that Rubber Ed had half-turned away from him. He was looking into the street, although not much was happening out there. Richler could suspect, but suspicion was the best he could do.

Unless there was some sort of concrete evidence binding Todd to the old man.

Exactly the sort of evidence Rubber Ed French could give.

Ridiculous man in a pair of ridiculous sneakers. Such a ridiculous man hardly deserved to live. Todd touched the barrel of the .30-.30.

Yes, Rubber Ed was a link they didn't have. They could *never* prove that Todd had been an accessory to one of Dussander's murders. But with Rubber Ed's testimony they could prove conspiracy. And would even *that* end it? Oh, no. They would get his high school graduation picture next and start showing it to the stewbums down in the Mission district. A long shot, but one Richler could ill afford not to play. If we can't pin one bunch of winos on him, maybe we can get him for the other bunch.

What next? Court next.

His father would get him a wonderful bunch of lawyers, of course. And the lawyers would get him off, of course. Too much circumstantial evidence. He would make too favorable an impression on the jury. But by then his life would be ruined anyway, just as Dussander had said it would be. It would be all dragged through the newspapers, dug up and brought into the light like the half-decayed bodies in Dussander's cellar.

"The man in that picture is the man who came to my office when you were in the ninth grade," Ed told him abruptly, turning to Todd again. "He purported to be your grandfather. Now it turns out he was a wanted war criminal."

"Yes," Todd said. His face had gone oddly blank. It was the face of a department-store dummy. All the healthiness, life, and vivacity had drained from it. What was left was frightening in its vacuous emptiness.

"How did it happen?" Ed asked, and perhaps he intended his question as a thundering accusation, but it came out sounding plaintive and lost and somehow cheated. "How did this happen, Todd?"

"Oh, one thing just followed another," Todd said, and picked up the .30-.30. "That's really how it happened. One thing just . . . followed another." He pushed the safety catch to the off position with his thumb and pointed the rifle at Rubber Ed. "As stupid as it sounds, that's just what happened. That's all there was to it."

"Todd," Ed said, his eyes widening. He took a step backwards. "Todd, you don't want to . . . please, Todd. We can talk this over. We can disc—"

"You and the fucking kraut can discuss it down in hell," Todd said, and pulled the trigger.

The sound of the shot rolled away in the hot and windless quiet of the afternoon. Ed French was flung back against his Saab. His hand groped behind him and tore off a windshield wiper. He stared at it foolishly as blood spread on his blue turtleneck, and then he dropped it and looked at Todd.

"Norma," he whispered.

"Okay," Todd said. "Whatever you say, champ." He shot Rubber Ed again and roughly half of his head disappeared in a spray of blood and bone.

Ed turned drunkenly and began to grope toward the driver's-side door, speaking his daughter's name over and over again in a choked and failing voice. Todd shot him again, aiming for the base of the spine, and Ed fell down. His feet drummed briefly on the gravel and then were still.

Sure did die hard for a guidance counsellor, Todd thought, and brief laughter escaped him. At the same moment a burst of pain as sharp as an icepick drove into his brain and he closed his eyes.

When he opened them again, he felt better than he had in months—maybe better than he had felt in years. Everything was fine. Everything was together. The blankness left his face and a kind of wild beauty filled it.

He went back into the garage and got all the shells he had, better than four hundred rounds. He put them in his old knapsack and shouldered it. When he came back out into the sunshine he was smiling excitedly, his eyes dancing—it was the way boys smile on their birthdays, on Christmas, on the Fourth of July. It was a smile that betokened skyrockets, tree-houses, secret signs and secret meeting-places, the aftermath of the triumphal big game when the players are carried out of the stadium and into town on the shoulders of the exultant fans. The ecstatic smile of tow-headed boys going off to war in coal-scuttle helmets.

"I'm king of the world!" he shouted mightily at the high blue sky, and raised the rifle two-handed over his head for a moment. Then, switching it to his right hand, he started toward that place above the freeway where the land fell away and where the dead tree would give him shelter.

It was five hours later and almost dark before they took him down.